ALMOST DEAD

Also by T. R. Ragan

Abducted (Lizzy Gardner Series #1)
Dead Weight (Lizzy Gardner Series #2)
A Dark Mind (Lizzy Gardner Series #3)
Obsessed (Lizzy Gardner Series #4)

Also by Theresa Ragan

Return of the Rose
A Knight in Central Park
Finding Kate Huntley
Taming Mad Max
Having My Baby
An Offer He Can't Refuse
Here Comes the Bride

ALMOST DEAD

T.R. RAGAN

THOMAS & MERCER

Text copyright © 2015 T. R. Ragan
All rights reserved.

Published by Thomas & Mercer, Seattle

www.apub.com

Amazon, the Amazon logo, and Thomas & Mercer are trademarks of Amazon.com, Inc., or its affiliates.

ISBN-13: 9781477819654
ISBN-10: 1477819657

Cover design by Cyanotype Book Architects

Library of Congress Control Number: 2014949133

Printed in the United States of America

DEDICATION

Joe, Jesse, Joey, Morgan, and Brittany.
Each of you is a constant reminder of what's really important.
I am so incredibly blessed.

When you've lost everything,
There's nothing left to lose . . .

CHAPTER 1

After work, the first thing Jenny Pickett did when she walked into her house off Glen Tree Drive in Citrus Heights was carry the mail to her office. Her sturdy heels clacked against the wood floor as she made her way down the hall to her study, adjusting picture frames as she went. She then sat down at her desk and turned on the lamp.

Using a letter opener, she sliced open one piece of mail after another. All junk. She then carefully slid each slip of paper into the shredder, one at a time.

Jenny was a creature of habit. She couldn't help it.

She looked at the far right corner of her desk. The article she'd clipped from the *Journal of the American Chemical Society* was like a magnet, begging to be read again and again. She had brought the article home three weeks ago, read it hundreds of times already, even crumpled it in her fist and threw it into the garbage. An hour after tossing it, though, she'd pulled it out, smoothed most of the wrinkles from the glossy paper, and then left it leaning against a stack of books—where it was now. She didn't need to bring it closer to know what it said. She had most of the article memorized.

She glanced at the clock. In a couple of hours, Brandon Louis would be paying her a visit, making this day one of the most important days of her life. For this reason, she refused to allow herself to continue on her recent downward spiral into depression—a dark mood she'd found herself in ever since she'd learned that Terri Kramer, an old college classmate, one of the few people she had considered to be a friend, had betrayed her.

Unable to help herself, she reached for the article and stared at the small picture of Terri. Her dark-brown hair was tied back, revealing the same round face and cobalt-blue eyes.

The entire industry had been abuzz about Terri Kramer's supposed discovery of a new antiaging serum. Terri Kramer had been quoted as saying, "Of course this discovery wasn't mine alone, but the result of the hard work of my team."

Jenny felt a rush of heat swoosh through her body. Three weeks had passed since she'd heard the news, and yet she couldn't look at the article without feeling as if she was sliding deeper into a seething funk.

It wasn't a bad dream. Terri stole my formula.

You knew she would. You don't have any friends. Nobody likes you.

Ignoring the voice in her head, Jenny inhaled, noticed the time, and then carefully placed the folded piece of paper back against the books. Brandon would be here in two hours. She didn't have time to think about any of this now.

Tonight was the night Brandon would propose. Woman's intuition had her body thrumming with excitement. Brandon was a pilot, and, although he didn't call often, he'd left a message with the receptionist at her work: we need to talk.

Only four words, but she knew. He wanted her to be ready. And boy, would she be. Although their time spent together was usually a quick romp in bed, she'd been seeing him for almost a year now. He was going to propose. It was time.

Don't be an idiot. Nobody loves you. You know that.

"Not tonight," she said aloud. "Leave me alone."

After one more glance at Terri's picture, she came to her feet. She walked into the bathroom, turned on the faucet, and sprinkled the water with lavender bath salts.

As the tub filled, she examined her recent purchases laid out on the bed. The formfitting red dress was beautiful. The undergarments made her blush. Should she wear the sexy mesh-and-lace corset with lace V-string or the red bombshell garter slip?

Tonight would be special—different from all of their other nights spent together.

Brandon was smart and funny and ridiculously charming. Every so often he would take her to dinner. Then they would return to her place to sip wine and talk—about everything.

Time raced, and although the next two hours felt like minutes, when the doorbell rang, she was ready. Giddy with anticipation, she opened the door. Before she could wrap her arms around him, Brandon made his way inside without so much as a hello.

She shut the door and swiveled around, her heart pounding. His hair was slicked back, the smell of his cologne woodsy and familiar. Tonight he had taken the time to change out of his uniform. He wore dark slacks and a white buttoned-up shirt.

"What's with all the candles?" he asked.

She waited for him to notice her, wanted him to take a good long look. She'd taken her time with her hair. Soft silky curls fell over her shoulders. There wasn't one part of her body that hadn't been pampered. She had to remind herself to breathe as she moved toward him, hoping to hypnotize him with the sway of her hips.

He didn't say a word. He was speechless—exactly the effect she'd hoped to have on him.

As she brought her lips to his, she untucked his shirt so she could slide her hands over his warm skin. Brandon's body felt like chiseled marble. Her breathing quickened. When she pressed her breasts against his chest and her lips to his, swirling her tongue around, his breathing quickened, too.

Much too soon for her liking, he pulled back and said, "We need to talk."

Those four words again. Her heart hammered. She'd keep it light, playful. Looking at him through dark lashes that had taken much too long to apply, she pouted. "Seriously, Mr. Louis? It has been weeks since I saw you last, and you just want to talk?"

He reached under his shirt, took hold of her wrists, and pulled her hands away.

This time when she looked into his eyes, she saw something she hadn't seen before—a dash of something she couldn't quite read. "What's wrong?"

He scratched the back of his head and then gestured with his chin toward the table she'd set for two, complete with candles and crystal glasses. "What's this all about, Jenny?"

"I've missed you. I wanted to surprise you." She tried to step closer, but he clasped his fingers around her forearms to keep her at bay. She looked at his hands. "You're hurting me."

He let go. "I don't know how to tell you this, Jenny, but under the circumstances I think it's best if I just blurt it out."

"Please do. You're scaring me. I have no idea—"

"I'm engaged."

"Engaged," she said, slowly enough to let the word wrap around her brain. "Engaged to be married?"

He nodded.

Cocksucker.

She rubbed her temples, tried to think, but his words did not make any sense. "I don't understand. How can that be true? When did you meet her?"

"The truth is I was engaged when I met you."

4

Nervous laughter escaped her. "That's ridiculous. We've been dating for nearly a year."

"I hardly call what we've been doing dating."

"What do you call it, then?"

"Fucking. We've been fucking, Jenny. You've got an amazing body. You're great in bed. You have the mouth of a porn star. How could I resist?"

That's why he never talked about marriage or kids or past relationships. Two minutes after you met him, I told you he was an asshole. Maybe you should start listening to me.

A flash of electricity whizzed through her head. The searing pain nearly brought her to her knees. She turned from him and went to the kitchen in search of aspirin.

He followed close on her heels. "I'm sorry."

He's not sorry. Look at him. He's a cocky son of a bitch who's been fucking someone else the entire time you've known him.

She fumbled with the bottle of pills. "Why are you here?"

"I had a few hours to kill. I figured I might as well tell you face-to-face."

She opened the bottle of aspirin, swallowed the pills, and then held on to the granite counter for support. "Is this why you could never give me your number? This is why you didn't want to be seen in public?"

No shit, Sherlock.

He didn't answer.

"Were there others besides me?"

Do bears shit in the woods?

"Of course not, baby. Only you."

This was not happening. They were meant to be together. She turned around and fell into him. She wrapped her arms around his waist and rested her head against his chest. "Please don't do this to me."

Unlatching her arms, he released a disgusted moan as he gently pushed her away from him. Then he carefully tucked his shirt back into his pants and smoothed back his hair. "Don't make this more difficult than it needs to be."

"I want to understand." She took hold of his hand and rubbed his knuckles against her cheek. "You said I was easy to talk to and that we had a special connection. What changed?"

"Nothing changed."

"Then tell me why you didn't pick me. Why am I not the one you're marrying?"

"You really want to know?"

She kissed his hand. "I do. I really do."

"Look at you," he said. "You're clinging to me as if I'm some sort of lifeline. What sort of woman sits at home, night after night, waiting for a man to stop by once a month?

"A desperate one," he said before she could answer.

The counters are covered in fingerprints and germs. This place is a mess! The butcher block is covered with bacteria and fungi. The sink is disgusting. No wonder he doesn't love you.

Letting go of his hand, she turned toward the sink. She grabbed a clean sponge, put it under water, and began to scrub. Everything was so dirty. There were smudges and germs everywhere.

"Here we go," Brandon said. "Hurry! Grab the disinfectant."

Usually she moved the sponge in small methodical circles, but at the moment, every movement was frantic.

He groaned. "I'm not going to finish what I was saying unless you stop cleaning."

Seconds passed before she dropped the sponge in the sink and told him to go on. She wasn't ready to turn around and face him, though. She couldn't bear to look at him.

"How many times have you told me about the people who taunted and bullied you throughout your life?" he asked. "Every time we get together, you complain about how people at work treat you with little or no respect, but do you ever do anything about it? No. You have zero confidence. You're like a scared little trapped mouse. You need to get a spine, Jenny Pickett. Stop bitching about your sorry life, for Christ's sakes, and do something about it. For once in your life, stand up for yourself."

The cocksucker has a point.

Her vision blurred. He was right. She needed to stick up for herself.

There's a knife right there in front of you, lots of them. Shut the man up, for God's sake.

"Does your fiancée know about us?"

"No," he said.

"I thought you came here tonight because you were going to ask me to marry you. I spent the past two hours getting ready."

His laughter echoed off the walls, causing every muscle in her body to tense.

"You see a man once a month, and you think he wants to marry you?"

She reached for the biggest knife from the wooden knife block, whipped around, and thrust the blade into his chest, pushing as hard as she could, surprised by her strength and the ease with which his flesh gave way to the sharp steel.

The surprise in his eyes, the open mouth, the stunned expression: *that* was the look she'd been hoping for earlier when she'd greeted him at the door.

Slow clap. Wow, I didn't know you had it in you. This is more like it!

Brandon's eyes had grown big and round. Both of his hands were clamped around the handle of the knife protruding from his chest. His eyes rolled to the back of his head, and he stumbled forward.

She jumped out of his way.

Thunk.

For a moment, she just stared at him, wondering if she had really just killed Brandon Louis. It took a little while for her breathing to return to normal, but it did, and she felt powerful and in control.

He was right. He really was. Standing up for herself was downright empowering. She felt invincible.

Blood seeped from his body and onto the floor, sending her anxiety into high alert. Careful not to step in the pool of blood, she ran to her bedroom, pulled off her clothes, and put on a pair of sweatpants and a T-shirt. She ran through the laundry room to the garage, where she gathered cleaning products, including a pair of thick rubber gloves and a bucket. She also grabbed a tarp she'd planned to use when she painted the guestroom, then headed back for the kitchen.

She needed to work quickly. She needed to be smart.

Rolling his body onto the tarp took more strength than she'd imagined it would. Once she mopped up the blood, she put on a clean pair of gloves and emptied his pockets.

The bastard had a cell phone. He'd told her he didn't have one, and she'd believed him. He'd told her cell phones were bad for the environment.

His phone had been powered off. *Perfect,* she thought, although she was dying to turn it on so she could check his messages and read his texts. But that would be stupid.

She looked through his wallet, found a picture of the woman she assumed he was engaged to. The hair was nice enough, but she had angry eyes and a pointy nose.

Do not take the picture.

Next she found the key to his rental car parked in her driveway.

She was an accomplished research chemist known for her organizational skills, intelligence, and ingenuity. Now was the time to act like it. She needed to be careful and methodical. She could not leave behind any evidence.

Once his body was rolled tightly in the tarp, she used duct tape to secure both ends. She would drag the body through the laundry room to the garage. Her father was a pig farmer in Elk Grove. He sometimes had to get rid of dead animals. She knew just what to do. Tomorrow was Friday. After work, she would pack up the body and head for the farm.

Right now, though, her priority was getting Brandon into the trunk of her car. Trussed up as he was, he wasn't as hard to maneuver as he might've been, but still, he was heavy as hell and unwieldy. A two-stage process would do it: turn him over onto the low furniture dolly stored behind her freezer and wheel him to the garage door; then drive her car into the garage and transfer him into the trunk. The transfers would be awkward, but she'd take her time. After that, she would clean herself up and get rid of the rental car.

CHAPTER 2

Lizzy had been seeing her therapist, Linda Gates, for eighteen years now, beginning when she was a teen and had just returned from three months of hell. In all those years, the office had hardly changed: same couch, same executive-sized desk, same ergonomic chair—everything, including the walls, was in neutral colors. The best part was the large paned windows overlooking downtown Sacramento. If you stood at just the right angle, you could even glimpse part of the American River.

"Why don't you tell me how you're feeling."

Lizzy crossed her legs. "My sister is driving me nuts. Why she let that asshole move back in, I'll never know. It makes no sense. My niece shouldn't have to listen to their constant bickering. It's—"

"Lizzy."

"Yes?"

"You're avoiding the question."

"I am?"

"Yes. How are *you* feeling?"

"Feeling?"

"Yes."

Lizzy's shoulders dropped. "Under the circumstances, I'm doing fine. I'm exercising and eating OK. Between work and my self-defense program, I'm keeping busy. The teenagers I'm teaching right now are great."

Linda sighed.

"What?" Lizzy asked. "Why do I get the feeling there are right and wrong answers to your questions?"

"There are no right or wrong answers, you know that, but I've known you for a long time and I'm concerned that you may be trying to move on as if nothing has changed. And that's not moving on at all."

"You think I'm in denial."

Linda nodded. "I know you are. In a matter of weeks you killed a man in self-defense, then lost your father, and now your fiancé lies comatose in a hospital bed and you're being asked to make a difficult decision."

"The decision was made before the first bullet hit Jared's chest," Lizzy said. "The advance directive Jared signed putting me in charge of his care was for exactly this purpose. But Jared's family has decided to bring the matter to court. They want to keep Jared on feeding tubes and ventilators, everything Jared didn't want."

"It doesn't help that his family and you don't see eye to eye," Linda said. "I think it would be in your best interest—"

"Don't say it," Lizzy said, cutting her off. "I have too many people as it is telling me how to handle the situation. I'm dealing with things the same way I've dealt with everything that's happened in my life." She uncrossed her legs and sat up straight. "I take it one day at a time. I get out of bed, get dressed, brush my teeth, and go to work. I can't say I'm stopping to smell the roses, but I'm here, aren't I?"

A deafening silence came between them.

"I'll be fine," Lizzy added.

"When are you planning on moving back into your house?"

"I don't know if I can."

"Why not?"

"Too many memories."

"You can't run from them forever."

Lizzy looked at the clock on the wall. "I need to get going." She stood. "I'll see you next week." Lizzy pointed a finger at Linda, who still sat on the couch, unmoving, her brow severely puckered. "I'm not holding back," Lizzy told her. "I will be fine. We'll all be fine."

CHAPTER 3

Tonight, Hayley was working with Kitally on the Steven Dow case.

His wife, Mrs. Beverly Dow, had hired Lizzy Gardner Investigations to find out if her husband was cheating. Lizzy didn't usually take on infidelity cases, but for whatever reason, when Beverly Dow had shown up at the downtown office, Lizzy hadn't balked. She had merely drawn up a contract, asked the woman to sign on the dotted line, and forgotten all about her.

If Lizzy's work ethic continued on this way for too long, Hayley knew she would be forced to talk to her about it. But for now, Hayley kept track of every move Lizzy made and did her best to clean up after her.

After watching Mr. Dow on and off for the past two weeks and getting nowhere, Hayley and Kitally decided to do things a little differently tonight.

Hayley sat in her Chevy, slumped down behind the wheel, her gaze set on the club across the street. Kitally was tonight's bait, and she had been inside the dimly lit place for forty-five minutes already. Lizzy would not be pleased to know what they were up to—their plan to catch Mr. Dow in the act might be considered entrapment by some—but Hayley really didn't give a shit. The man was a skank. Period. He needed to be taught a lesson.

According to Beverly Dow, at least twice a week, Mr. Dow told his wife that he had to meet a business client. Sometimes he wouldn't return home until sunrise. Beverly wanted to know what her husband was up to—that meant recordings and pictures, too.

Boredom set in, and Hayley's thoughts drifted back to Lizzy. She'd shown up at the office every day, in between funerals and hospital visits. If she wasn't in the office, she was teaching kids self-defense and trying to act as if nothing in her world had changed. She was obviously just going through the motions, and it was difficult to watch, knowing that any moment now she was going to slam into a wall and it was going to hurt bad. Nobody could keep his or her emotions bottled up forever.

But Hayley didn't think she should be the one to tell Lizzy it might be a good idea to let some of those emotions out instead of hoarding them all inside, pretending everything was just fine. That would be hypocritical—Hayley herself wasn't exactly in touch with her own feelings, and she was fine with that—so she said nothing.

She'd just arrived at this conclusion when she saw Kitally stumble out of the nightclub. Her body swayed; the long dreadlock hanging down her back did, too. She bumped into the side of the building and had to catch herself. Hayley was about to go after her when she saw Mr. Dow exit the bar, rush forward, and put a hand around Kitally's waist, leading her away, keeping her from falling on the sidewalk.

Figuring Kitally was putting on a show, Hayley grabbed the camera, zoomed in, and took a couple of pictures. When Kitally nearly toppled completely over, the sleazeball scooped her into his arms, his hands all over her as if he were trying to steady her.

Something was wrong with this picture. Kitally could handle her alcohol and this was no act, which meant Mr. Dow had slipped something into her drink. *Shit.*

Hayley took another picture, then set her camera on the passenger seat and turned on the engine. When Mr. Dow pulled out onto the road, she was ready to go. She followed his black Mercedes to a stoplight. Although this had been the plan all along, the plan had not included the man slipping something into Kitally's drink.

Her nerves were jangled. More than anything, she wanted to slam her car into the back of his shiny black luxury car. Instead, she held in her anger, determined not to lose her cool or, more importantly, Kitally.

When the light changed, the Mercedes shot away from her with a screech of wheels.

He was wise to her.

Hayley's Chevy Impala was a piece of shit, but the tires and the suspension were solid, taking curbs as if they were nothing more than a rough patch of road. He was going close to sixty on a narrow street packed tight with cars parked on both sides. Usually she wouldn't worry so much about Kitally. She was a tough girl. She could handle herself when she was sober, but not like this.

Hayley sped up, almost caught up to him when he took a sharp left.

More screeching of tires. She yanked hard on the wheel. Her Chevy felt as if it might topple. The road took her straight up a ridiculously steep hill. On both sides of her the landscape was open fields dotted with trees and shrubs and covered in waist-high grass after the recent rains. She knew this area. Although she'd never come this way, at the top of the small mountain was what the kids called Makeout Hill.

Her Chevy puttered a bit on the incline, and she lost sight of his taillights. She leaned forward, as though that might give the old car a little help.

As she continued up, she caught sight of a dark shadow heading downward through the middle of the hill to her left where there was no road to speak of, just a foot trail. His lights were off. *That son of a bitch!*

An old, dilapidated wood fence was the only thing stopping Hayley from being able to do a little off-road driving and follow him. *To hell with it.* She turned off her headlights, then turned toward the fence, surprised when she was able to plow right through. The terrain was bumpy, but if she was careful not to hit any trees or rocks, she might be able to catch up to the asshole.

There he was. She caught a glint of chrome in the night and then could see the shadowy silhouette of his Mercedes hiding in the blackness beneath an oak tree with wild, gangly branches that shot out in every direction. Her lights still off, she banked sharply and shot toward him through the tall grass. She didn't let up on the gas. Her body felt like a broken piston as she was joggled over the uneven ground; she could only hope nothing big enough to stop her was hidden in the grass. If he saw her coming, he certainly didn't do anything about it. She ground her teeth together right before she rammed into the driver's side of the Mercedes.

In the last instant before impact, it occurred to her that Kitally was in the car. She hit the brakes. Then the crash. And then silence and a bit of steam curling out from under the hood of her Chevy. Its engine stayed on, though. The thing was a tank. She threw it into park, grabbed her baton, and leaped from the car.

The air bag had not deployed, and she could see Dow behind the wheel. She tried to open the driver's door, but it was locked.

The window had cracked upon impact, and she only needed a little help from her baton to shatter glass.

Dow appeared dazed. A trickle of blood oozed down the side of his face, either from the Chevy's impact or the flying glass from the shattered driver's window.

She reached through the window, unlocked, and then yanked open the door. She grabbed a fistful of shirt and heaved him out onto the ground. For a few seconds, he remained facedown, eating dirt. He pushed the upper half of his body upward, seemed to gather his wits enough to feign outrage. "What the hell do you think you're doing?"

It was all she could do not to permanently crease his head.

Instead, she pulled his keys out of the ignition and tossed them into the high grass. Then she opened the back door and saw Kitally crumpled on the floor.

Hayley touched her shoulder. "Kitally, are you all right?"

Kitally moaned.

She was alive. A spurt of relief was quickly replaced with raging hot fury.

Mr. Dow had managed to get to his feet.

"You sick fuck," she said as she extended her baton and whipped him across the cheek. More blood. She didn't care.

He held up both hands.

She smacked him across the wrist.

He was back on the ground, screaming in pain.

She raised the stick high in the air. "What did you give her?"

"Nothing, I swear."

"Bullshit. Was it Rohypnol? Tell me what you gave her or I swear I'll break both your legs." She sighted down the baton at one of his knees, then raised the stick high again, ready to strike.

"Gamma 10. I didn't give her much."

Leaving him alone, she returned to Kitally, hooked the strap of her bag over her shoulder, and then pulled her outside into the fresh air. With one arm around Kitally's waist, she led her, stumbling, through the high grass to the Chevy's passenger door. Once she had Kitally inside and the seatbelt latched, she got behind the wheel, turned on the headlights, backed away from the Mercedes, and drove slowly away, following the trail of flattened grass until she found the spot where she'd knocked over the fence.

Back on the road, she stopped to take a breath.

Kitally opened her eyes and groaned. "Did we get him?"

"Yeah," Hayley said before driving off. "We got him good."

CHAPTER 4

Jolted awake, Lizzy sat up in bed and looked at the clock on the nightstand. It was almost eight in the morning. She hadn't fallen asleep until well after three.

She could hear shouting downstairs. Cathy and Richard were fighting again.

Her eyelids felt heavy from lack of sleep. She couldn't take any more of their crazy fights. Her sister's ex-husband, Richard, was a bona fide dick. Her sister, Cathy, had zero confidence and couldn't stand not having a man, so she'd allowed the two-timing son of a bitch back into her life. It was hard to conjure up much sympathy for her sister, though. No wonder her niece spent most weekends at her friend's house.

Lizzy slid out of bed, went to the door, and opened it so she could hear what they were fighting about this time.

"I'm not going to tell you again," Richard shouted. "You're not going anywhere!"

"Please keep your voice down," Cathy said. "Lizzy's been to hell and back, and she's finally resting."

"I don't give a shit. She's been trying to drive a wedge between us since the beginning of time. And if you really want to end this discussion, all you have to do is call your friend and tell her you're not going."

"I don't understand what your problem is. Just because *you* had an affair doesn't mean I would do the same thing. I'm going shopping with Stella. You've met her before. You have nothing to worry about."

"Stella is a slut. The only thing she's shopping for is a man."

"So what if she is? She's single."

"My mind's made up. You're not going."

With a shake of her head, Lizzy turned back to the room where she'd been living for the past three weeks. What was she doing here? She needed to get out of here, find a hotel—anything but this. She thought about the house she'd shared with Jared. She wasn't ready to go back there yet. Her therapist might think she was in denial about everything that had happened, but that wasn't the case. She wasn't in denial. She just had zero desire to spend time in a house that would bring back nothing but memories of her time with Jared. Despite wanting to hold out hope like everyone else, she knew what the deal was—Jared was in a vegetative state and would most likely never awake from a coma. As soon as the doctors made that official, she would do what they'd each promised the other they would do if this situation arose: sign the necessary papers that would let him slip away. Until then, though, she just wasn't ready to think about a future without him. Given the line of work they were both in, she and Jared had talked many times about the possibility of something bad happening to one or the other. But that didn't mean she wanted to live in the house they'd once shared and have the memories thrown in her face every time she turned around. When she was ready to deal with those emotions, she would go back to the house. Until then, she would find somewhere else to stay.

She replaced her T-shirt with a fresh one and slipped on a pair of jeans. She retrieved her suitcase from the closet, then opened the dresser drawers one at a time, gathered her belongings and tossed them into the luggage. Once her toiletries were packed up, she was ready to go. If Cathy wanted to live with the douche bag, let him boss her around and tell her when she could take a pee or go to the store, that was her problem. Lizzy refused to stay another minute under the same roof with that man.

She went to the window and looked out.

The street was quiet.

He wasn't there.

She had no idea who the dark figure was. She'd seen him watching her at Heather's funeral and then at the hospital just the other day. All she knew about him so far was that he stood well over six feet, and that he was following her. Which gave her one more reason she needed to leave, since she didn't want to put her sister or her niece in danger.

Lizzy snapped on her holster and gun, grabbed her suitcase, and headed down the stairs. She took quiet steps, figuring she wouldn't bother saying goodbye since she didn't want to get in the middle of their squabble. But the *SMACK* followed by glass shattering against the tile floor stopped her cold.

She set her suitcase at the bottom of the staircase and headed for the kitchen.

Richard had Cathy shoved against the refrigerator.

Red in the face, Cathy beat her fists against his chest, trying her best to get him off her.

A frenzy of emotion curled up inside Lizzy as she unlatched her gun from its holster.

"Lizzy, don't."

She shoved the barrel into the back of Richard's head. "Get your hands off my sister or I'm going to blow your fucking head off."

Seemingly unafraid, he let go of Cathy and turned on Lizzy instead. "You're a psycho freak. Get out of my house or I'm calling the police."

"This is my house, too," Cathy said. "She can stay as long as she wants."

Lizzy kept the gun aimed at him, but then she saw a family picture, Brittany front and center, smiling, happy to be with both of her parents. She sucked in a long breath and counted to three, something she often did when she needed to regroup and focus. Feeling defeated, she put the gun away and went to the phone instead. "I'll call the police for you."

"Please don't," Cathy said, her voice a whisper.

"What are you doing?" Lizzy asked her sister. "Do you really want this man knocking you around and telling you how to live your life?"

"This right here," Richard said, motioning between the two sisters, "is what's really fucked up." He pulled his keys from his pants pocket. "I'm going for a ride so I can cool off. If you're not here when I get back," he told Cathy, "I'm having the locks changed."

They watched him walk out the front door and slam it behind him.

Lizzy looked at her sister. "He's hitting you now?"

"No, of course not."

Lizzy shook her head. "Of course not. You have red indentations from his fingers on your neck after that little scene. And you don't think I've noticed the fingerprints he leaves on your arms or the black-and-blue eyes beneath the dark sunglasses?"

Familiar silence fell between them.

Lizzy walked to the front door, picked up her suitcase, and added, "Brittany isn't stupid, either. Your daughter knows exactly what's going on. And this is *your* house, Cathy, not his. He gave up his rights a long time ago. Kick his ass out of here before one of you does something you'll both regret."

CHAPTER 5

In the dead of night, Hayley no longer hung around the old house she'd once shared with her mother.

She had a new place to watch: Apartment 8C off Cornerstone. The place belonged to a known rapist. Like all rapists, he had a name, but she preferred to call him *Almost Dead*.

She never understood why perverts like this particular guy were released after a couple of years, only to set out and find someone else's life to destroy.

He would rape again.

That was a no-brainer. Eventually he would get caught again, serve a few more years behind bars, and then get out to do it all over—a vicious circle.

Yeah, she knew two wrongs didn't make a right. She also knew Almost Dead might get his just due in another life, but that wasn't good enough. It wasn't right that pricks like the guy living in 8C could go on destroying lives and get away with it.

Not under her watch.

Ever since Brian's death, she'd known what she needed to do.

Things were going to change around here. She couldn't get them all. Couldn't save the world. But she could and *would* do her best to rid Sacramento of one scumbag at a time.

The lights inside the man's apartment had been turned off a while ago, so she put out her cigarette and made her way back to her car and drove off. Although she planned to take him out eventually, she needed to be patient. In fact, she had rules that she intended to follow:

a) Catch him in the act; *then* kick his ass.
b) Do whatever it takes to make sure he would never be able to strike again.
c) Don't get caught.

It was quiet and dark, and her thoughts, as they often did, went to Lizzy's wedding. Tonight was Thursday night. Almost three weeks had passed since Jared and the others had been shot down.

Hayley and Kitally had headed for the shooter the moment they heard shots fired. Hayley had managed to get in the shooter's blind spot, but Kitally hadn't been quite so lucky. She was fast and managed to drop to the floor mostly out of firing range—but only mostly. A bullet had grazed her head, leaving a noticeable indentation in her hairline that Kitally had already managed to turn into a fashion statement. Not exactly a lightning bolt across her hairline, but close.

Magnus Vitalis, DEA, had been even less lucky. He'd taken a bullet in the spine and might never walk again.

Jared, the target of the shooter's rage, had taken a total of five bullets and was all but dead.

And then, at the farthest, darkest reaches of the luck scale came the four people who had died that day.

Hayley had brought the shooter down, but not before all that blood had been shed, not before all those lives had been wrecked or lost. So, no, not a hero. At least not as far as she was concerned.

Not ready for sleep, Hayley found herself driving down J Street. It was two o'clock in the morning, and Lizzy's car was parked outside the investigative office.

Hayley parked behind Lizzy's car.

The night was dark and the air was brisk. Through the front window, she saw Lizzy sitting at her computer, both feet propped high on her desk.

When Hayley opened the door to the office, she got a whiff of alcohol.

Lizzy's head rested on the back of the chair, both eyes closed, an empty shot glass in her right hand.

Hayley cleared her throat.

Seemingly unsurprised by Hayley's appearance, she opened her eyes and said, "Hey."

"Hey."

A half-empty bottle of Scotch with a red bow stuck to the label sat on the desk.

"Grab a cup and help yourself."

"No, thanks," Hayley said. "What's going on? You're not sleeping here, are you?"

A throaty laugh erupted. "What if I am?"

Hayley took a seat in one of the two chairs facing Lizzy's desk. "I thought you were staying with your sister."

"Not any longer. Longest three weeks of my life."

"I guess your brother-in-law was there?"

Lizzy's head drooped, her chin nearly hitting her chest. "*Ex*-brother-in-law," she drawled. "I wouldn't be surprised if Cathy marries him again, though. My dumbass sister likes being pushed around and told what to do."

Lizzy's feet dropped to the floor. She sagged over her desk and somehow managed to fill her glass and swallow the contents in one gulp. Then she lifted the bottle and gave it a little shake.

"A wedding gift from one of Jared's college friends. According to the card, it was Jared's drink of choice back in the day. Who knew?"

"Why don't you come home with me and we can talk."

Lizzy wasn't the type to laugh easily, but she laughed now and she laughed so hard she fell back, causing her chair to almost topple over. Hayley jumped to her feet, but Lizzy managed to grab hold of her desk and regain balance. In the process, though, she knocked her elbow.

"Ouch and fuck."

Hayley sat down again. Lizzy met her gaze straight on. "You want to talk, Hayley?" She pointed a finger at her. "That's a new one. Hayley Hansen wants to talk. Everyone hear that? I'm all ears, Hayley." She filled her glass again. "Oh, by the way, thanks for taking out my wedding crasher. I keep meaning to thank you for that."

Hayley said nothing.

"You know, if I hadn't sliced off that bastard's head, I might be Mrs. Jared Shayne right now. Jared would be in Virginia discussing one case or another with criminologists and psychologists or whoever. Better yet, if I had quit this fucked-up business . . . that's all I had to do." Still clutching the shot glass, she leaned forward, her eyes unblinking. "If I had any sense at all, Jared would be sleeping next to me tonight, holding me close, telling me he loves me. But, no, I'm a glutton for punishment. That's how the sayin' goes, right?" She frowned.

Lizzy sat up straighter and took a sip of Scotch. "This shit really is good. You should try some." She sighed. "Enough about me. What are you up to tonight? Just making your usual rounds? Seeing who's been naughty and who's been nice?"

"Pretty much."

"What's the deal with you, anyhow?" Lizzy asked.

27

"What do you mean?"

"What goes on in that head of yours day after day?"

Hayley scratched her chin. "Not much. Nothing good, anyway."

"So how do you keep going, you know, living day after day in this shit-for-nothing world?"

"I guess I don't really know. It seems I wake up and before I know it, the sun disappears and another day has passed."

Lizzy appeared to be letting that soak in for a moment.

"It's not your fault," Hayley told her.

Lizzy swayed a few inches to the left, then put the glass to her mouth and drank up. She slammed the shot glass hard on her desk and said, "Bullshit."

"If it's bullshit," Hayley said evenly, "then everything you've been telling me for the past two years is also bullshit. If you could have prevented those deaths, then that means I could have prevented my mother's, too."

Lizzy looked sad. "Fuck. You're right. I'm a bullshitter. Just what we need . . . another goddamn bullshitter in the world." She folded her arms on her desk and laid her head facedown on top of her hands.

Hayley waited a moment before she said, "Lizzy?"

No answer.

Hayley came to her feet and walked around to the other side of the desk. She took Lizzy's purse and shuffled around until she found the keys to her car. Then she went outside and looked in the trunk. Lizzy's stuff was piled inside, just as she'd figured it would be. After transferring Lizzy's things to her own car, she went back inside to get Lizzy and take her home.

CHAPTER 6

A sliver of wintry morning sun snaked its devilish fingers through the blinds, its bright light clutching at the comforter and crawling up the bed until it pierced right through Lizzy's skull.

She pried her eyes open. Her efforts to lift her head were rewarded with more painful pinpricks to the brain. Where the hell was she?

The king-sized bed was covered in luxurious bedding. The headboard was cushioned with expensive cream-colored fabric that bordered on gaudy. The walls were painted a shimmering silver, making her feel as if she were in a Vegas hotel. The sheets and comforter were white and ultrasoft. The room was clean and neat, everything in its place.

The last thing she remembered was sitting in her office downtown, drinking a bottle of Scotch.

Hayley.

Bits and pieces of last night slowly came back to her. Hayley had shown up at the office at some ungodly hour. That's it. That's all she remembered.

A good fifteen minutes passed, maybe longer, before Lizzy was able to will her body out of bed. She caught a glimpse of herself in the mirror above the bureau. Not a pretty sight. Stringy, dirty-blonde unwashed hair, hollow cheeks and eyes: the ghost of someone she once knew. Wearing an extra-long purple T-shirt that she didn't recognize, she plodded her way into the bathroom. Hayley had gone to the bother of setting up her toiletries? The thought of Hayley organizing her toothbrush and toothpaste didn't compute, which meant somebody else had done it. She washed her hands and brushed her teeth, then left the room in search of answers.

This was no hotel—it was a house. A ridiculously large house. Halfway down a long stretch of carpeted stairs, she got a whiff of bacon. Her stomach rumbled in a bad way.

Despite the never-ending square footage, the kitchen was easy enough to find. Kitally stood in front of the stove, flipping pancakes.

"You're just in time. Bacon and pancakes. If you prefer eggs, I can make them to order."

"Just coffee. I just need coffee."

"Cream and sugar?"

"No, thanks. Black." Lizzy walked past the kitchen table so she could see into the main living area. Everywhere she looked, she saw beautifully carved columns and a combination of rich wood and stone floors. Leather seating. Minimal furniture. No decorative items to speak of. "Is this your house?"

"Actually it belongs to my parents. Once I turned eighteen, they moved to a bigger place in El Dorado Hills and left this one to me."

"You live alone in this mansion?"

"Not any longer. Hayley's landlord is selling her house, so Hayley needed a place to stay. There's plenty of room for you, too."

"Thanks, but no thanks."

"Why not?"

"I have my own house."

"Yeah, but you wouldn't be living at the office if you were ready to move back home."

The kid had a point, which was annoying as hell.

"Why don't you just think about it? I'll give you a key, and that way you'll have a place to stay if you need it." Kitally handed Lizzy a mug of coffee. "Hayley is in the office if you want to say hi. It's down the main hall. Last room on the left."

"Thanks. I'll do that." Lizzy found herself in a sewing room before she finally found the main hallway. Like every room in the place, the office was spacious. Hayley sat at a large mahogany desk in the center of the room. She was buried in papers, but she looked up and said, "Morning."

Lizzy grunted. "What are you working on?"

"Just trying to catch up on all the paperwork. We've got a half-dozen workers' comp claims that need serious attention. If you're feeling up to it later, we also need to meet with a very persistent woman named Pam Middleton. She sounded panicky on the phone and said it was an emergency."

Lizzy eased herself into a cushioned chair, propped her feet on the matching ottoman, and sipped her coffee. Was it possible for hair to hurt? Her hair hurt. "OK. So what does this Pam . . . whoever need?"

"She wants us to find the baby she gave up twenty-five years ago."

"Do we know why?"

"She said it was a matter of life and death. And she wants *you* to be there."

Lizzy sighed. "What time is it?"

"Ten fifteen."

"How about noon today?"

"Sounds good," Hayley said with a nod. "Did Kitally invite you to stay here at the house with us?"

"She did, but I'm not so sure it's a good idea."

"I disagree. You've been through some incredibly fucked-up shit. All you have to do is look in the mirror to see that much. You shouldn't be alone right now. Go ahead and drink yourself into oblivion, but do it here where we can watch out for you."

Lizzy looked around. "It's not a bad setup. I'll give you that."

"No rent, and breakfast is included. You can't beat it."

Lizzy took another swig of coffee. "I'll think about it."

CHAPTER 7

Jenny Pickett returned home from work, parked in the garage, and walked through the laundry room to her study. As a senior research chemist, she did consulting work for various health-care, pharmaceutical, and food manufacturers, helping both small and large companies with product development and testing. Depending on which company she was working for, five days a week, usually from eight to four, she could almost always be found in a lab, wearing goggles and a lab coat over her work clothes, which consisted of a skirt or slacks with matching jacket, unless the company had a low-key dress code. In that case, she might replace the jacket with a sweater.

She made her way down the hallway, straightening picture frames on the wall as she went. She liked order, structure, and symmetry. After setting the mail in a neat pile on the desk in front of her computer, she went to her bedroom and hung her purse on the wall hook. Robotically, she removed, examined, and then finally hung up her dark-blue jacket.

After that, she headed for the kitchen, where she washed her hands twice, making sure to get the areas between every finger before using a clean towel to thoroughly dry her hands. The last thing she did was pour herself a glass of cold water from the filtered pitcher in the refrigerator. As she held the glass to her lips, she spotted the knife block. Her right hand trembled slightly.

Back in her study, she sat at her desk. Usually the first thing she did each day was look through the mail, sorting bills from junk, but not today. Ever since she'd killed Brandon, she'd been unable to concentrate. Her moment of empowerment had been short-lived.

She reached inside her purse, unzipped the side pouch, and pulled out a small plastic container. Inside was one capsule, the size of a pea, filled with concentrated potassium cyanide. The pill was not to be swallowed whole. She would need to crush it between her molars.

She wouldn't suffer. There would be minimal pain, if any.

Coward. You shouldn't be the one to die for what happened to Brandon.

Her eyes watered. Her entire life had been filled with so much anguish and torment. But after all this time, she'd killed a man. Why now?

Long overdue.

She shook her head.

It's time to make a list, Jenny.

She stared at the pill within the container. The fast-acting poison would cause brain death within minutes. Her heart would stop soon after.

Put that away and make the list. Trust me. You'll feel better if you just make the fucking list!

OK! OK! She'd make the damn list. She put the pill to the side and set about finding a notebook and pen. She stared at the blank paper for a few minutes before finally reaching over and grabbing the article she'd been saving. She examined the picture of Terri

Kramer, her supposed friend—the woman who had stolen her antiaging formula and made headline news.

On the first line of the notebook, she wrote *Brandon Louis* and then drew a line through his name. Next, she wrote *Terri Kramer.* Beneath Terri's name, she wrote *Stephen White.*

The names came easily after that, one after another. With each came memories: insults, snickering, nasty words whispered in her ear. Every push and every shove came flooding back to her in vivid detail.

She swallowed the knot in her throat, surprised by the emotions so easily conjured, spilling forth, as if it had all happened yesterday. Not a day had gone by in high school that she wasn't pointed at, called names, and made fun of. One particular group of kids had been relentless in their taunting. The harder she had worked at becoming invisible, the more they had picked on her. Their actions had never made any sense to Jenny since she'd done nothing to earn their wrath.

She was the geek, the kid with no friends. All she wanted was to be left alone. The bullying had gotten so bad that there had come a point where she figured she deserved to be punished. Why wouldn't she be made fun of? She was the poor girl who lived on a pig farm, the girl with crooked teeth and thick glasses. She was the oddball with the bangs chopped off at odd angles, the kid who wore hand-me-down clothes and flimsy shoes without laces.

The teachers were no better. They knew what was going on, but they never lifted a finger to help her in any way.

Some memories of what the other kids did to her were too painful to bring forth: recollections so awful, she kept them locked tight in her memory banks; things that made being kicked and shoved into a locker seem like child's play; occurrences so horrifyingly humiliating and repulsive, she didn't dare call them up. Not now. Not yet. Preferably never.

After college, and after she'd started earning a decent paycheck, she'd gotten braces, contacts, ridiculously expensive haircuts, and new clothes. Even before the mini-makeover, she'd possessed a decent body, but in the end none of it mattered. One thing she'd learned very quickly was that no amount of scrubbing and perfume could hide the fact that she would always be the poor girl from a pig farm.

Always had been.

Always would be.

Mirror, mirror on the wall . . . who's the ugliest of them all? Jenny Pickett, that's who.

She reached for the small canister, and this time she removed the lid. One tiny pill could end it all. Put her out of her misery forever.

For a moment in time, Jenny had thought things could be different. She'd thought hard work and success would show all her haters that she didn't deserve their disdain.

But now she knew better.

All of those people who fucked with you are the pigs, not you! Why can't you see the truth? Don't you dare take that pill!

Jenny clamped her hands over her ears.

Look at the list again. Don't be a fool. They're the ones who deserve to die!

She didn't want to listen to the voice. She wanted to end her misery and be done with it.

Read the list, Jenny!

Jenny dropped her hands and forced herself to look at the names. This time, she read each one slowly, letting every syllable roll over her tongue. Each person on her list had done horrible things to her. It wasn't her fault they did what they did. They had a choice. It was them, not her. The hatred and disgust she'd felt for herself had been misplaced.

The realization caused her to feel a hundred pounds lighter.

Why hadn't she seen it before?

She put the lid back on the container and put the suicide pill away.

It's about time you stood up for yourself. Maybe you're not so spineless, after all.

~~Brandon Louis~~
Terri Kramer
Stephen White
Debi Murray
Gavin Murdock
Rachel Elliott
Melony Reed
Ron Jennings
Louise Penderfor
Mindy Graft
Aubrey Singleton
Claire Moss
Chelsea Webster
Dean Newman
Gary Perdue

After reading the names over and over, confident that these were the worst of the offenders, she sucked in a deep breath of air and then slowly exhaled.

This is your kill list. It's beautiful.

Yes . . . her kill list. Each and every person on the list would die, but she would need to follow a set of rules:

a) be smart,
b) be patient, and
c) do not get caught.

Making the list had been easy. Now she needed to work things through and put some thought into how she would end their lives.

She'd gotten lucky with Brandon. He'd kept their relationship a well-guarded secret, which turned out to serve her well. He'd never shared his private numbers with her, always calling her from airport pay phones.

But in the end, stabbing him had proved to be quite messy. Cleaning up all that blood wasn't easy. Getting rid of the rental car and Brandon's body had taken the entire night. Lining the trunk of her car, driving to her parents' farm, and then digging a hole in the middle of their fifty-acre parcel had been beyond exhausting.

How could she kill them without getting caught?

It can't be that difficult. You're a chemist.

She couldn't exactly bury any more dead people on her parents' farm. She needed to make the deaths appear to be random accidents. But how?

Do I have to repeat myself? You're a chemist. Poison.

She straightened in her seat. It couldn't possibly be that easy. She went to the wall of books lining the shelves and brushed her fingers over the spines: *Organic Chemicals, Pharmacotherapy: A Pathophysiologic Approach, The Pharmacological Basis of Therapeutics, Handbook of Pharmaceutical Excipients,* and—there it was. *Toxicology: The Basic Science of Poisons.* Perfect.

CHAPTER 8

Pam Middleton walked into Lizzy's office downtown at exactly twelve noon. She wore dark slacks, a white sweater, and a strand of pearls. Her blonde hair, streaked with auburn, was pulled back with a clip. Her face looked pinched, her eyes tired. Her lips appeared as a thin red line.

After introductions were made, Lizzy gestured for Mrs. Middleton to have a seat in the empty chair next to Hayley.

"Thank you for meeting with me on such short notice."

"Not a problem. Hayley told me that you need us to locate someone for you. Why don't you give us the specifics?"

The woman's hands were clamped tightly on her lap. "Everything we talk about today will remain in the strictest of confidence?"

Lizzy and Hayley both agreed.

"Twenty-five years ago, at the age of sixteen, I had a baby girl. My boyfriend, Dillon, and I struggled with the decision to give our baby up for adoption, but in the end we felt we had no choice. We were young. My parents threatened to throw me out of the house. His parents were devastated. It was a horrible time. Neither of us had a job. There was no way we would be able to provide for our child."

The woman took a steadying breath before continuing. "So the decision was made, and, because we thought it was only fair to the adoptive parents that we stay out of the picture, we never looked back."

Mrs. Middleton toyed with her pearls before she found her voice again. "Seven years later, I married Dillon and we went on to have another child. A daughter."

The woman's eyes watered and her bottom lip quivered. She took a moment to gather her thoughts while Hayley and Lizzy exchanged looks, both waiting for the other to offer words of comfort and support. Instead, they merely sat there, unmoving and blank-faced.

"Recently," Mrs. Middleton went on, "our sixteen-year-old daughter developed severe stomach cramps and was rushed to the hospital. Within twenty-four hours of bringing her to the hospital, we learned that she had a rare form of leukemia."

"I'm sorry," Lizzy said.

A tear dripped down the side of Pam Middleton's cheek.

Lizzy offered her a tissue.

The woman dabbed at her eyes and then said, "After my daughter is given radiation and chemo, she'll need a bone marrow transplant to replenish her red blood cells."

"What happens if she doesn't find a donor?" Hayley asked.

"She'll die."

"You need the daughter you gave up to save your younger daughter," Hayley stated.

"Yes," the woman said. "Can you help me find her?"

CHAPTER 9

As Kitally sat in the car, slumped down low, her eye on the house across the street, she couldn't help but think that all three of them—Lizzy, Hayley, and herself—were in way over their heads.

They had never been busier.

They had so many workers' compensation cases that Kitally and Hayley were forced to divide up the cases and go out on their own. There was no reason to have two people during long days of surveillance sitting in the car, but that did make for a tedious day.

Right now, Kitally was working on three different cases.

Howard Chalkor was one of them.

According to his claim, he couldn't lift his right arm due to an on-the-job injury. The worst part of this particular case was that Kitally had thought she was done with Mr. Chalkor after she'd gotten some great shots of him and his son loading a truck with furniture. But the insurance company, picky sons of bitches, said the photos were blurry and unacceptable, which was ridiculous. She had a top-of-the-line camera and her photos were on par with Hayley's and Lizzy's.

At last, Mr. Chalkor came through the front door, looked over his shoulder, and shouted to someone inside the house. He then slammed the door shut and lit a cigarette as he made his way down the path leading to the sidewalk.

He didn't get far before a woman came running after him. Towing a dog, a Samoyed, she handed him the leash. They exchanged heated words before she turned and marched back to the house.

Mr. Chalkor did not look happy. The frown lines in his face were deep, making him look much older than forty-two. With the smoke in his left hand and the leash in his right, he stalked off, heading away from where Kitally was parked.

Every time Chalkor yanked on the leash, Kitally gritted her teeth. Not only was he using the arm that was supposedly injured; he was hurting the dog. More than anything, she wanted to take that leash and wrap it around the man's neck—show him what it felt like to be yanked and pulled.

As he rounded the bend, she thought about pursuing him by car but opted to shadow him on foot. She grabbed her camera, locked her car, and followed his trail.

Once Mr. Chalkor and his dog were back in view, she took a picture every time he yanked on the leash, which happened a lot, since he wouldn't allow the poor dog to even smell a bush, much less take a pee.

She watched Chalkor join a group of people and their dogs in the dog park. It wasn't long before he'd singled out the prettiest woman and struck up a conversation with her, forgetting all about the dog at his side. No wonder the woman back at the house wasn't happy with him.

Figuring now was a good time to check the pictures she'd already taken, she found a bench and took a seat. The pictures were good, but yanking on a dog's leash wasn't exactly the same as lifting heavy furniture. She would have to call the insurance company and see what they thought. Maybe if she got video of

Chalkor yanking on the leash instead of still pictures. She sighed. More than likely, she would have to come back again.

"Hey you."

Kitally looked up, surprised to see Mr. Chalkor standing right in front of her. He was a stocky man—five-ten and well over 250 pounds.

"Yeah you," he said.

"Can I help you?"

He lifted a stubby finger. "I'm going to give you a warning, but only one. Stay away from me."

"I don't know what you're talking about."

"Next time I see you sitting in your car taking pictures of me and my family, I'm going to make you wish you had minded your own business."

"Are you threatening me?"

"Damn right I am."

CHAPTER 10

Jenny parked her car a few blocks away from the apartment building. The clothes she had on were recently purchased from Goodwill: a tight-fitting beige V-neck sweater, pleated skirt, and two-inch heels. She was going for the librarian look. She would need to find out where to get more wigs like the red one she was wearing today. It was fine, but the selection at Goodwill had been too sparse for her needs.

She'd also bought a used computer from a guy on Craigslist because she planned on researching the people on her kill list—find out where they lived and what they were up to. If they lived out of state, she put them aside for now.

After everyone on her list was exterminated, she would destroy the computer. Although she sort of liked being a redhead and looked forward to being a blonde, she'd have to get rid of all the wigs and accessories, too.

In the center of the plate she carried was a chocolate cake. She'd made it herself using unbleached all-purpose flour, eggs, sugar, the best-quality dark chocolate she could find, rich European butter, and a healthy dose of cyanide.

Her shoes clacked against the cement stairs as she made her way to the third floor of the apartment building. She had checked out the place a few days ago. There were two cameras: one outside the main office and another one on the front of the building facing the main parking lot.

Standing outside Apartment 32B, she drew a deep breath, then rapped her knuckles against the door. As she waited, her heart pounded against her chest, a little bit harder with each passing second.

She'd been sitting in her car a block away, waiting and watching, when she saw Terri Kramer pull into the parking lot.

She knew Terri was home.

Jenny was about to knock again when the door opened. Terri Kramer in the flesh. She'd gained a few pounds since college, but overall she still looked young and confident. Her hair was darker than Jenny remembered and was cut short. She had big eyes and red, kissy lips stolen right off a *Betty Boop* comic strip.

Terri still looked the same, but Jenny didn't. There was no possible way Terri would recognize her. She didn't look anything like the Jenny Pickett from their college days.

"Hi! My name is Kasey Trumble, and I just moved into the apartment building last week. When I heard that a famous chemist lived in the building, I decided to bake a cake and take a minute to introduce myself."

"I'm sorry," Terri said. "I really don't have time to talk right now. I'm rushing off for a business trip. Another day maybe?"

She's not falling for it. I told you it was a dumb idea. You better get your ass inside that apartment before someone sees you.

"Oh, I see," Jenny said. "I just thought since we're both research chemists and being that you are everything I aspire to be, well . . . gosh, never mind."

"You're a chemist?"

Jenny nodded.

Terri bit down on her bottom lip. "I really am in a hurry. How about next week?"

"Does the trip you're going on have to do with the antiaging serum you developed? If so, you better get your people to make sure your patent is airtight."

The corners of Terri's red bow lips turned downward. "Why do you say that?"

"Like I said, I'm a chemist. A woman I work with showed me a write-up on you in the *Journal of the American Chemical Society*. She swears on the Bible that she knew you in college and then worked with you at Pfizer, and that she came up with the formula first."

Terri's face turned a shade of green. "What's her name?"

"Jenny Pickett."

Jenny gave the news a minute to settle into Terri's brain waves. Then she said, "Don't tell me you really know Jenny Pickett?"

"I do," Terri said. "Why don't you come in and tell me what else she said."

"Are you sure? I know you're busy."

"I'm sure, and, besides, that cake looks delicious."

"Great," Jenny said, making quick work of getting inside the apartment, relieved when Terri shut the door behind her. "I'll just give you the details," Jenny told her, "and then skedaddle out of here."

Terri Kramer seemed to be in a daze, which was understandable, considering the news Jenny had just dumped on her.

Get this show on the road! Get some plates.

The apartment was small. The kitchen, dining, and living areas were all lumped together. Jenny pointed to the kitchen. "Where do you keep your dishes?"

Terri pulled two plates from a cupboard. "Would you like hot tea or milk?"

"Milk would be great," Jenny said as she took a seat at one of four chairs surrounding the dining room table. There was no time for awkward silence. "Wait until you get a taste of this chocolate miracle. My grandmother passed the recipe on to me. It's to die for."

Really?

Terri seemed to be in her own world as she poured them both glasses of milk and then took a seat at the table across from Jenny. Since she hadn't cut into the cake yet, Jenny took the knife and did the honors.

In a matter of minutes, Terri's demeanor had transformed from a confident woman in a hurry to an apprehensive woman awaiting execution.

"Are you all right?" Jenny asked. "You look sort of pale. If it's about Jenny Pickett, I wouldn't worry too much about anything she says. Everyone at work thinks she's a bit strange, if you know what I mean."

"No, I guess I don't understand."

The cake. Make her eat the cake and then get out of here!

"Before I explain further," Jenny said, "I insist you try a bite of chocolate heaven. I want to know what you think."

Terri did as she was told. She nodded her approval and even took a second bite before chasing it down with some cold milk. "That is quite good."

"I'm glad you like it."

As Terri ate, Jenny rambled on, making up stories about her coworker. "Jenny is so reserved. Beyond reserved, really. Strange, like I said. She doesn't have any friends that I know of. She brings a brown paper bag lunch to work and keeps to herself."

Terri shrugged as she took another bite and followed it with a sip of milk. "I've met a lot of chemists over the years and most seem to be introverted."

"Really?"

Terri nodded. "I don't think Jenny Pickett ever realized how brilliant she really was and is."

"Brilliant?"

"Definitely. But the one thing she always lacked was confidence. It was sad, really, the way she let people walk all over her." Terri took another bite. "This cake is delicious—dense but so moist."

"I'll give you the recipe before I go."

What's taking so long? Why isn't she dying? Don't tell me you fucked this up.

"Shut up," Jenny said under her breath.

"What?"

Jenny touched her throat. "Sorry, I was just trying to clear a tickle."

It was quiet for a moment. Terri had put her fork down and appeared to be staring at her plate.

"I'm sorry if I upset you. I never should have told you about Jenny Pickett in the first place."

"No, I'm glad you did."

"You didn't really steal the formula from her, did you?"

Terri looked across the table at Jenny. There was a defeated look about her. "I think I need to call Jenny. You wouldn't happen to have her phone number, would you?"

"Why? What would you tell her?"

"I would tell her—" Terri put a hand to her chest. "I don't feel good." She pushed her chair away from the table and stood. "You'll have to excuse me. I think I'm going to be sick."

Jenny watched her stagger away. She got halfway across the living area before beginning to topple. She took hold of a cushioned chair and was able to fall gracefully back on the carpeted floor. As she lay faceup, her gaze fastened on the ceiling, the muscles in her body contracted and then relaxed, again and again, until finally her legs and arms began to shake uncontrollably.

The next few minutes were excruciatingly long. Jenny didn't move from her seat. She just wanted it to be over.

Quit being a baby. You're finally sticking up for yourself. She deserves to die, and you deserve to watch her do it.

Another moment passed before Jenny stood and walked over to Terri. She hovered over her, knowing she couldn't leave until she was certain Terri was dead.

Terri stopped shaking long enough to reach both arms upward toward Jenny. "Please help me."

Jenny's plan had been to pull off her wig and reveal herself while she watched Terri die. Jenny had even gone out of her way to look into the mirror and practice what she would say: *Who's the clever one now? Who has the last laugh?* But she couldn't do it. She walked back to the kitchen and picked up the phone, ready to dial 911.

Don't be stupid. The bitch stole your formula and took all of the credit. If she had any respect for you, she would have contacted you months ago. Nobody likes you. Brandon treated you like a whore. The people on your list all treated you like trash. It's time to stand up for yourself. It's time to take control.

Jenny looked over her shoulder at Terri and saw that she was no longer moving.

She set the phone down and slowly, methodically retrieved gloves and a plastic bag from her purse. She took all the dishes from the table. Poured out the milk, washed and dried every dish, wiped fingerprints from the phone, table, and chairs. She dumped the cake along with the plate into the plastic bag, making sure to seal it tightly before putting it inside her oversized bag. When there was nothing left on the table or in the sink, she wiped down all the furniture one more time. She then removed and folded the gloves, tucked them into her bag along with everything else. She peeked out the peephole to make sure nobody was outside. It was all clear.

She stretched the sleeves of her sweater over the fingers of her right hand, making sure not to leave prints on the door handle. And then she dared one last look at Terri, whose eyes were wide open. One thin trickle of blood seeped from the corner of her mouth.

It'll get easier. I promise.

CHAPTER 11

Two o'clock Thursday, while Lizzy taught her defense class downtown, Kitally and Hayley continued the search for any clue that might lead them to the daughter Pam Middleton gave up twenty-five years ago.

"I think I found the man who adopted Mrs. Middleton's baby," Hayley told Kitally. "Dan Blatt of Rocklin, California. He's fifty, which would be the age of the man we're looking for. He works at Ramsland Realty." Hayley stood. "Let's go."

Kitally raised a brow. "Why not just give him a call?"

"People are more apt to give out information if we talk to them face-to-face."

"You don't think he'll tell us where his daughter is living?"

"Not over the phone."

"Maybe she still lives at home."

"If so, we'll find out. Let's go."

"Can we take my car?" Kitally asked.

"You have a problem with my Chevy? The vehicle that almost gave its life rescuing you from the slimy clutches of that creep Dow?"

"The vehicle that almost took my life, you mean! You could've launched me through the back window with that heap of metal."

"That's gratitude for you," Hayley muttered.

Kitally shrugged. "I seriously think it's time for you to put that thing to rest."

"Come on—let's go," Hayley urged. "This has taken too much time as it is."

"Should we leave Lizzy a note?"

"No. She'll call if she needs us."

"Do you think Lizzy will be OK?"

"I know she will be."

"There must be something we can do for her," Kitally said.

"We're doing it. We just need to give her space."

It was quiet for a bit before Kitally changed the subject and asked, "When we see Mr. Blatt, what's the plan?"

"I'll know what to say when I see him."

Twenty minutes later, Hayley and Kitally walked in and then right out of Ramsland Realty after they were told Dan Blatt sometimes worked from home. Today was one of those days.

"Let's take a ride to his house," Hayley said. She looked at her notes and then punched his home address into the navigation system on her cell. "It's less than ten miles from here."

Dan Blatt's white stucco house looked like every other house on the block: two-car garage, front window, shutters, a small square of newly mowed front lawn, and a stone pathway leading to the door.

Hayley rang the doorbell.

The woman who answered was all dressed up: charcoal pencil skirt, white blouse, and black heels. Her head was angled as she worked at putting on an earring.

"My name is Hayley Hansen, and this is Kitally. We're looking for Dan Blatt."

"I'm his wife." Finished with the earring, she straightened for a better look at who was standing at her door. "What's this about?"

"We're looking for Dan Blatt's daughter."

"Sorry, girls. You have the wrong Dan Blatt. We don't have any children."

A heavyset man with a bald head and a bird's nest of a mustache came to the door. "What's going on?"

"These girls are looking for the daughter of Dan Blatt. I told them they had the wrong man."

"Sorry to bother you," Kitally said before turning to head for the car.

Hayley looked into the bald man's eyes. "Did you adopt a little girl twenty-five years ago?"

He opened his mouth, closed it, and then looked at his wife.

"I told you—we never had children," the woman repeated.

"Is your name Barbara?" Hayley asked.

The woman frowned. "That was the name of Dan's first wife, but she passed away a few years before Dan and I met."

"Who exactly are you looking for?" Dan asked Hayley, obviously shaken up, nervous. "Do you have a name?"

"We were hired by Pam Middleton to find the daughter she gave up twenty-five years ago. It was a closed adoption, but Mrs. Middleton saw the names Dan and Barbara Blatt in the file at her attorney's office."

"I don't think I can help you," Mr. Blatt said, his face pale, his eyes downcast as he reached past his wife for the door, clearly ready to get rid of them.

Kitally was back at Hayley's side. "Mr. Blatt," she said flatly. "Your adopted daughter has a biological sister. She's sixteen and she has leukemia. There's a real possibility she'll die unless she can find a match. Your daughter might be her only hope for survival. Are you sure you can't help us?"

His wife's face was pinched, her body stiff. "Dan, what's going on?"

He sighed as he rubbed the top of his head. "Barbara and I adopted a little girl. We named her Debra. Four years later, Barbara was dead." His head bowed. "I was grief-stricken. So was Debra."

Debra Blatt. They finally had a name. Hayley was about to ask about Debra, but his wife saved her the trouble.

"What happened to your daughter? Where is she?"

"I called the adoption agency and told them I couldn't take care of a child on my own." Dan Blatt's gaze caught Hayley's. His jowls shook as he said, "I couldn't even take care of myself."

"They took her back?" his wife asked him. "Can they do that?"

"No," he answered. "It's complicated. Barbara's mother took Debra, and I haven't seen her since."

Hayley's stomach churned. Just one more misplaced kid. It never ceased to amaze her. People treated children worse than dogs. The child no longer suited his lifestyle, so he gave her away—decided to let someone else deal with her? *Unbelievable.* "You gave your four-year-old daughter away without—"

Kitally stepped in front of Hayley, cutting her off. "Please, Mr. Blatt. Can you give us information about Barbara's mother— tell us where we can find her? We need to talk to her as soon as possible."

"Of course he will," his wife said. "You girls stay here. I'll be right back." She shut the door. Through the decorative glass, they watched her usher Dan back into the main part of the house until they couldn't see either of them.

"Sorry about that," Kitally said. "I didn't want to interrupt, but I didn't think ripping the man apart was going to get us the answers we need."

"People like Mr. Blatt need to grow a fucking pair. Who does he think he is? The only person in the world who's had someone die? Jesus." Hayley turned around and headed down the path. "I'll wait for you in the car."

As she had done every day since the shooting, Lizzy walked into the hospital room at Sutter General and sat in a chair pulled up close to the bed. She clasped her hand around Jared's fingers and proceeded to talk about whatever came to mind. "I miss you." She paused. "Did I tell you that I'm living with Kitally and Hayley?" She forced a laugh. "I couldn't live with Cathy and Richard for another moment," she told him. "You're probably wondering why I moved in with my sister to begin with. It was a stupid idea, I know." She paused, smiled at Jared, then leaned closer and brushed the back of her hand over his cheek.

He looked so peaceful.

"Open your eyes, Jared. Talk to me."

She watched him. Waited.

"Squeeze my finger so I know you're here with me."

Nothing.

A nurse came in. She checked Jared's vital signs, wrote down numbers on his chart. "He looks good," she said in a cheerful voice that grated on Lizzy's nerves. "It says here that Dr. Calloway wants to speak with you."

Lizzy stared at Jared, willing him to wake up, praying for a miracle.

"Did you hear what I said?" the nurse asked.

"No."

"Dr. Calloway would like to talk to you."

Lizzy looked up at the nurse, then followed her gaze, which was directed at the door. She was surprised to see Jared's sister, Lynn, standing there.

Lizzy stood and gathered her coat from the back of the chair.

"You don't have to leave," Lynn said.

"I'm afraid I must. I'll come back later."

Lynn stepped into the room and released a long, drawn-out breath. "I realize my father never warmed up to you, Lizzy, but surely you understand why he's fighting you on this. Jared is his only son. The two of you weren't even married—"

"Jared signed an advanced directive," Lizzy said calmly. "This was Jared's decision. Not mine. He did not take any of this lightly."

"But you're not family."

Lizzy stiffened. "When was the last time you called your brother?"

Silence.

"Exactly. Why don't you ask your mother and father the same question. The three of you didn't even have the decency to call Jared after wedding invitations were sent out. And yet you can stand here now and tell me you know what's right for a man you haven't seen in years?"

Lynn shook her head. "You don't know about our family, Lizzy. You certainly can't judge us."

"Too late for that."

Lynn narrowed her eyes, then heaved another sigh. "Jared always had a blind eye when it came to you."

"And what exactly does that mean?"

"He had the whole world at his feet. He could have done so much, gone so far, but you probably have no idea what I'm talking about."

"Why don't you tell me."

"Before you came back into his life, Jared was gearing up to go into politics."

Lizzy snorted. "That's the most ridiculous thing I've ever heard."

"It's true. Ask Jimmy Martin if you don't believe me."

Lizzy inwardly counted to three. "Even if it were true, what's your point, Lynn?"

"The moment you came back into my little brother's life, I knew Jared's future would be a dark one. We all knew."

That blow landed, but Lizzy didn't let on, just lifted her chin a notch. "You're all so selfish. You don't give a damn about Jared's wishes. This is all about *you*. This is about *you* and your parents wanting power and control over Jared, something you all never had while he was growing up." Lizzy raised her hands in frustration. "I get it now. I know why Jared picked me to make this horrible decision . . . He knew I loved him and that I would put his wishes before mine. He also knew his family would always put themselves first."

Lynn closed the distance between them and slapped Lizzy's cheek. Lizzy could've stopped her—could've done a lot of things—but she let it happen, maybe even welcomed it.

Lynn stepped back and put a hand to her mouth, seemingly stunned by her actions. Then she whirled about and left the room as quickly as she'd come.

After turning back to Jared, Lizzy fixed his hair, then leaned over and kissed his forehead.

When she looked up, she saw the same nurse still standing on the other side of the bed. The scene she'd just witnessed was more than likely going to give her a lot to talk about at the nurses' station. Lizzy looked at her and said, "Do you think you could give him a sponge bath?"

"That was taken care of this morning. It's right here on—"

"I'll be back tomorrow."

"What about Dr. Calloway? He did ask me to—"

"Please tell him I'll have to talk to him some other time. I'm sure he'll understand." Lizzy walked out of the room before the nurse could protest further. Lizzy wasn't ready to hear what Dr. Calloway had to say. Jared's family would probably be surprised if they knew that they weren't the only ones clinging to the irrational idea that Jared could still somehow pull out of this.

CHAPTER 12

Jenny Pickett pulled into the garage, closed the roll-down door, then took the long way around the side of her house to gather the mail. On her way up the walkway, she took a good long look at the house she'd bought two years ago and even found herself looking at it in a new light. It was small, but it had a lot of potential. The house could use a new coat of paint. She'd never had a green thumb, but for some reason she thought it might be time to hire a landscaper, too—clean the place up a bit. Maybe plant some roses or a couple of nice-smelling camellia bushes.

She inserted her key and opened the door. Two weeks after killing Brandon, it seemed to her she was morphing into a whole new person. She was learning to break away from the same old routine. She held her head high at work and made eye contact with coworkers. She had even dared to join another table of people in the cafeteria during her lunch break today. Although she didn't say much, nobody had seemed to give it a second thought, nor did they appear to be put off by her existence. One of them, Dwayne Roth, even smiled at her and took her tray from the table when she finished eating.

Jenny left the pile of mail on her desk, and then changed into comfortable clothes before walking back to the kitchen. In celebration of the changes she'd made, she set the table, complete with a crystal glass, candles, and a cloth napkin. When dinner was ready, she admired the table setting, then turned on the television and rolled the TV table to a place where she could watch the news while she ate. Before sitting down, she went to her office to get her list.

~~Brandon Louis~~
~~Terri Kramer~~
Stephen White
~~Debi Murray~~
~~Gavin Murdock~~
Rachel Elliott
Melony Reed
Ron Jennings
Louise Penderfor
Mindy Graft
Aubrey Singleton
Claire Moss
Chelsea Webster
Dean Newman
Gary Perdue

She sat up taller when she heard the Channel 3 anchorman say Stephen White's name. That was fast! Apparently Stephen barbecued more often than she'd dared hope.

"The thirty-one-year-old Auburn man is dead, and three others were also injured after a quantity of gunpowder exploded at Oakhaven at approximately 8:30 p.m. last night."

Access to the property was blocked, but a Detective Quincy said the incident was most likely a "freak" accident. "Just friends getting together for a barbecue," he said.

"We believe Stephen White was killed instantly. He was pronounced dead at 8:45 p.m."

Jenny couldn't believe it. Her idea had worked.

Even back in high school, everyone had known that Stephen was an avid gun collector. He used to brag about his and his father's collection of muskets and what skilled muzzleloader marksmen they were. A ridiculous passion, but Jenny felt certain it wasn't something he'd give up.

She was right.

After learning where Stephen lived, it was easy enough to make some flyers about Christian life and then dress up in a short black wig with bangs that swept over one eye. She'd done her homework and she already knew Stephen was in construction and was working on a remodel in Granite Bay. After knocking on his front door and getting no answer, she pretended to be looking for the occupant of the house and walked around to the back. She didn't even have to break in. There, in an unsecured shed—Stephen was no brighter now than he'd ever been—she found shelves loaded with bags of gunpowder. She made quick work of setting up the barbecue using her own mixture of the stuff and nitroglycerine.

The only thing she'd left to chance was the timing. She had no idea when Stephen White would use his barbecue next, especially since summertime was months away. She hadn't been sure if Stephen had children, and the idea of harming an innocent child had weighed heavily on her mind.

You were innocent once. Nobody worried about you. Don't be an idiot.

She continued to listen to the anchorman. Investigators had spent the day talking to neighbors and family members who were inside the house when the explosion occurred. Investigators were analyzing gunpowder from the scene, confused by the rarity of such an odd event ever occurring.

Jenny picked up the knife and fork in front of her and took a bite of perfectly cooked chicken, chewing as she listened to the rest of the report.

Three of Stephen's friends had minor injuries, but they would be OK. Bully for them. She had no intention of hurting anyone who was not on her list. But accidents did happen and could not always be avoided.

Stephen was dead. She set her fork down, picked up the pen, and drew a straight black line through his name.

Her thoughts turned to Terri Kramer. She still hadn't seen anything on the news about her death. It was a little annoying. Surely word would've gotten out if her body had been discovered.

Let her rot.

Jenny shrugged. She supposed it wouldn't hurt for whatever evidence she might've left behind to degrade a bit.

As she looked over her list, she took another bite of savory chicken, making sure to chew at least twenty-five times before swallowing.

Rachel Elliott was up next on her list.

What about Debi Murray and Gavin Murdock? Why are their names crossed off the list?

"Where have you been? Easy smeasy." The minute Jenny had discovered that Debi drove an old car, she'd parked next to Debi's heap in the lot at her workplace, then pretended to be fixing a tire when really she was cutting into Debi's brake line. Just a small leak, mind you. Although Jenny wasn't sure if the idea was based on old Hollywood fantasy, she figured it was worth a shot. The accident was in the paper the other day. The poor woman had taken the highway home and went right over the side of the road. Died instantly.

Clever.

To say the least, Jenny thought. As for Gavin Murdock, he was a football coach for a bunch of peewee third graders. Built up a whale of a thirst, she noticed, and wasn't too careful about where he set down his Gatorade. Next game, she'd swapped his for one laced with antifreeze. Terrible thing. First he'd seemed drunk on the sweet stuff. Really made quite a scene. Parents were already shepherding their precious boys away from him when he started vomiting. And then the heart failure. She'd read his obituary the other morning. The paper had been gentle about it, glossing over his obvious drinking problem and focusing on the heart attack angle. "Doesn't get much easier than that," she said with a smile.

Don't get cocky. You still have Rachel to worry about.

According to Rachel's Facebook page, she liked to run after work. Jenny had already driven through Rachel's Folsom neighborhood on three different occasions and confirmed that this wasn't just Facebook showboating. Rachel was serious about her exercise. Every night, like clockwork, she exited her house and then jogged past her neighbors' homes before turning off a private trail that led to Folsom Lake.

Jenny sipped her water and tried to come up with another perfect murder.

There's no such thing. You're not exactly a criminal mastermind.

True. She was new at this. Fingerprints used to be the big deal. A murderer who didn't use gloves was an idiot. Now she had other things to worry about, like tire tracks, ballistics, mobile phones, blood, hair; you name it. Most criminals got caught because they didn't strategize. Bodies turned up eventually, which was why she planned to make sure Brandon's body decayed at a rapid pace. She usually had dinner with her parents once a month. Next time she visited, she intended to take some lime. Dead animal burials on the farm used to be covered with hydrated lime for pathogen reduction. With all the rain that was expected in the coming days, she worried that Brandon's body might eventually float to the surface. She also needed to worry about rats, coyotes, and dogs carrying off a foot or a bone.

Brandon is old news. What about Rachel? What are you going to do, trip her while she's running?

She swallowed another bite of chicken and nearly choked from excitement. Trip her! That's exactly what she would do. She would make a spear, a wood spear—plenty of them, just to be sure. She would rub the ends with aconite, also known as monkshood or wolfsbane. Back in the day, before the nineteenth century, *Aconitum napellus* was thought to have some toxicological importance. In her line of work, research chemists often used the plant for drug testing and treatment, regardless of the fact that there were much safer herbs and medicines to experiment with.

She could barely contain her excitement.

Rachel usually took her runs right before dark. There were plenty of trees on both sides of the trail. Jenny could tie a vine, camouflaged by nature, from one tree to the other. Rachel would trip and fall on the poisonous tips of tiny wooden spears protruding from the soil.

She had her work cut out for her, but Brandon was right. Standing up for herself was the best thing she'd ever done. Sure, she'd experienced misgivings at first, but that was in the past. She'd come to terms with what needed to be done. She was sleeping better than ever, refreshed, ready to begin each new day. For the first time in her life, she was finally taking control. And she liked it.

Out of the corner of her eye, a picture on the television screen caught her attention. Her next breath hitched in her throat. *Oh, my God! They finally found her.*

Terri Kramer, famed research chemist, found dead.

Jenny stopped laughing when the news station showed the video, then showed it again. A woman crossing the street near Terri Kramer's apartment building. The ten seconds of video was out of focus, but there was no mistaking the red wig and pleated skirt.

You dumb bitch.

The newscaster asked anyone who might recognize the woman shown in the video to call in. Then they plastered a 1-800 number across the screen. Following the announcement was a prerecorded video of the crime scene: cop cars, a dozen of them, yellow crime tape across Apartment 32B, and a body bag brought out on a stretcher and lifted into an ambulance.

Only two cameras, huh? How stupid could you be?

Deflated, Jenny took her plate and glass to the kitchen, dumped the food into the garbage, and then put on a pair of rubber gloves and began to scrub.

CHAPTER 13

"You worry too much," Lizzy told Jessica as she kept her hands on the wheel and her eyes on the road.

"I'm going to see if I can get a few days off and come for a short visit."

"It's been sort of hectic," Lizzy told her. "I appreciate the thought, but it's really not necessary."

"Class is starting in a minute," Jessica said. "I have to go, but we're not finished with this conversation, OK?"

"Whatever you say. Go to class. We'll talk again soon." Lizzy hit the Off button on the console, shutting off their Bluetooth connection. Jessica Pleiss had joined Lizzy Gardner Investigations as an intern when she was attending Sac State. They had been through a lot together. Recently, Jessica had been accepted into the FBI Academy, located on a Marine Corps base in Quantico, Virginia. She was enrolled in a twenty-week training course, and, as far as Lizzy was concerned, she needed to stay in Virginia and focus on her studies.

Parking was tight around Melony Reed's house off Fuller in Granite Bay, so Lizzy parked at the junior high school across the street and walked the half block to her place. Melony had called, told her it was an emergency. Lizzy didn't plan to be in the office today, so she'd told Melony she would stop by this afternoon.

The only thing Lizzy knew about her was that she was newly divorced and more than a little bitter toward her ex-husband, who had run off with his secretary and taken everything with him, including her pride.

A light rain sprinkled the walkway as she made her way to the door.

Melony Reed greeted her before she could knock. The woman was tall and thin. Her cheekbones were sharp, and a thick layer of foundation was losing out to the gray circles under her eyes. She looked like a Stepford wife: a little too perfect in her sleeveless pink formfitting dress and pearl necklace.

Melony opened the door wide and said, "Thank you for coming."

Lizzy followed her inside. The interior was traditional: calm, orderly, and predictable. Everything was impeccably tidy.

Melony bent down to pick up an invisible piece of lint from the hardwood floors and said, "Excuse the mess."

After Lizzy turned down an offer of tea and coffee and they were seated in the living room, Lizzy said, "If you don't mind, I'd like to get right down to business. It's been a crazy week."

Melony agreed.

"During our phone conversation, you said that you were afraid for your life."

"That's correct."

"You also said that you talked to the police, but they can't help you."

"Correct."

Lizzy pulled out paper and pencil and peered into a pair of cat-shaped eyes. "Why don't we start from the beginning?"

The woman's hands were clasped in her lap, her spine as straight as a post. "In the past three weeks," Melony said, "four people from my high school have died."

Lizzy waited for her to go on, but Melony seemed to think that bit of information was enough to sound the alarms. "And?"

"And I'm afraid I might be next."

"People die all the time." Lizzy knew that firsthand.

"You sound like the police."

Ouch.

"One freak accident might be overlooked, but four so close together? The odds are astounding."

"How did they die?"

"Stephen White was blown up while barbecuing a steak. People barbeque every day. Tell me that's not a little peculiar? Debi Murray was the next to go. She was driving on the highway when her brakes went out. She hit a divider and went over an embankment. Died instantly. And then Gavin Murdock, a health freak, had a heart attack on his thirty-first birthday. Concerned, I called my friend Rachel Elliott. She didn't have time to talk for long, but I asked her if she'd heard the news about the others, which she had. We set a time to meet for coffee the next day, but she didn't show up. It turned out, thirty minutes after I talked to Rachel, she was dead—tripped and fell during her evening run."

"How? Did she hit her head on a rock?"

"No. Get this—she fell on a cluster of punji sticks, the same sort of sharp upright bamboo sticks that were used in the Vietnam War."

"What did the police say about that?"

"They're still looking into it, of course, but they believe kids in the neighborhood were playing around. The police report indicates that the sticks weren't sharp enough to kill anybody and therefore they believe Rachel died of a heart attack before she even hit the ground. Absurd."

It was quiet while Lizzy made notes.

"I'm scared," Melony said. "I don't know what to do."

Lizzy looked up from her notes. "Were you close to any of the other people who've died beside Rachel Elliott?"

"At one time . . . yes. We were all very close, which is why I'm worried. We were in the same club back in high school." She stood and went to another room. When she returned, she handed Lizzy a thin spiral notebook. "If you open it up, you'll see that I wrote down the names of everyone in the Ambassador Club. There were thirteen of us."

Lizzy flipped the notebook open. Thirteen names, just as she said. A few phone numbers and addresses were scribbled in the margins. "You believe everyone on this list is in danger?"

"I do. I haven't been able to locate three of the people on the list. They could have moved away or maybe they're dead, too. As you can see, I've made notes—anything I thought might be helpful to you."

"Have you called every name with a number?"

"No. Rachel was the only one on the list who I contacted. After she died, I went to the police. Then I called you."

"How did you get my name?"

"Detective Chase."

Lizzy tried not to grimace, but it wasn't easy. Did Detective Chase think this was amusing? That man was a walking, talking asshole. He obviously didn't take the woman seriously. And, well, Lizzy could hardly blame him. Melony was definitely skittish; although it was difficult to tell whether she was nervous or scared. She kept crossing and uncrossing her legs, making Lizzy think she might be feeling guilty instead of frightened. Was she doing this for attention? It happened, far too often.

"Why don't you tell me more about your club," Lizzy said. "I'm having a difficult time figuring out why you believe anyone would want to do you or anyone else in your group harm."

Melony stood and then walked around a bit before white-knuckling the back of her chair. "Because we were mean," she blurted, then slumped forward in defeat.

Lizzy lifted a brow. "Mean as in *Mean Girls*?"

"Yes, but our club included boys, too. There were eight girls and five boys."

"Was that the club's intention? To be nasty to other students?"

"No. The group was originally formed with the idea of making an exclusive club for VIP students."

"VIP students?"

Melony looked heavenward as if she were exasperated, which annoyed Lizzy. Getting any real information out of the woman was like waiting for water to boil.

"Rich kids," Melony said. "Kids who simply preferred to hang out with like-minded people."

Lizzy set her notebook aside so she could rub the bridge of her nose. Detective Chase was going to get an earful.

"I know what you're thinking."

"No," Lizzy said. "I don't think you do. If you did, you might see how very silly your group sounds to an outsider."

"You shouldn't be so quick to judge. Rich kids are taunted, too. We were treated like outliers, so we decided to band together and do something about it."

"Are you saying that kids picked on you?"

"In the beginning, yes. But our group rallied together quickly. They didn't have a chance after that."

Lizzy pulled in her emotions. Her mother used to tell her that two wrongs didn't make a right. But she wasn't here to lecture the woman, so she kept that one to herself. One thing she never understood or cared for, though, were bullies. "OK, so you started this exclusive group, but it somehow became more of a mean-kid group?"

"Yes," Melony said. "More or less."

"And now you think somebody on the other side of the Ambassador Club's backlash is coming after every single one of you?"

"I do."

"Any idea who that might be?"

Melony began to pace the room. "It's not easy to narrow the list down. I'll be the first to admit that we got carried away. By the time our class graduated, I would chance it to say that there weren't too many people who liked us."

"That must have been painful."

"Not really. We had each other. At least in the beginning."

"And then what happened?" *Please tell me you all grew up.*

"It wasn't until our ten-year reunion two years back that I realized how deeply the scars ran. Dean Newman, one of the boys in our club, talked to me at the beginning of the night. He wanted to know how I was holding up and whether or not the guilt was getting to me. He went on to tell me that he had become an alcoholic and recently joined AA. A few weeks ago, I heard from Dean again. As part of his treatment, he'd vowed to apologize to every single person he might have caused harm."

"And he just called you out of the blue recently to let you know?"

"Not exactly. He called me because he wanted names."

"Of the victims of your abuse?"

"Yes," she managed, unable to look Lizzy in the eyes.

"Did anyone in your group cause verbal *and* physical harm?"

"A few."

"Did you?"

"A shove there, a push into the locker every once in a while. Nothing to get worked up about."

Lizzy held in a moan.

"Mostly just the usual kind of stunts kids pull in high school."

Lizzy cocked her head. "Could you fill me in, please? What are the usual stunts?"

"You know, taking someone's clothes while they're in the shower or taking the older kids' keys and moving their car to a spot a few blocks away. Things like that."

Lizzy was making notes. When she looked up, Melony was chewing on her bottom lip.

"There's more, isn't there?"

"I wasn't involved, but two of the guys and Rachel did kidnap a girl once and take her on a ride."

Lizzy tried to remain calm. "What was the girl's name?"

"I don't know. I was going to ask Rachel when we met up, but like I said, she was dead by morning."

"Do you know what happened to the girl you're talking about?"

"I just know it was bad."

Lovely. "Anything else?"

"It all happened so long ago. I'm sure there were other incidents, but I'll have to think some more."

"You do that. As things stand right now, if someone really is causing these accidents, from what you said it could be almost anybody."

Melony pointed at the notebook next to Lizzy. "I also included a list of students who I believe were picked on the most, including people I consider to be unstable, based on things I've heard."

Melony disappeared for the second time. This time she returned with an envelope and handed it to Lizzy.

"What's this?"

"A thousand dollars. A deposit. If my douche bag of an ex-husband wasn't hiding all of his earnings, I would be able to give you more up front. As it is, I was planning on remodeling the kitchen, but that will have to wait. For now, I'll have to set my budget at ten thousand dollars."

Lizzy held up the notebook. "You've given me a long list of names of people who were affected by the Ambassador Club's tormenting. This could take forever and a day to reach out to all of these people, let alone narrow the list of suspects down to ten . . . or one. In two or three months' time, your money could be spent and you might not be any closer to the truth than you are right now."

"Are you saying you won't take the job?"

"No. I'm just letting you know that you might be better off spending that money on security around here. An alarm, perhaps a camera installed outside. Keep your car in the garage. Be vigilant about locking your doors and windows."

"I could move in with the chief of police and I still wouldn't feel safe. I need to know who's behind these killings. I need you to say yes. If you agree to do this, I'll feel safer knowing that every time we take someone off the list of suspects, we'll be one step closer to finding the person responsible."

Lizzy stood and gathered her things. She held up the envelope. "I'll get started right away."

"I appreciate it."

Lizzy shook her hand. It was a done deal.

She disliked Melony Reed, and she wasn't sure she even wanted to take on the job, but the idea that Detective Chase was responsible for this woman coming to her for help spurred Lizzy onward.

Somehow, someway, she'd make the big man eat crow. Again.

CHAPTER 14

Eighty-year-old Donna Kingsbury talked faster than an auction-eer on speed. And louder, too, although she needed to talk loudly if she wanted to be heard over the television blasting in the other room. Mrs. Kingsbury stood in the middle of the kitchen in her trailer home wearing a flowery muumuu, nylon knee-highs, and slippers. The place smelled like old dishrags and cat pee, which made sense when an orange-and-white cat appeared from the other room and began to weave around her thick ankles, its tail curling around her calves.

Hayley had been listening to her talk for ten minutes non-stop. Her cavernous mouth just kept running like a faucet that couldn't be turned off.

She couldn't remember it ever being so difficult to get infor-mation out of someone. Adoption searches were usually easy. Hayley could do them with her eyes closed. But getting anything useful out of this crazy lady felt never ending.

The good news was Donna Kingsbury lived in Citrus Heights. At least she hadn't had to drive too far.

Kitally and Hayley had learned from their short visit with Dan Blatt that he'd been unable to handle all the grief stemming from the death of his first wife and had asked his mother-in-law, now ex-mother-in-law, to take care of his daughter for a few weeks. A few weeks turned into a few months and a few months turned into years. At least, that's what Mr. Blatt had told them. The man was slime. How could you give away your daughter as if she were a cat or dog and then never look back?

"That child was the devil's offspring," the old woman assured her. "I always wondered if Barbara and Dan made a trade with some new-aged gypsies."

Hayley opened her mouth to speak, but she wasn't fast enough.

"I don't have too many good things to say about Dan, either, you understand. That man couldn't take care of a cactus, let alone his own wife and daughter. My Barbara deserved better. She would probably still be alive if it weren't for that man taking advantage of her, forcing her to slave over him day and night.

"As Mrs. Kinsbury droned on, Hayley found herself wishing she'd waited for Kitally to return from her morning surveillance, another workers' comp claimant with an alleged neck injury. Kitally had patience, and she knew how to handle people like Mrs. Kingsbury.

When the old lady finally paused for breath, Hayley jumped in. "Please, Mrs. Kingsbury, I need to know what happened to Debra Blatt."

"I told you already. I gave her away."

The words came out so fast, Hayley thought maybe she heard her wrong. "You gave her away?"

"Damn straight," she said, lifting her chin, daring Hayley to judge her. "She was nothing but trouble."

Another cat appeared. This one was solid black.

"I had four cats at the time, and she used to pull on their tails. Once she started peeing in the bed, I couldn't take it any longer."

"How long did Debra live here with you?"

"Two hellish years. She must have been five or six when I finally called social services and told them they needed to take the girl or I was throwing her out on the street." The woman snorted. "That did the trick."

"Do you know where she is now?"

A spider skittered out from under the carpet and onto the linoleum. The woman was fast, though—she jumped on the thing, putting her whole body into killing it with the bottom of her slippered foot. "What do you mean do I know where she is?" She guffawed. "It's been close to twenty years."

"You haven't stayed in touch with your granddaughter?"

"No. Why should I? She wasn't my blood. I only took her in because Dan promised to pay me, which he never did."

Having heard enough, Hayley started for the exit.

"She must be close to twenty-five years old now," the woman shouted after her. "Wait. Did she die and leave me some kind of inheritance? Is that why you're here?"

Hayley had never been much for words, but it took everything she had not to turn and verbally rip the old hag to shreds.

"That's it, isn't it?" the woman screeched after her. "My granddaughter died and she wants to help out her ol' Grandma."

Hayley stepped outside without bothering to shut the door behind her. Away from the stench, she inhaled.

"You come back here right now and tell me how much she left me!"

Hayley pulled a tape recorder from her back pocket and pivoted so that she was facing the old woman, who'd skittered after her as far as the doorway. "It's true," Hayley told her. "Debra married well. She had millions when she died, but her will specifically states that we can only disperse monies to the people who loved her most." Hayley smiled and held the recorder in the air for her to see. "I'm so glad we had this talk. I can't thank you enough for being so frank with me. I've got everything the estate attorney needs right here."

It was a ludicrous lie, but this was a ludicrous, awful old woman. It felt sweet to watch her mouth fall open, and sweeter still to hear no words come out of it.

CHAPTER 15

The house was a fortress, Lizzy thought, with never-ending hallways and a lot of unused rooms, wasted space. She had no idea where Kitally and Hayley were, but she wasn't their mother and she wasn't about to call and check up on them.

She was a visitor, a temporary guest, nothing more.

Lizzy left the office at the end of the house and headed for the kitchen. She wasn't hungry, but she hadn't eaten all day. She would force something down. Maybe some soup. She walked across the hallway, each step echoing off the polished wood floors.

She felt suddenly very alone.

A sharp creak froze her blood.

She took a step backward. Right there, where the hallway transitioned from wood to stone.

CREAK.

A loose board. That's all it was. Nothing to worry about.

She stepped into the living room. Moonlight spilled in through high windows, shedding an eerie light over still unfamiliar terrain. Most of the furniture, in her opinion, was cold and uninviting. She'd never claimed to have any sort of flair for interior design, but the place needed a makeover—a throw rug and a few decorative pillows.

In the kitchen, she looked out the window above the sink. One of the girls usually turned on the outside lights, but since neither of them was home, the lights weren't on. It was pitch-black out there.

A *tap-tap* on the window nearly brought her out of her skin. Instinct kicked in. Both hands shot up, her gun clasped unsteadily between them, her finger on the trigger.

She saw nothing but the dark expanse of the lawn and the black trees beyond.

She took a few breaths before finally pointing the gun at the floor. Hadn't even realized she was carrying her gun around until that moment.

Her heart pounded against her chest. She'd heard a tap; she knew she had.

"Hayley, is that you?"

No answer.

She needed to calm down.

She locked her gun in her holster and concentrated on finding a damn light switch. Once she located the first switch, she flipped on every one she could find in the place. By the time she was done, the front yard was lit up like Christmas.

Better.

She could see past the front lawn all the way to the mailbox.

She unlocked the door and stepped outside, leaving the door open. A couple of acorns and a branch lay on the ground in front of the window. She looked up. A tall oak was the culprit.

Back inside, she sucked in a deep breath.

The cat circled her legs. Hannah. *Where did you come from?* She'd forgotten all about the cat. Never once in these past few weeks had she wondered or worried about Hannah's fate.

Lizzy sank to the floor and scooped the cat into her arms, holding her close. Hannah purred against her chest as Lizzy ran her fingers through soft fur. "I'm sorry," she whispered. "I'm not good at taking care of animals. I warned you right from the beginning, you know."

More purring.

"Let's get you something to eat."

Lizzy stood, leaving Hannah to follow her to the kitchen. Like the outside, the entire house was lit up, giving plenty of light as she searched cupboards and finally the pantry, where she found everything she needed.

After feeding Hannah, she warmed up some vegetable soup. It had no taste, but she ate it because she'd told her therapist she was eating every day.

Her cell phone rang. She pulled it from her back pocket and hit Talk. "Hello?"

"It's me . . . Kitally."

"Hey, where are you guys?"

"I don't know what Hayley's up to, but I should be home in thirty minutes. I just thought I should let you know."

"Are you checking up on me, Kitally?"

"No, of course not. Why would I?"

"No reason," Lizzy said. "Thanks for taking care of Hannah. I didn't realize she was here until two minutes ago."

"She likes to hang out in my room. I keep dry food, water, and a cat box in my bathroom."

"Oh."

"How's it going over there at the house?"

"Fine," Lizzy answered. "Everything's fine."

"Well, OK, I'll see you soon. If Hannah starts meowing, that means she's ready to go down for the night. She sleeps in the bed with me. And she likes it if you turn on the television."

"You sleep with the cat?"

"Yeah, why? Is that a problem?"

"No. Not a problem."

"OK, well, see you soon."

After Lizzy hung up the phone, she realized she didn't know what to do, didn't know what to say, didn't know what to think. Nothing made sense any more.

The cat wouldn't stop meowing, something Hannah never did before. Lizzy snapped her fingers as she led Hannah down the long hallway to the room where Kitally slept. The master bedroom was bigger than an apartment. The bed could fit an entire family in it. She leaned over, picked up Hannah, then settled her gently on the middle of the down comforter.

Lizzy sat on the edge of the bed, even found herself smiling as she watched Hannah curl into a ball and settle down for the night. Lizzy picked up the remote from the nightstand and then joined Hannah on the bed. She rested her back against the soft pillows as she scratched Hannah between the eyes and pushed the Power button.

Channel 10 News came on, the images on the screen a blur as she thought about Jared lying alone in the hospital. Nighttime was always the worst. Lizzy had asked the doctors and nurses if she could stay with him, but the hospital had rules and strict visiting hours.

Jared was in coma.

At times like this, the idea of it seemed surreal.

During the first week that Jared was in the hospital, she'd left a portable radio close to his pillow, but the nurse told her he couldn't hear anything. It wasn't long before she'd overheard the nurses talking in private: Jared's body was shutting down, one organ at a time. They were losing him. But before she'd had a chance to talk to Dr. Calloway and sign the necessary papers, Jared's family showed up and chaos quickly became the norm. His dad started making threats, unable to comprehend that his only son had signed his life over to Lizzy. At least that's how Mr. Shayne saw things. He had petitioned the court for guardianship over Jared's health. Until the court decided what to do, it didn't matter what Dr. Calloway had to say about Jared's condition.

Lizzy tried to think of happier times but saw nothing—a blank slate. It wasn't happening, and she couldn't seem to force it. She felt nothing. All of her senses had deserted her. No taste. No memories. No emotions.

"Freak accident," the on-site reporter said into the microphone. "Melony Reed died after slipping on her kitchen floor and landing upright on a cutlery basket."

Lizzy sat up and turned up the volume.

A picture of Melony Reed, the same woman she'd met with flashed across the screen.

"Melony Reed managed to get to the phone and dial 911," the reporter said from outside Melony's home, a house Lizzy recognized because she'd sat inside the living room with her just over forty-eight hours ago, "but she died shortly after arriving at Sutter General."

As soon as a commercial aired, Lizzy rushed to the other room to grab her laptop and the list of names Melony had given her. Back on the bed, Hannah curled up closer. Lizzy's fingers clacked against the keyboard as she got to work. Melony Reed graduated from Parkview High School in 2002. There were over six hundred in her graduating class. Some of the school's notable graduates included politicians, athletes, and a journalist. Lizzy scoured the Internet for anything she could find on Melony's personal list of suspects.

She read the scribbled notes next to each name: mentally unstable, suicidal, abused by parents, et cetera, et cetera, which in Melony's narrow-mindedness made these particular people capable of murder.

And now Melony was dead.

As much as Lizzy hated to admit it, the woman had been onto something. The coincidence of another "accident" was just too damned far-fetched. Having access to a much broader database than Melony made it easy to cross a few people off the list. If someone had moved out of state, Lizzy put a dark line through their names and jotted down their new locations just in case she'd need it down the road.

By the time she heard a car pull into the garage, half of the names had been crossed off the list.

Big deal, Lizzy thought. No matter how many names she eliminated, it didn't change the fact that once again she had failed someone. Melony had been right when she'd said Lizzy sounded like the police. Lizzy had taken the case for all the wrong reasons. Melony was dead, and Lizzy hadn't done a damn thing to help her.

CHAPTER 16

A sliver of a moon shone above him, shedding little light. Not enough light to leave a shadow as he emerged from the depths of tall oaks. He made his way around the house, careful not to make any noise as he checked each door and window.

He felt neither excitement nor fear. No emotion whatsoever.

Sometimes he wondered if he was human.

Since being released from prison, he'd been living outside among the stars and trees. He'd slept in parks and playgrounds, on rooftops and in abandoned buildings. Deep in the woods was where he kept his few belongings. To keep up appearances, he made a weekly trip to the public library, where he used the bathroom to shave and wash up. Food was easy enough to find if you knew where and when to look through Dumpsters.

He was a Dumpster diver.

He was a survivor.

He was a killer.

The truth was, he was also human, but his needs were mostly animalistic. He possessed an indifference to all but his physical needs . . . and now Lizzy Gardner, and his need for vengeance.

When he was younger, when he actually cared what other people thought, when he had hopes and dreams, he was what one teacher called socially awkward. He was excessively shy, and he had a lot of anxiety back then.

Retarded, moron, loser. He'd been called a lot of things in his lifetime, but that was because nobody had ever understood him. Nobody knew who he really was. Nobody cared.

People liked to say that everyone in the world had a mother and everyone had a father. What a joke. Some people just weren't meant to procreate. Period. He used to think his mother was a magician: one minute she was there and the next she was not. His father was the embodiment of anger and fear—a raised hand, a harsh voice, pain and suffering tied to everything he said and did. Together they raised a paranoid, confused kid who seldom went to school. Every once in a while, a nice young lady or man from the state would stop by to check up on him. They would ask his mother or father, or whoever the hell was around, a few questions as they filled out some forms. They always left with concerned expressions on their faces, but the same person never came twice. There was a short time, maybe a week or so, when he'd been dropped off at his grandparents' on his mother's side, and there was a golden moment in time when he'd hoped that they might be his saviors. But no sooner had his grandmother fondled him under the pretense of wanting to be sure he was healthy and whole than he'd found his grandfather down at the lake, drowning the kittens they'd found that very morning at the end of their driveway.

That particular day was forever engraved in his mind.

That was the day he'd lost *all* hope.

Putting old memories behind him, he withdrew into the dark among the tallest trees in the backyard of the large house, where a creek ran along the back of the property. Everything was locked up tight, including the windows framing the downstairs bedroom, the only room with the lights on.

She was in there.

He was sure of it.

He'd followed her here from her downtown office the other day. It seemed he'd been watching Lizzy Gardner for most of his life, or at least had known of her. In fact, he thought he knew everything about her, but he had to admit, he wasn't exactly sure why she was staying at this particular residence. After the death of her fiancé, it made sense that she'd moved in with her only sister. But it made even more sense to see her move out, away from her brother-in-law. The man had the innate sort of stupidity that came from being born with inferior genes. He'd thought about killing him just for sport, but that would only serve to make Lizzy happy. The last thing he wanted to do was make her happy.

Lizzy Gardner had ruined his life.

She was a bitch, and he planned to fuck with her, starting with her students. He had one picked out. The one she obviously cared for the most. His greatest regret was that someone else had tried to kill her fiancé before he had a chance to. Lizzy deserved everything she got. She liked to meddle in other people's business. His business.

He closed his eyes, breathed in nature's scent. His name was Frank Lyle.

Frank's first kill was an accident, more or less. Happened when he was having sex with a girl. First time in his life. She'd gotten all bitchy, called him impotent and shit like that. He had wanted to shut her up . . . quick. So he'd killed her. Strangled her. Then he'd shoved his dick down her throat and it was amazing how hard he got.

He never got caught for that one.

He'd killed two more girls after that, and it was the second whore who sent him to prison. Two days after he killed Jennifer Campbell and left her body in Folsom Lake, the second whore, the one he'd strangled and left on the side of the road, managed to trick him. She'd played dead, and, after he left her, she had found a way back to civilization. When he was brought in for questioning and told that the girl was alive and well, he didn't believe it until he saw her in the courtroom. There she was, sitting at the witness stand looking prim and proper, whining and crying as she recounted the horrors he'd put her through. She sure could tell a story. Made him sound like Jack the Ripper. Not once did she mention that he'd washed her up each night and heated her up some soup, even fed it to the bitch.

The jurors took less than an hour to come to the conclusion that he was guilty and should be locked up. They gave him ten years without parole. And they didn't even know about the first two chicks he'd killed. The woman he'd thought he'd killed had told such a titillating story, word got around fast that, as far as rapists went, he was about as bad as they got.

It made no sense. He was put away for what? He didn't even kill the bitch!

But that was nothing. Next thing he knew, rumors were flying and every dead body that floated to the surface of a lake or body of water was being attributed to him. He was being called "Spiderman," a serial killer everyone was in a lather about.

Prior to Frank's incarceration, at least four young girls had been abducted and murdered, their bodies left in various locations throughout Sacramento. Each child was held captive for months before being killed. The string of deaths had triggered a murder investigation, one of the largest in the history of the state. Hysteria reigned. Parents stopped dropping off their children at bus stops. Young people were afraid to walk outside without an escort. Playgrounds were empty.

Until somebody got the bright idea to hang the crimes on mad rapist Frank Lyle, since he was handy.

At first he didn't like the crush of attention being thrown his way. Suddenly, everybody wanted to interview Frank Lyle. But as it snowballed, it started growing on him. He was a celebrity, even wound up on the cover of *Time* and *People*. For the first time in his life, he was somebody. Everyone knew his name. Everyone wanted to talk to him. His face was all over the news. Over the next decade, Frank aspired to have his image on serial-murder trading cards, comic books, T-shirts, and calendars. Book deals were in the talks—even a fucking movie!

And then, poof! Lizzy Gardner came onto the scene and told the media that Frank Lyle was merely a wannabe and a copycat. After that, every doctor in California was saying that he had a pathological need for notoriety and that he was delusional.

He passed the damn polygraph. Didn't that mean anything?

Saying he bore a grudge would be downplaying his feelings toward Lizzy Gardner. He resented her. Hated her. Abhorred her. For the first time in his life, he'd had an identity . . . He'd been somebody. And she took it all away.

As it turned out, the real Spiderman had indeed come back to town to take care of unfinished business. But Lizzy Gardner proved resilient and took care of Spiderman once and for all.

Having served his time, Frank was promptly released. With his newfound anonymity, he quickly became unrecognizable. People didn't look twice when he walked by. His book deal had crashed and burned. Nobody cared what he did or where he went.

He was back to being what he'd always been—a nobody.

But not for long.

As he planned and plotted, he felt a stirring of excitement building within. He felt alive again. He'd risen from the dead, and this time he would make them all pay. Nobody was safe. Not the granny walking less than a block from the bus stop. Not the jogger

on American River trail or the speed-walker taking a quick break
from work. Over the years he'd been watching, learning. Random
acts of killing kept the police in the dark. And nobody liked the
dark better than Frank Lyle.

CHAPTER 17

Jenny Pickett looked around her old bedroom at her parents' farmhouse. The yellow walls were faded and chipped. Every time she came home, the room appeared so much smaller than she remembered. The mirror her mother had made for her when she was little, framed with wood and feathers and lots of glue, still hung above a three-legged dresser.

The mirror had been purposely cracked because at the time her mother thought that would give it a unique, vintage look, but what it did instead was freakishly distort the reflection of anyone who looked into it. Jenny had always hated the thing, thought it was the ugliest gift any parent could bestow upon their only child, but looking at it now, with new eyes, she thought differently.

Turning, she viewed her profile. Her shoulders were no longer hunched over. When had that changed?

Facing her reflection straight on, she leaned forward, peered into the broken pieces of mirror, and smiled. Even the cracks couldn't hide a straight white smile and killer eyes. Pun intended. She smiled at her own wittiness. The pitiful farm girl was transforming, growing more confident with every passing day.

You're not the fairest of them all. You came here for a reason. Now get busy.

She made her way down the hallway, the wood floors creaking and shifting beneath her feet. In the kitchen, Mom stood at the stove, using a wooden spoon to stir all the leftovers from their meal in a giant banged-up pot. Leftover stew. Mom had been making it for as long as Jenny could remember. Only one burner on the stove worked, but somehow Mom had managed to cook a lot of meals.

The blue curtains framing the small window above the sink, the scarred trestle table, and the mismatched slat-back chairs—everything was the same. Nothing had changed.

A sigh escaped as she watched her parents for a moment longer. Mom had never been considered a good cook, but whatever she served up on any given day always did take care of the hunger pains.

Don't forget how many times you got food poisoning. You'll be sick by midnight, guaranteed.

Dad was sitting at the table, fiddling with his napkin. He wasn't all there these days, but he still had random moments of clarity. Mom had been forty-five when she'd given birth to Jenny in the back room of this very house. Dad had been fifty. Now he was eighty and sliding downhill fast.

Usually she visited her parents once or twice a month, but for reasons that couldn't be helped, she hadn't been to the farm in nearly two months, not counting her midnight jaunt into the field to bury Brandon's body. That was the reason she'd come tonight. After the recent rains, she couldn't stop worrying about his body floating up to the top of his makeshift grave.

You better get moving. Brandon's corpse could be resting in the neighbor's yard.

"I'm going to take that bucket of scraps to the pigs," Jenny told her mom.

"No need to do that, dear. Harry will be here to feed all the animals in the morning."

"That's OK—I *want* to do it. I want to see the pigs before I go."

"You'll get your nice clothes dirty," Dad said.

"You both need to stop worrying about every little thing. I'll go to the barn first and slide into one of Dad's old painting garments before I head for the pen." She looked at Mom. "Do you mind finishing up the dishes by yourself?"

"Not at all. You go have fun with the pigs. Rosa is about to have her litter any minute now. Oh," she said before Jenny got to the door, "watch out for the new boar. He's eight hundred pounds and mean as they come."

"A boar? Why do we have a boar?"

"Mr. Higgins is moving away soon, and he knew how much your dad always liked the big boar, so he gave it to him. Maybe you should go say hello to Jack before he moves on to greener pastures. He's always been fond of you, you know. Talks about you as if you were his own daughter. Such a sweet man."

About as sweet as a bite of sour apple with a squirt of lemon juice, Jenny thought but kept it to herself. The last person in the world she wanted to talk to or think about was the next-door neighbor. Mr. Jack Higgins was rotten to the core. Of course, Mom had no idea of the things he'd done to sabotage Jenny's relationship with his eldest son, Bobby. As it turned out, Mr. Higgins had had big plans for Bobby, and those plans had not included Jenny Pickett.

Without another word, Jenny grabbed the bucket of slop and headed outside.

Inside the barn, she made quick work of stepping into overalls and a pair of rubber boots, grabbed a flashlight, and then headed out to the field. Figuring Mom might be watching from the kitchen window, she held the bucket of scraps high in one hand as she headed for the pigpen. As soon as she rounded the corner, though, she set the bucket down and ran toward the place where she'd buried Brandon.

After scouring the muddy fields for a while, she'd just decided she might be in the clear when she tripped over a half-eaten foot and nearly face-planted in the mud.

Damn. Could have been coyotes or raccoons—or maybe her dad's new prize boar. In fact, that was pretty damned likely. She passed the flashlight's beam around the field. Its batteries were fading. She couldn't help but wonder if the old boar was watching her.

She hurried back for the barn and tossed a shovel and an axe in the wheelbarrow. Before she got halfway across the twelve-hundred-square-foot barn, though, Mr. Higgins, stepped inside and even went to all the bother to slide the creaky metal door closed behind him. "Well, well. If it ain't the one and only Jenny Pickett. How ya doin', pretty gal?"

"I'm busy right now, Mr. Higgins, and I really don't have time for small talk."

His eyes opened wide. "Jenny Pickett has gone and grown a voice. Ain't that a kicker?"

His scrutiny of her felt heavy as a wet blanket on her shoulders, just as it used to feel when she was younger and he stared at her like he was doing now. His gaze rested somewhere close to her thighs before working upward to her bosom.

She felt exposed.

She didn't like it.

Leaving the wheelbarrow, Jenny walked to the back of the barn, grabbed an empty bucket, and started to fill it with grain, anything to get his prying, ugly eyes off her.

"I'm sure you saw it in the paper," Mr. Higgins began. "My Bobby went and married himself a pretty girl named Jenny. Ain't that a coincidence? You remember her. Jenny Rowe. Voted most popular girl in your class. Then she won all sorts of awards in college."

Jenny gritted her teeth. The last thing she wanted was to make a scene at her parents' house. "I can't imagine why you would think I would care, other than to thank my lucky stars I didn't get stuck with Bobby myself," she told him, unable to stop herself. "Everybody knows about poor Jenny Rowe, and I mean *everyone*. For years after college, she couldn't get a job and she had to give massages to men she'd never met just to keep a roof over her head and food on the table. And I'm not talking about foot massages, Mr. Higgins. I'm talking about the kind of massages that include a happy ending. Poor sad Jenny must have been pretty desperate to go and marry big ol' Bobby."

Jack Higgins's round, droopy-jowled face paled. "You, you—"

"Jesus Christ, Mr. Higgins. Get a clue. Your son weighs at least four hundred pounds and he can't lift a fork to his mouth without sweating. Does he have a job? A house? How the hell is he going to fuck that new wife of his if he can't find his penis?"

Higgins pointed a fat, stubby finger at her. "You better watch that mouth of yours. Your father is lucky he has dementia because he would not be happy to know what's become of his only daughter."

Jenny dropped the bag of grain and walked toward Mr. Higgins, grabbing the axe from the wheelbarrow as she passed by. She marched through sawdust and shavings until she stood directly in front of him. Her hands shook as she stared him down, holding the axe in front of her chest, ready to raise the sharpened edge and strike him down if she felt the need.

Do it. Do it.

Jenny's voice trembled as she spoke. "You think I don't remember spending the night with your daughter, Jill, only to have you creep into the bedroom in the middle of the night so you could slide your dirty, filthy hands beneath my shirt and touch me?"

His bloated lips hung open. One of his big hands rose to them, then slowly fell to his giant barrel of a stomach. His wiry gray chest hairs curled around the buttons of his plaid shirt like the kind of weedy vines that were impossible to eradicate.

"I'm not the only one who knows what you did," she continued. "Jill knows it, too. Why do you think your daughter moved away before she turned eighteen? She hated you. She was disgusted by her own father. I bet Bobby knows what you did, too. Probably the reason why he eats so much, anything to mask the pain . . . So he just eats and eats and eats."

Mr. Higgins turned away and headed for the exit. His steps were slower than before and his shoulders hung low.

If you're not going to kill him right now, at least add him to the list.

No. I'm not going to add him to the list. Sometimes living with the truth is worse than dying. "That's right," she called out to Mr. Higgins. "Run along now. And don't you ever come back here again, or I *will* call the police and fill out a long-overdue report. I wonder what would happen if word got out? How many little girls in the neighborhood would come forth?" Jenny let the heavy end of the axe drop to her side and used her free hand to rub her chin. "I really do wonder."

Even after Higgins left the barn, the putrid smell of him remained. She tossed the axe back into the wheelbarrow, ignored the deafening clang, and then headed through the barn door back toward the field.

She had a body to take care of and pigs to feed.

CHAPTER 18

"What's wrong with Lizzy?" Kitally asked. "Is she going to be all right?"

Hayley followed the direction of Kitally's gaze. Lizzy sat on the edge of a cushioned chair in the darkened living room, leaning forward as she stared out one of the many floor-to-ceiling windows. It was dark out. A couple of spotlights dotted the landscaping, shedding light on countless oak trees with crooked, outstretched branches. Beyond the oaks, grass, and mossy rocks was a creek. If you stood anywhere near the property line, you could hear the steady trickle of water.

Hayley stepped into the room with her.

"Somebody's out there," Lizzy said as she approached.

Hayley walked past Lizzy and stood inches from the window, peering into the night, trying to see what Lizzy saw, figuring it was most likely Lizzy's imagination getting the best of her again. This wasn't the first time she'd caught Lizzy staring into the darkness. And it wouldn't be the last.

"I don't see anything."

"To the right of the biggest rock. I can see the faint outline of his head and shoulders."

Kitally joined them. "What are you guys looking at?"

"Lizzy thinks she sees someone out there."

"I don't *think* I see anything. He's right there, mocking me."

"Who is it?" Kitally asked.

"I'm not sure, but I've had enough. I'm going to find out." Lizzy pushed herself from the chair.

Kitally followed her to the French doors leading to the backyard. She glanced back at Hayley, who merely shrugged.

Hayley watched the two of them walk outside and make their way across the grass toward the back of the property until they separated and slipped into the trees and she could no longer see them at all.

The moonlight against the trees tricked her, making shadows out of air.

And then she saw it—an undeniable flash of movement in the trees between the points at which Lizzy and Kitally had entered the woods.

She stood still, unblinking, daring whatever it was to move again. Somebody or something was out there.

And then it did move. It was a man, openly skirting the edge of the trees for a moment and then taking off into them.

She ran for the open door.

She was halfway across the grass when Kitally burst from the woods.

"Did you see him?" Kitally asked. "I thought he went this way."

"Where's Lizzy?"

They looked at one another. They both knew: she'd gone off after him on her own.

Shit. Hayley charged into the woods with Kitally on her heels. They weren't as impenetrably dark as they'd seemed from the house, but they were plenty dark enough. She tripped over something, caught herself, then nearly fell again before finding a trail that weaved through the trees along the creek. Then, after maybe half a minute, the two of them popped out of the woods and there was Lizzy, standing in the middle of the street with her hands on her knees, breathing hard.

"Which way did he go?" Hayley asked.

Lizzy pointed into the utter blackness of the denser wooded area across the street.

"What was he doing out there?" Kitally panted.

"He was watching me."

"How long has this been going on?"

"Since I moved in. He was watching me at Cathy's house, too."

"What about before?" Hayley didn't elaborate. Everyone in their little circle knew what that meant—*before* the shooting or *after* the shooting. It was all still too raw for there to be anything else.

Unsure if Lizzy had heard her, she reworded the question, "How long has he been watching you?"

"I think forever."

Lizzy didn't want to call the police, and she didn't want to talk about it. But she damn well refused to put Kitally and Hayley in danger, too. *Packing my things is becoming an all too familiar event*, she thought as she scrambled around the bedroom, gathering her belongings into one big pile in the middle of the bed.

"Please don't leave," Kitally said for the tenth time.

Lizzy shoved everything into the suitcase and zipped it shut. "Don't you get it, Kitally?"

"No, I guess I don't. Everything has been so much better since you've been staying with us. It feels like a family, living here with you guys. I like it."

Lizzy walked into the bathroom, gathered her toiletries into a pile on the sink, and then came back into the bedroom and looked around for something to put it all in. "I never said I was going to be staying indefinitely. You're damned if you do, damned if you don't," she muttered as she searched through the closet for her backpack.

Once that was done, Lizzy exited the closet and found one very dejected young woman standing marooned in the middle of the room. She walked over to Kitally and placed her hands on her shoulders. "Kitally, listen to me. You don't understand. I can't put your life in danger. I just can't do it. If something happened to you because of my living here . . . how am I supposed to live with that?"

"You're the one who doesn't understand," Kitally said. "We need each other. All three of us need each other. God forbid, not forever, but now. Right now." She took a deep breath, then released it. "You could leave," she went on. "Hayley could leave, too. I could get hit by a car tomorrow and die. We all know shit happens. But what good would your leaving have done me then?"

Lizzy dropped her hands from Kitally's shoulders.

"And what about Hayley?" Kitally asked. "She's been out trolling the streets of Sacramento every night since Jared was kill—" She stopped herself midsentence.

Lizzy moved to the window. "His sister believes he's going to make it," Lizzy said.

"What about you? What do you believe?"

"I know what needs to be done. At least I thought I did. His sister and his parents are hanging on tight to the belief that Jared will make it . . . They still have hope." Lizzy put a hand to her chest. "What if they're right? Maybe I just haven't hung on to enough hope to bring him back."

"Hopes and prayers are important, but they don't bring people back to life."

Lizzy peered out into a vast expanse of nothingness. And that's exactly what she felt. Nothing. She felt nothing. Not scared. Not sad. Not anything. Her therapist was right. Something was wrong with her.

She was defective. Broken.

She was surprised when she realized Kitally was still talking.

"And then you moved in," Kitally was saying, trying to sound cheerful. "Since then, Hayley's been sticking around more. I think it's because she's worried about you." Kitally laughed. "Imagine that? Hayley Hansen worried about another human being? It defies logic and understanding. And yet it's true. I've seen it, and I know you've seen it. You can't leave us. Not yet. Certainly not tonight."

Lizzy expelled a breath as she turned back toward Kitally.

"If we split up," Kitally went on, "we're all more vulnerable. If you're really concerned about my well-being, you'll stay. I'm not saying that you need to protect me, but we're all better off with each other."

"I'll stay for now," Lizzy told her. "But you, young lady, better watch your back, because if something happens to you under my watch, I'm gonna be pissed."

CHAPTER 19

The next morning, Lizzy poured herself a cup of coffee and then took a seat at the kitchen table, where she'd already placed her notebook. Hayley was hunting for leftovers in the refrigerator while Kitally stood at the stove, whipping up omelets for anyone interested.

"We've got another case," Lizzy announced.

"Another workers' comp case?" Kitally asked.

Lizzy shook her head. "Our first missing dog case."

"Seriously? Someone wants to pay you to find their dog?"

Lizzy nodded. "It's a purebred. A pug."

Hayley grunted.

"I can do it," Kitally said. "I just sent in the completed file for that Baxter woman with the supposedly debilitating back and neck injuries from her spill in the ladies' room. I got some great pictures of her jumping her horse."

"Good job," Lizzy said. "All the information you need to get started on the missing dog case is in the office under PUG. The woman is frantic and she's convinced that someone took him right out of her backyard. She said he's an indoor dog that never leaves her sight except to do his business in the yard once in the morning and once at night. If that's true, then whoever it was had a very short time frame in which to take the dog."

"Maybe the dog just dug his way right under the fence."

"No," Lizzy said. "The woman told me she has a sturdy iron fence and her dog is too fat to fit through the rails."

"Why would somebody go to all that bother to steal a dog?"

"People are crazy," Hayley told Kitally. "You know that."

"Take a turn through the neighborhood," Lizzy suggested. "Talk to a few neighbors. See if anything smells suspicious."

"Find out more about the owner, too," Hayley said into the open refrigerator. "See if you can flush out any enemies. Maybe an ex-husband or disgruntled boyfriend took the thing."

Lizzy looked at her notebook and then lifted her chin toward Hayley. "Any leads yet on Pam Middleton's daughter?"

Hayley straightened and shut the refrigerator, empty-handed. "I forgot to tell you guys. As you know, Dan and Barbara Blatt adopted Pam Middleton's baby. Kitally and I did find Mr. Blatt, but it's a sad story. They named the little girl Debra. When she was four, her mom, Barbara Blatt, died of cancer. Dan Blatt was so overcome with grief he couldn't take care of his daughter, so he offered to pay Barbara's mother to watch her for a while."

"He had to *pay* his mother-in-law?"

"You bet. It gets worse. The mother-in-law is an old lady who had nothing good to say about her granddaughter. After watching Debra for two years, she turned the little girl over to Child Services."

"Why?" Kitally asked.

"She didn't like the kid bothering her cats, for one thing. When Debra began to wet the bed, she'd had enough. And it turns out Dan Blatt never paid her, which is a good thing."

"Why is that a good thing?" Lizzy asked.

"Because the old bat might have kept Debra, and that would have been a shame."

Lizzy shook her head. "Have you talked to Child Services to find out what happened to the little girl?"

"I've called twice. No response yet, which means I'll have to pay them a visit."

"Keep me updated." Lizzy turned again to her notes and heaved a sigh. "OK, I got a call recently from Beverly Dow. She sounded upset. Do either of you know anything about that?"

Kitally looked at Hayley.

"She hired us to follow her husband," Hayley said. "She wanted to know if he was cheating."

"I saw the file," Lizzy said. "I know what we were doing for her. I just don't know why. We don't do infidelity cases."

"That's what I thought," Hayley answered. "That's why I was a little surprised when Mrs. Dow came to the office and you drew up a contract right then and there."

Lizzy sank back in the chair. "I do sort of remember that. Was that the woman who wore a bottle of perfume?"

Hayley nodded. "That's the one."

"I could hardly breathe. She's going to stop by the office next week. I want you both to be there."

Hayley and Kitally caught eyes, then both looked away.

"Is that a problem?" Lizzy asked.

"Nope," Hayley said. "Let us know when she'll be coming and we'll be there."

Lizzy nodded. "Moving on . . . I'll be out all this week visiting schools, giving kids the usual safety spiel."

"What about the man who's watching you?" Kitally asked. "Maybe we should have Tommy place a couple of surveillance cameras in the front and back of the house."

"I think that's a good idea."

"I'll take care of it," Kitally said.

Lizzy pointed at Hayley. "Let me know the second you learn anything about Debra Blatt's whereabouts. Her sister is back in the hospital, and it's crucial we find her as soon as possible."

"Will do."

CHAPTER 20

The moment Jenny Pickett opened the door, regret slithered up her spine. She should have stayed in the kitchen until whoever was at the door went away.

The man standing on her front porch looked familiar. Under the glow of the outside light, she guessed him to be in his thirties. He wore khaki pants and a newly ironed buttoned-up dress shirt. His dark hair was thinning, but there was something glimmering within his blue eyes that told her he'd been a charmer in his day. Grasped in his hands was a letter-sized envelope.

He looked at her with sorrowful eyes. "Sorry to bother you. I was told that Jenny Pickett lived here."

"I'm Jenny Pickett."

He looked hopeful and doubtful all at once. "Jenny?"

"Who gave you my address?"

"Your mother."

"Should I know you?"

"I'm not surprised you don't recognize me. It seems like a lifetime ago that we graduated high school. I'm Dean Newman."

The name rattled something deep within, something foul. Dean Newman. Quarterback.

The boy who raped her and then held her down for his friends to take turns.

Her instincts screamed for her to slam the door on him, but the voice in her head demanded otherwise.

Let him in. Now!

"I came to tell you how sorry I am, Jenny," he said, his voice hoarse, "and to ask for your forgiveness."

Dean Newman, on her doorstep. It was dizzying. He wasn't just on her kill list; he was one of its unquestioned stars. Close to the bottom of the list because she'd been saving the worst for last. As she peered into his eyes, she had a difficult time swallowing. Memories of her time with Dean Newman had been buried deeper than most.

"Can I come in? Just for a moment?"

She glanced past him and saw his black SUV parked in front of her house. It was past nine and already dark.

She didn't want to hear one word of what he had to say to her. What would she do? Listen to his bullshit and then forgive him?

Don't even think about it. You've got him right where you want him. Let him in and then take care of business.

How? What will I use? I can't keep him here and—

What about the muscle relaxant in the refrigerator? Use that.

Not a bad idea. It would only last for another five days. She'd planned on using it on the next victim on her list . . . but she just wasn't prepared for Dean Newman. Was she? She needed to think for a minute.

"Are you all right?" Dean asked.

"Um, no, not really. I'm a bit stunned to see you, actually."

"I understand. I can't believe I expected you to invite me into your home. If I could leave this envelope with you, though, it would mean a lot. If you—"

Get him in the house now!

"I was just about to eat dinner," Jenny blurted. "If you agree to come inside and have some chicken and rice, I'll listen to what you have to say."

"Are you sure?"

"Of course. It's cold out. Come on in."

As soon as he stepped inside, she shut the door behind him and then led him into the kitchen nook, insisting he take a seat in one of the four chairs surrounding the glass table.

He slid the envelope back into his pocket and did as she said.

Jenny quickly set the table for two. "If you'll excuse me for a moment, I need to grab my sweater from the other room."

In her office, she unlocked her desk drawer and looked through the different bottles of pills she'd been collecting over the past few weeks. She needed something strong. Something that would knock him out fast so she could figure out what to do next. The muscle relaxant would be used later.

The Rohypnol caught her eye.

That should do it.

Then what? This is crazy. I need more time.

Feed him to the eight-hundred-pound boar.

No. Jenny took in a breath. And then it came to her. "I'll slip him the Rohypnol," she muttered, "then pull his car into the garage and lead him out to it. Get him into the passenger side and then inject him with halothane. That should give me about forty minutes to get to the canal. I'll make it looked like he drove into the water on purpose. I've got a bottle of whiskey that I'll leave with him. Everyone will think he fell off the wagon and just couldn't live with himself."

I still like the boar.

"The pig's not happening. Mom or Dad sees me, then what?"

No reply.

With the pills she needed in her possession, Jenny was half-way down the hall before she remembered what she'd gone to the back of the house to get in the first place. Her sweater.

"Sorry about that," she said when she finally returned. She went to the kitchen to prepare dinner.

"Not a problem," Dean said. He came to his feet. "Can I help you with anything?"

"No," she snapped.

He looked taken aback.

She smiled. "I want to do this. You're my guest."

He took his seat again and seemed to relax. "I can't thank you enough for allowing me inside your home. It's beautiful. From the look of things, you've done well for yourself."

"I can't complain," she said as she crushed the pills and mixed them into a small portion of rice. "How about you? What are you up to these days?"

"The truth is I'm doing better now. I've been sober for a few years now."

She brought him a cup of hot tea and set it in front of him. "Well, good for you." Back in the kitchen, she pulled out two plates, used the tongs to grab a chicken breast from the pan in the oven. Next came the rice, topped off with a mushroom sauce. "Here you go—chicken and rice with my famous mushroom sauce." She set the plate in front of him.

"I really can't let you feed me. It doesn't seem right."

"If you don't eat every bite on your plate," she stated firmly, "I'll never forgive you. *Ever.*"

Convinced, once she joined him at the table he didn't waste any time devouring everything on his plate. When he finished, he said, "That was the best meal I've had in a very long time."

"You're being too kind."

"I'm serious. And you look amazing, Jenny. You really do."

She didn't care what he thought, but she said playfully, "Stop it now. You're just trying to make me blush."

He put his napkin on the table. "I hate to ruin this wonderful evening, but I need to tell you, Jenny, that a day hasn't gone by that I haven't thought about what I did to you."

"It's in the past," she said, praying the pills would soon take effect so she wouldn't have to listen to his half-assed apologies.

He used his napkin to wipe perspiration from his brow.

He looked flushed. *Thank God.*

"Are you all right?"

"Just a little dizzy. I must have eaten too quickly. And sitting here with you . . . I don't think you understand how much I appreciate you inviting me inside and then feeding me. I'm overwhelmed by your generosity."

She stood. "Why don't we have a seat in the living room where you'll be more comfortable?"

"I should probably go."

Her eyes narrowed. "Not before you have a seat in the living room and tell me what you came here to say. It's important that I hear it."

He made it to the other room without trouble, but then all but toppled into a seat on one end of the couch. His body sank into the cushions. He wasn't going to last five minutes. If she couldn't lead him into the car, maybe she could at least find a way to get him closer to the garage.

"I've got an idea," she said cheerfully. She held out her hand. "Give me the keys to your car."

"Why?"

"I'm going to pull your car into the garage, and then I'm going to drive you home. You don't look well."

"I can't let you do that."

He could hardly move. She just hoped she hadn't put too many pills in his rice. He couldn't die yet. She had bigger plans for him, and they had a lot to talk about. She reached into his jacket pocket, retrieved his keys, and held them up for him to see. "I insist."

CHAPTER 21

For over ten years now, Lizzy had been volunteering her time teaching defense strategies to young girls and boys. High schools in Placer and Sacramento Counties were accommodating, opening up their gyms and cafeterias after school for a few hours a month. No charge.

Tommy had been a regular volunteer for the last couple of years. He was fantastic with the kids—super energetic, with an infectious passion for self-defense. They loved him. He'd turned twenty-five last week. He owned his own karate school, which is where he could be found most days. No matter how busy Tommy got, he always took the time to help Lizzy out. As far as Lizzy was concerned, he was one of the good guys.

A good guy with tough romantic instincts, though. Tommy had a thing for Hayley. Everyone knew that. The part that surprised Lizzy, though, was that he hadn't given up yet. Hayley wasn't an easy person to gauge, or get along with, for that matter. It was true that since Brian Rosie's death, Hayley seemed different. She was still far from chatty, but not as silent as she used to be. Still, if you looked close enough, it was easy to see that a subtle darkness continued to simmer and brew just beneath the surface.

Today's class had been held at Crestmont High, not far from her office on J Street. Lizzy had been holding self-defense classes at this particular school for years, so she knew most of the regulars. Her class size had grown from an average of seven kids to double that in the past few years. Some of the kids invited her to birthday parties and other family events.

It was almost five. Time to lock up. She was surprised to see Tommy still there, talking to a group of girls in the far corner of the room. He'd recently opened a second karate school and therefore he usually hurried to his car the moment class ended.

But not tonight.

One of the girls was crying. Something was wrong.

Lizzy joined their small circle, made eye contact with Tommy, and lifted a questioning brow.

"It's Shelby," he said as he stepped out of the group and pulled Lizzy with him. "She's missing."

"Since when?"

"According to her friends, Shelby was at school yesterday and everything seemed fine. Apparently Shelby tutors math and so when she didn't come straight home from school, her mom figured she'd be home later. By dinnertime, her parents knew something was wrong. That's really all I know. One of the girls over there said that all of Shelby's friends were being questioned by authorities at school today. Rumor has it that they found her car on the side of the highway."

"OK, thanks, Tommy."

"Are you all right?"

"I don't know," Lizzy said. Her ears were buzzing. This couldn't be happening. "I just can't imagine Shelby putting herself in a situation where this could happen. She's been coming to my classes for years. She's smart, tough, and she's a fighter."

Tommy started to pull Lizzy into his arms, then backed off when she stiffened. "I'm sorry. You looked like you could use . . ." He trailed off.

Lizzy shook her head. "I'm the one who should be apologizing. I didn't mean to get all weird on you."

"Don't worry," he said. "I get it. You've been put through the wringer. No need to explain. You need time." He waved a hand through the air. "Look around. You're a decent person doing a decent thing by helping these kids. They look up to you. Hayley and Kitally do, too. So do I."

"Thanks. I'm going to go talk to some of the girls, see what I can do to help. See you next week?"

"I'll be here."

After Tommy walked off, Lizzy talked to the remaining girls. They were all just as baffled as Lizzy. Shelby had just turned seventeen. She was a junior and had been dating the same boy for three years. A nice boy, they all said. Lizzy had met him a couple of times when he picked Shelby up from class.

Then Lizzy remembered. The buzzing in her ears was back. Last week—maybe the week before that, Lizzy wasn't sure—Shelby had tried to talk to her after class. She'd asked a few questions about relationships and love, and Lizzy realized now that she hadn't really listened to her. She'd been caught up in her own thoughts, could hardly remember a word of what Shelby had said.

After everyone left the gym, Lizzy locked up and then made her way across the parking lot, keeping an eye on her surroundings as she went.

Goose bumps crawled up her arms. He was out there . . . watching her.

She stopped. Looked at the row of windows in the building across the street. Shadows danced within. Her gaze roamed the area, darting from tree to tree, building to building, then to every car parked on the side of the road.

"Who are you?" she said out loud. "What do you want from me?"

There was no answer.

She got to her car, climbed in behind the wheel, locked the doors, and started the engine. *There's nobody out there*, she told herself.

Nobody out there, in all the world.

"Jared," she said suddenly, surprised by her own outburst. "Come back to me."

She tried to imagine him sitting in the seat next to her, but no image of how things used to be came to her. No matter how hard she tried, she couldn't remember happier times. When she wasn't sitting in the hospital with him, it was as if he'd never been. These non-feelings didn't make any sense. And yet every once in a while, she would feel a glimmer of hope, and for a moment, never longer, she shut her eyes and dared to imagine that everything would be all right. It was pure insanity. She was living in a tornado of confusion, a constant war between logic and irrationality.

A white Volkswagen Passat rolled into the parking lot. Behind the wheel was a young man. Clearly not a threat. Lizzy watched him drive up close to her car, stop, and roll down his window. She cracked her own.

"Ms. Gardner? My name is Derek Murphy," he said. "I've been trying to reach you for days."

Before she could tell him to get lost, he said, "I work for *Channel 10 News*, and we want to do a human interest story on you. You know, the story behind the story."

She hit the Roll-Up button on her window and drove off.

Forty-five minutes later, after being told she could go ahead and enter Detective Chase's office, Lizzy opened the door, but then started to back out when she noticed he was on the phone.

Detective Chase waved her in, gesturing toward the chair in front of his desk.

Lizzy shut the door and took a seat. While he finished his conversation, she glanced around, taking note of the framed certificate on the wall. Apparently he'd graduated from George Washington University in Washington, DC.

If she were trying to figure out what sort of man he was, judging by the pictures, she would guess he liked to fish and golf with his buddies. A man's man. Her gaze left the wall and settled on the bronze trophy sitting on the credenza to the right. Apparently Detective Chase received a Top Cop Award and was honored by the president of the United States. Shocker. She didn't think Chase had it in him.

Chase hung up the phone and said, "Gardner."

"Detective Chase."

"How are you holding up?"

The big man was trying to come across as if he cared. "I'm doing OK."

"You don't look OK."

"Thanks."

"What brings you here today?"

She had two reasons for the visit, but she decided to start with, "Melony Reed."

Blank face, no expression. "Haven't heard the name."

"She came to see you because she was scared."

"About what?"

"All her friends from high school were dying. Does that ring a bell?"

"That happens, you know—people's friends die."

"Yes. I know. Thanks for the reminder."

He shrugged.

"Melony Reed hired me to investigate why so many of her friends are disappearing."

"So have you solved the case? It's been at least a week, hasn't it?"

"So you do remember."

Another shrug.

"Did you know Melony died recently, slipped and fell on the knives sticking straight up out of her open dishwasher?"

No shrug this time. Instead Chase appeared a bit uneasy.

"You can't deny that that's a lot of accidents in a short period of time."

"Quite a coincidence. I'll give you that."

"Why did you send her to me?" Lizzy asked.

"Because I know how you like to solve murder mysteries."

Detective Chase, it seemed, was back to his old dickish self. Lizzy didn't flinch. "You sent her to me because you thought she was a joke. You didn't believe her."

"You're wrong. I believed her when she told me that her friends died. But as I said, people die all of the time. Melony Reed was going through a divorce. There were a lot of contested financial issues, and she ended up losing everything. It was easy enough to see that she was experiencing some kind of midlife crisis—"

"She was only thirty."

Chase sighed. "Listen. If you add up all of the homicides, rapes, robberies, and aggravated assaults, we're talking thousands of crimes every year. And that's just right here in Sacramento."

"Ahh, you're busy, so you just decided to brush her aside."

"Not every death is a murder."

"She came to you for help, and you did nothing."

"Sounds like she went to you, too. What did you do to help Melony Reed?"

Lizzy didn't have an answer.

"Am I supposed to drop everything anytime Lizzy Gardner walks into my office?" He leaned back in his chair. "Though you do seem to have some clout around here. I wouldn't be surprised to get a call from Jimmy Martin any second now."

"Stop being an ass."

"Are we done here?"

"Not yet," Lizzy said. "What do you know about Shelby Geitner?"

"Now I know we're finished. There's the door." He leaned forward and began shuffling through the papers on his desk.

"I *know* Shelby personally. I've been to her house. She would never run away, let alone put herself in a position to be kidnapped."

"Who said anything about being kidnapped?"

"I heard it through the grapevine, Detective. You should get out there, hit the pavement—you learn things that way."

"Listen, Gardner. I don't care if you and Shelby talked on the phone every day and had coffee on Sundays. Keep your nose out of my case."

"Is that a threat?"

He took in a breath. "Listen. I want to find Shelby as badly as you do. I know Shelby's father. We've played golf together. We're in the process of locating and interviewing witnesses, re-canvassing the crime scene and booking evidence, searching criminal databases. In other words, we've got it covered. I'd appreciate it if you stayed out of my way."

"Wow. Detective Chase is being polite and asking nicely."

"Is it working?"

"Maybe. Answer four questions and I'll think about backing off."

He actually smiled. "Ask the questions and I'll think about answering them."

"Any suspects?"

"Not yet."

"Did you find her car?"

"Yes."

"Do you think someone was waiting for her in it after school?"

"Looks that way."

"Did she put up a fight?"

"Absolutely."

CHAPTER 22

Jenny disconnected the tube from the needle sticking in Dean Newman's forearm. Then she wrapped the whole kit and caboodle up and shoved it all inside her handy-dandy bag. Next, she peeled off the tape, along with a few of his arm hairs, and then yanked the needle out. "Sorry," she said. "Did that hurt?"

Dean didn't say a word. He looked like a wet noodle. He just sat there in the passenger seat of his SUV, slumped against the door like a rag doll.

"I bet you're wondering how you got an IV in your arm."

"No," she said, answering Dean's unasked question, "I'm not a nurse. I'm a chemist. But making a homemade IV turned out to be no big deal. There's a good chance you might get an infection, of course, but no need to worry about that because you'll be dead soon."

Once she had all her things packed away, she took hold of Dean's arm and pulled him toward her, trying to drag him over the console and into the driver's seat. This wasn't going to be easy. She opened the driver's door, turned her back to it, braced her feet against the console, and heaved. Good God, the man was a load, but she was making progress. She had to stop a few times to take a breath and then try again. His shoulders were across, then his trunk—and then, finally, all in a rush, she was flying out of the car and he was coming out of the SUV after her, hanging up at the last second or he would've crushed her beneath him.

"Jeez. How much do you weigh, Dean?"

He couldn't answer her, of course, but she had to admit she was having fun with him. Well, if you could call pulling a two-hundred-pound man from the passenger seat to the driver's seat fun. It was slow going tucking his legs down where they needed to go and hoisting him up behind the wheel, but she managed.

"I was surprised you showed up tonight," Jenny told him, panting beside the open door with her hands on her knees. Even in the cold night air, she was sweating like mad. "Despite not being prepared, I put a lot of thought into how I might get rid of your body. I thought about chopping you up and feeding you to the big boar on my parents' pig farm but decided against it. Besides, I don't even think the eight-hundred-pound boar would enjoy nibbling on you, Dean. You don't look anything like the big hot stud who used to throw the ball across the field every Friday night. Those tight pants of yours always made the cheerleaders work extra hard for you."

She had her breath now. She straightened his clothes and his hair as best she could, then fastened his seatbelt nice and tight and walked around to the other side of the vehicle. She climbed into the SUV's passenger seat and pulled the bottle of whiskey she'd brought from beneath the seat.

She wore rubber gloves and a hairnet. She was on her game.

After opening the bottle of booze, she slid close enough to reach over and put it to his lips.

One of his fingers twitched.

The alcohol drizzled from his mouth and down his chin. She put his hand around the bottle, making sure his prints were there in case they found him sooner rather than later.

"I don't have much time, Dean. The muscle relaxant I gave you only works for so long. In case you didn't know what was going on, you're paralyzed. If you could speak, I wonder what you would say right now. Maybe one more apology?"

Jenny laughed. "Nah, just kidding. I don't care one iota about what you're thinking. I just hope you're feeling even a tiny bit of what I was feeling when you held me down, naked and cold out on the muddy field, while your friends had their way with me. I hope now you might *really* understand what you did to me."

She took a breath, even found herself enjoying the view of the murky canal—Dean's watery grave. "How does it feel to have zero control, Dean? It's not fun, is it? In case you were wondering, it never took much to trigger memories of that day. Every time I see a football game, I have flashbacks. Certain smells bring me right back to the night that you and your friends raped me. I wish your pals were here now so I could watch them do to you what they did to me after you were finished. Two guys at once. A dirty shirt stuffed so far into my mouth I thought for sure I would suffocate. Your big, strong hands are what kept me from being able to scratch their eyes out. You do realize that, right? Your fingers were clamped so tightly around my wrists, I had bruises for a month. Did you know that I had nothing to look at but *you* while your friends poked and prodded? I bet you didn't realize that your breathing quickened in excitement as the minutes ticked by. Did you know that not one time during that incident did you have the nerve to look me in the eye?"

Another finger twitched.

"What were you thinking would happen tonight, Dean? Did you really think you could ruin my life and then just expect me to forgive you? Are you kidding me? You just decided one day that it was time to come clean? You thought you would just travel through the city, knocking on every one of your victims' doors and say you're sorry? I don't know about everyone else you messed with, but I, personally, don't care if you've changed or even if you spent the last ten years drinking yourself into oblivion. You did what you did because you're heartless and cruel and now you're finally going to pay for your actions."

Jenny sucked in a breath as she worked to get her anger in check. "I better get the show on the road. I don't want you waking up too soon. Once you drive your car into the water, it should only take a few minutes for you to drown."

He'd fallen over against the driver's door. She did her best to haul him upright and clamp his fingers around the steering wheel. She made sure every window was open, too. "Everyone's going to think you started drinking again. You couldn't live with yourself, so you drove into the canal."

Jenny sat back so she could survey her work. Everything was in place. She leaned over and turned the engine on. Then she examined the passenger window, hoping she would have enough time to jump out before they hit the water. She really didn't feel like getting wet.

After tossing her bag out the window and making sure there was nothing else left in the car that might incriminate her, she used both hands to pick up his right leg and plunk his foot hard on the gas pedal. The SUV's engine roared.

"Easy, now," she said, pulling on his leg so he wasn't flooring it. This might be trickier than she'd thought. If she just had him drift down into the water, the vehicle might stop before he went under. She pushed down on his leg again, then slipped the SUV into gear.

The surge of power caught her off guard. Jenny fell back against the leather seat and was sent soaring into the frigid water right along with Dean Newman.

CHAPTER 23

"I think I found Pam Middleton's long-lost daughter," Hayley told Kitally. "If this is the right woman, the girl's name is now Christina Bradley."

Kitally headed across the room and hovered over her. "How the heck did you find her? I've called every child-care service provider in Sacramento. Most of them wouldn't give out any information unless I was a parent or an attorney. The few people who didn't care about rules and regulations had no one in their records by the name of Debra Blatt."

"I decided to use the hospital where she was born and her birth date instead of her name," Hayley said. "Then I followed a paper trail of foster homes and sent out a dozen emails. I just received a response from a woman who said all the information I gave her matched a girl she roomed with named Debra Blatt. She said that when Debra turned eighteen, she had her name legally changed to Christina Bradley."

"Lizzy is going to be happy about this. You might have just saved a young girl's life."

"Don't get too high and don't get too low," Hayley said. "Even if we find Christina Bradley, we don't know if she'll be a match."

Hayley continued to clack away at the keyboard. A Facebook page for Christina Bradley popped up on her screen.

"Looks like she put herself through college," Kitally said.

Hayley nodded. "Look at all the congratulations. She's engaged to be married."

"Considering how rough her life started out, she looks like she's gotten it together."

Hayley shrugged. "Everybody's life looks shiny and happy on Facebook." She scrolled down. "She runs a day care center in Citrus Heights."

"I have to run another surveillance on Mr. Chalkor," Kitally said. "Do you want me to stop by the day care on my way? See if she's there?"

"No, I've got this. You take care of Chalkor. I'll talk to Christina."

Hayley pulled her Chevy into the parking lot of a strip mall off Birdcage and quickly found an empty spot. The battered beast of a car sputtered and jerked before the engine fell silent. The day care center was dark blue with white shutters. Long blades of bright-green grass had been painted all around the base at the front of the building, making it appear as if grass were growing right out of the pavement.

The moment Hayley walked inside she was assaulted by noise.

A half wall, three feet high and painted the colors of the rainbow, separated the front desk from a thousand-square-foot room filled with small tables and chairs, games, and *lots* of kids. Hayley had never been in a day care center before. It wasn't anything like Child Services. These kids were actually having fun.

A woman in her early twenties stood near the front desk. She was on the phone and held up a finger to let Hayley know she'd be a minute.

A high-pierced scream caused every nerve inside Hayley's body to tense. Pain or joy? Who the hell knew?

The girl finished her phone conversation and said, "How can I help you?"

"I'm looking for Christina Bradley."

"She's around here somewhere. Let me find her for you."

By the time the young woman helped a little girl with her drawing and then stopped two boys in the middle of a tug-of-war over a toy car, two other ladies had entered the room through a back door. The three women exchanged a few words, and then one of them looked over the sea of little heads and caught Hayley's gaze. She was about five-four, wore a rainbow T-shirt and jeans, and had her light-colored hair pulled back in a ponytail. Even before she headed Hayley's way, Hayley knew she'd found Christina Bradley. She looked just like Pam Middleton.

Christina introduced herself, then said, "If you're looking for a job, we don't have any openings right now."

"That's not why I'm here," Hayley said. "Is there somewhere, a room maybe, where we could talk privately?"

"I'm unusually busy right now. Why don't you tell me why you're here?"

"It's about your biological mom, Pam Middleton. She's looking for you."

Christina paled.

"Are you all right?"

Christina's hand fell to her chest. "You caught me off guard, but I'll be fine. Why don't we go to my office, after all?"

Hayley followed her through a door and into a small windowless office. "Have a seat," Christina said.

Hayley did exactly that.

"Pam Middleton," Christina said. "Is that her name?"

Hayley nodded.

"What's she like?"

"I've only met her once, for less than ten minutes. She looks a lot like you. She talks fast, and she comes across as a little uptight."

Christina appeared to be holding back a smile. "Do you work for the adoption agency?"

"No. I'm with Lizzy Gardner Investigations in Sacramento."

"How did you find me?"

"Yours was a closed adoption, which made things more difficult. I talked to your father, Dan Blatt, and your grandmother—"

"He's not my father. I'd prefer it if we didn't talk about those people."

"I understand."

Christina folded her arms in front of her. "So how long has this Pam Middleton been looking for me?"

"As far as I know, at least a couple of weeks."

Christina audibly exhaled. "Do you know why?"

"Yes."

"That bad, huh?"

Hayley didn't know what to say to that, so she kept her thoughts to herself.

"Go ahead and tell me. I'm a big girl. I can handle it."

"The whole story or just the bottom line?" Hayley asked.

"Sum it up nice and neat for me, if you can."

Hayley obliged. "Your mother had you when she was sixteen. She and her boyfriend decided they weren't ready to raise a child, so they gave you up for adoption. Years later, they married and had another child. A daughter. She's sick and she needs a bone marrow transplant. If you're a match, you could be her only hope."

Christina came to her feet, seemed to struggle to take her next breath. "Wow, you sure know how to tell it like it is, don't you?"

Hayley remained silent.

After a long moment, Christina said, "So. Based on what you just told me, Pam Middleton would never have sought me out if it wasn't for her sick daughter."

"I wouldn't want to speculate."

Christina took a deep breath and then blew it out and began to pace the room. "Both my parents are together and they never looked for me." She looked at Hayley, her hands rolled into tight fists at her sides. It was easy to see that she was fighting all sorts of crazy emotions. "How old is she . . . the sick girl?"

"Sixteen."

"Have you met her?"

"No."

She nodded and kept nodding as she paced. "God, I just feel like screaming. This is so out of the blue."

The door opened, and the young woman Hayley had talked to when she'd first entered the building asked Christina if everything was all right.

"I'm fine, thanks, but I'm going to need a few more minutes. Is everything OK out there?"

"We're fine. Take your time."

After she left, Christina returned to her seat. Another minute passed before she propped both elbows on her desk and let her head fall into her open palms. When she looked up again, she apologized and said, "I don't know if I can do it."

Hayley put a business card on Christina's desk and slid it toward her. "Why don't you take some time to think about it?"

"Is the girl in the hospital?"

"Yes. Sutter General Hospital, on the fourth floor. Your sister's name is Kirsten Middleton."

"I don't have a sister."

Hayley nodded.

"How much time does she have?"

"Not much."

Christina stiffened. "I'm serious. I really don't think I can help her."

"I understand," Hayley said again.

"Do you really?"

Hayley took a moment to think about that. "No, I guess you're right. I don't."

"What would *you* do?"

Hayley hated these sorts of questions. Hypothetical bullshit, but she hadn't come all this way for nothing. "Not everyone gets a chance to be a hero," Hayley told her. "I'd like to think I would rise to the occasion and do whatever needed to be done, but who the hell knows? Maybe telling Pam Middleton to fuck off would feel a lot better than saving someone you've never met."

Silence.

"Ultimately," Hayley added, "nobody can make this decision for you."

"Is it dangerous . . . you know . . . donating bone marrow or whatever it is she would need?"

"From what I've read about bone marrow donation, it's mostly a time commitment. Every surgical procedure has risks."

"I'm getting married in four weeks."

"Congratulations."

"Thanks."

"Nobody is going to judge you if you don't do this," Hayley said.

"No? Cancel my wedding to save a life or let the girl die and find a way to think happy thoughts on my honeymoon?"

"You might not be a match," Hayley told her, "and then you won't have to make the decision at all."

"But what if I am?"

Hayley said nothing, let a solid minute of silence settle between them before coming to her feet. "I think you should do what's right for you and nobody else." She gestured toward the card she'd left on the desk. "If you need to vent or you want someone to go to the hospital with you or to set up a meeting with Pam Middleton, call me anytime."

CHAPTER 24

Lizzy walked to her car, frustrated and tired. She hadn't been sleeping well. The notion that someone had taken Shelby was too much for her. And then there were the people on Melony's list—targets, every one of them.

And the man who was watching her.

Fuck this life of hers.

Not a day went by that Lizzy didn't feel his eyes on her, crawling over her skin like a tick looking for its host—sensing body heat and vibrations.

And yet the cameras Tommy had hooked up in the front yard and backyard had yet to show anything tangible: deer, raccoon, the usual culprits you would expect to see on any given night.

Once she was inside her car, she looked over the list of names Melony Reed had provided her. She stopped at Dean Newman. According to Melony's scribbled notes, Dean had grown up in a wealthy family. His father owned Merrick's Lumber and Hardware. The way Melony told it, the things Dean had done in high school ended up being too much for him and drove him to drink. Sounded to Lizzy like this could just as easily be Melony's own guilt talking, but who knew? Whatever the reason, Dean was definitely a drunk. Kicked out of college in his junior year, he'd moved back home and even ended up on the street for a short time until he'd joined Alcoholics Anonymous. As far as Melony knew, he'd stayed sober since then.

A quick check with DMV records provided her with an address in Roseville. It was a nice house at the end of a cul-de-sac off East Roseville Parkway near the Galleria mall. It was past ten in the morning when she knocked on the front door.

A woman answered with a burp rag thrown over her shoulder and a baby in her arms. Judging by the dark shadows under her eyes, she hadn't slept any better than Lizzy had.

"I don't want any," she said.

"I'm not selling anything. I need to talk to Dean Newman. Does he live here?"

"You tell me," the woman said. The baby began to cry, and she moved the infant from one arm to the other. She started to walk away and said over her shoulder, "Come on in and shut the door behind you."

Lizzy stepped inside.

Big mistake. Had she known the woman was going to wheel around and plop the baby in her arms, she never would have followed her. "I'm not good with babies," Lizzy warned her. "I haven't held a baby in years. I might drop her."

"It's a boy," the woman said from the kitchen. She held a bottle beneath the water, waiting for it to heat up. "You're doing just fine."

Lizzy had to agree. The tiny human in her arms had stopped crying, and he was looking up at her with bright-blue watery eyes.

"Nobody ever told me taking care of a baby would be so hard," the woman said from the kitchen. "All of my friends made it look easy. They all said breast-feed, cuddle, change the diaper, and repeat. What a crock of shit. Blake refuses to breast-feed. He cries when I cuddle him. And he won't sleep for more than ten minutes at a time. I'm at my wits' end."

"I'm sorry," Lizzy said, wondering what to do now that Blake was grabbing fistfuls of her hair and pulling. He was stronger than he looked. It hurt, but she didn't want to make him cry, so she let him be. When his chubby fingers got a little too close to her nostrils, she made googly eyes at the kid and then lifted her chin. Blake must have found her amusing because he giggled.

"Did he just laugh?"

"I don't know," Lizzy said. "I think so."

"Oh, my God. Oh, my God. Stay right there. Don't move. I need to get my camera."

Lizzy's bottom lip was being twisted and pulled.

"Blake, that really hurts," she told him. "Maybe you should go back to pulling my hair."

He smiled.

"You're pretty cute, but you already know that, don't you?"

He started to coo and gurgle.

"OK," the woman said as she returned to Lizzy's side. "Do it again. Make him laugh."

"I don't think I can. I have no idea what I did the first time."

"Maybe it's your voice. I'll just keep the video running while you talk . . . about anything."

"Let's talk about Dean Newman."

As if on cue, the baby laughed.

"You did it! He laughed."

Blake did laugh. And then he proceeded to spit up on Lizzy's shirt.

The woman stopped recording and handed Lizzy a rag.

Lizzy cleaned herself as best she could, considering she still cradled the baby in her arms. She followed the woman back to the kitchen and tried to hand Blake to her, but she wouldn't take him. "I'm sorry," Lizzy said, "but I really don't have time for this. I need to get going."

"I thought you wanted to know about Dean."

"I do, but I've been here for almost fifteen minutes and I know more about Blake than I do Dean."

"Fine," the woman said in a huff, crossing her arms. "Dean and I have been living together for five years now. He's also Blake's father. Three days ago, Dean came home from work and told me he needed to deliver another one of his stupid letters apologizing to someone he feels he may have slighted in high school."

Lizzy waited for the woman to continue, but that seemed to be the end of the story. "Are you saying he never returned?"

"That's exactly what I'm saying. He's done this before. Every once in a while he falls off the wagon and doesn't return home for days."

"Did you report him missing?"

"Nah, what would be the point? He'll come back. It might be another day or two, but he'll come back to me with a bouquet of roses in his hands and a mountain of apologies. This is exactly why I won't marry him. He's not ready. It's sad, really," she said as she reached for Blake, took him into her arms, and held him close. "He's missing out on so much."

Now that Lizzy was empty-handed, she felt a strange sense of loss that confused her. It took her a moment to figure out what she wanted to say. "Could you let me know if Dean returns? I really do need to talk to him."

The woman reached up and smacked her forehead with her free hand. "Oh, my God! I'm sorry. Ever since Blake was born, I've been out of sorts. I haven't even asked you your name or why you're even looking for Dean."

"My name is Lizzy Gardner. I'm an investigator."

The woman's eyes narrowed. "I recognize your name. What could you possibly want with Dean?"

"A woman he went to high school with hired me to investigate a string of accidents."

"I don't understand. Does she think Dean was involved in these accidents somehow?"

"No, not at all. Dean is on the list of people she's concerned about. She and Dean and others had formed a group when they were in high school together—the Ambassador Club."

"I've heard Dean mention that club before."

"Melony Reed, the woman who hired me, was worried that people in the Ambassador Club were being targeted."

"So she thinks Dean could be in danger?"

"Yes. The list of letters you talked about Dean delivering . . . you wouldn't happen to know or recall the names of the people he's been apologizing to, would you?"

"No. I never asked. I feel like a dunce. I should have talked to him about it, asked him more questions. What if he's been hurt?"

"I'll leave my card right here on the kitchen counter," Lizzy told her. "If Dean returns or you remember anything at all about the people he was setting out to apologize to, I'd appreciate it if you could give me a call."

CHAPTER 25

Jenny sat in her car a few blocks away from the house that Dean Newman shared with his girlfriend and watched Lizzy Gardner make a quick exit.

This was more than a coincidence.

First, Lizzy Gardner had shown up at Melony Reed's house, and now she was talking to Dean Newman's girlfriend. The first time she'd seen Lizzy at Melony's place, she hadn't known who she was, so she'd followed her to her office downtown. As soon as she saw where the woman worked, it all made sense. Melony had always been the leader of the Ambassador Club. Of course Melony would be the one to notice that her friends were dying off.

It didn't take Jenny long to conclude that Melony must have hired Lizzy Gardner to investigate the series of recent deaths. The mistake Jenny made was in thinking that killing Melony would put an end to any possible investigation. Not so. Apparently Lizzy Gardner felt compelled to help her clients even after they were dead and buried.

Thanks to Ms. Gardner, she'd had no choice but to make quick work of doing away with Melony Reed. After Melony was asleep, Jenny opened the dishwasher, made sure multiple knives were sticking straight up, and then poured dishwasher soap on the floor. She also removed the lightbulb above the kitchen sink. Then she opened the refrigerator and unscrewed the bulb, leaving the place dark. The appliance would set off an annoying beeping alarm after being left open for too long. Melony would come out and flip on the lights to no avail. She'd then have to take the quickest route to shut the timer off and the rest was history.

At the time, Jenny hadn't been sure her plan would work, but it all fell together beautifully. Melony had tripped and impaled herself upon a variety of knives. Jenny had been watching and waiting. She beat the ambulance to the hospital and then listened to the nurses talk about the woman who came in with a fillet knife stuck in her neck and a carving knife that had pierced all the way through the woman's middle.

Every kill had gotten easier. Taking matters into her own hands, making these horrible people pay for what they did to her, left Jenny feeling a sense of accomplishment and pride.

After Lizzy drove away from Dean Newman's house, Jenny was tempted to knock on the door and ask Dean's girlfriend what the purpose of Lizzy's visit was, but there was no need. She knew exactly what Lizzy was doing. There was no other explanation.

Lizzy Gardner could ruin everything. Kill her.

Don't be silly. I'm going to stick to the people on my list—the ones who deserve to die. Besides, the Gardner woman intrigues me.

Jenny checked the time. She had an appointment with Ron Jennings at AutoNation in Roseville. It was time to park her car at home and take the bus to the Auto Mall.

Jenny chose the car farthest from the main building and then used one of her disposable phones to call Ron Jennings and let him know she was out in his lot and had found a car she was interested in taking for a test drive.

It didn't take the man long at all to find her by the SUV. It was definitely the same Ron from high school. He'd gained a few pounds and he now walked with a labored, irregular movement, but the round bowling ball head pierced with two squinty eyes hadn't changed a bit.

She greeted Jennings with a smile. Today she had gone for the edgy platinum-blonde wig that gave her a flirty look. "My good friend told me you were the best salesman in the area, so I thought I would come see for myself."

"What's your friend's name? I could give her a call and thank her for recommending me."

"Oh, no," Jenny said. "It's been too many years. She wouldn't remember."

He rubbed his hands together. "Very well. Let's find you a car. You told me over the phone that you needed something with power and lots of room."

"That's right."

"I have a beautiful red stunner, a Cadillac Escalade, right over here."

Jenny didn't budge from her chosen SUV. "I like this one."

"OK, this one it is!" He opened the door for her, and she climbed in. She clutched the steering wheel with both hands. Being that it was the end of January and the air was still nippy, she knew he wouldn't question her gloved hands. She poked a few buttons. "Oh, this one won't do. I don't see the On–Off switch to deactivate the air bag in the passenger seat."

"No worries," he assured her, then hustled around to the passenger side. With the cab briefly to herself, she pulled from her purse the pair of glasses and tube of lipstick she'd found inside his ex-wife's car and dropped them between the seat and the console.

Jennings opened the passenger door and pointed. "It's right here beneath the glove box. It's on the Off position. You just insert the key and turn it on whenever you want to activate it."

"That only deactivates the passenger side air bag, is that right? I have small children I'm worried about."

"That's right. The driver's air bag will remain on at all times. That's exactly why the manufacturers started making these switches—for busy mothers like you."

"Great."

"So, do you have a large family? Do you travel a lot? Will you need lots of space in the back for family outings? Well, you've come to the right place. This baby can do it all."

For the next five minutes straight, she listened to his high-pressure tactics. Ron Jennings was still a salesman. He used to be on the debate team in high school and would mock his opponents to throw them off their game. Ron hadn't raped her or held her down for his friends like Dean Newman had, but he used to pinch her when nobody was looking. Sometimes he yanked on her hair or poked her with a sharpened pencil.

He dug deep into his front pants pocket and pulled out a key. "Want to take this baby for a ride?"

"Boy, do I."

After they both latched their seatbelts, she turned on the engine and headed out to the main street, making a right on Sunrise and a left onto Eureka Road. "Am I allowed to take the car onto the highway?"

"Absolutely. Anything you want to do."

She stopped at the light. So far, so good. "So how's the car business these days?"

"I can't complain."

"Are you married?"

He laughed. "Are you flirting with me?"

"No," she said, trying her best to look bashful. "I was just curious."

"I was married once. No children," he said. "That woman put me through hell. She's still trying to get every dime out of me."

Jenny listened to him ramble on. She knew all about his failed marriage and acrimonious divorce, which was why she knew the cops would go straight to his ex-wife after they found him.

"I'm only thirty," he said. "I plan to keep my options open."

The light turned green, and she hit the gas a little too hard. "Oops, sorry about that."

Quit fooling around. You're never going to pull this stunt off.

Jennings settled back in the leather seat, appeared at ease. With his tight pants, wrinkled shirt, and ugly tie with a food stain front and center, not to mention his slicked-back hair, she knew he'd be single for a while.

"What do you think about financing?" he asked.

"What do you mean?"

"Are you looking for a larger monthly payment over a shorter duration of time or—"

"Cash," she said.

"OK, now we're talkin'. This baby isn't cheap, you know?"

"That's all right, Mr. Jennings, I've worked hard my entire life. I deserve a nice car."

"Well, good for you."

She didn't want him asking questions about her work, so she asked him about himself, and for the next ten minutes he talked and she drove.

She merged onto Interstate 80 and then cut over and headed toward Marysville on 65. She stayed at the legal speed limit all the way to the Blue Oaks exit. She was well on her way to a seldom used two-lane road where teenagers sometimes gathered on the weekends to drag race when he finally stopped talking long enough to realize that something might be a little off.

"Where are we headed?"

"You said I could go anywhere I wanted, so I thought I'd take us on a little joyride in the dirt, see if this car is as good as you say it is."

"I don't think that's a good idea, toots."

"'Toots'? Do you call all of your female customers toots?"

"Just the cute ones."

She turned onto the dirt road and pushed down on the gas pedal, bringing the speedometer to seventy. "Tell me, Ron. Do you still pinch and pull hair like you used to?"

"What?" One of his hands was clamped on to the grab-handle above the window. He cleared his throat. "Of course not. What are you talking about?"

"You're a liar." She sped up. The speedometer read eighty and then eighty-five—way too fast for the road. The SUV was swimming a bit over the dirt. It was exhilarating.

The bend in the road wasn't too far off now.

He let go of the grab-handle and placed both hands on the dashboard instead. "You need to slow down, ma'am. This isn't safe or legal."

When she failed to do as he said, he lunged for the steering wheel.

Jenny grabbed a sharpened pencil from her jacket pocket and stabbed his arm—once, twice, three times until he finally retreated.

Blood dripped from his arm. "What the hell do you think you're doing?"

She kept her eyes on the road. "Nothing more than you did to me in high school." She dropped the pencil. "How does it feel? Not too good, right?" Keeping her eyes on the road, she blindly reached for him and pinched him as hard as she could.

He shouted an obscenity as he yanked his arm back where she couldn't get to him. "Who are you?"

"Someone you messed with one too many times."

"You're crazy!"

The speedometer read ninety. The dirt road was long and straight with a gradual uphill grade. Finally, straight ahead, was the 60-degree bend she was waiting for.

"Slow down!"

As the SUV lifted into the air over the peak, just before a bare dirt bank with a stand of trees in the background, she reached over with her right hand and unclasped his seatbelt.

His hands were all over the place as he tried to connect the belt. But it was too late. Instead of turning the wheel, she slammed hard on the brakes. She knew the air bag was supposed to be activated by accelerometers, not by making contact.

BAM!

The air bag on the driver's side shoved her back with tremendous force. For two seconds, Jenny wondered if she'd broken her neck. Disoriented, she reached for the door handle. A strong acrid smell and a fine white mist floated around her.

She sat quietly for a moment.

Before climbing out of the car, she looked over at the passenger seat. The top part of Ron's head had gone through the window. From the looks of it, a jagged piece of glass had taken off the top of his head upon impact. She could see more than just his skull. After the collision, she'd planned on giving him a shot of cyanide to make sure he didn't survive, but there was certainly no need for that now.

She stepped out onto the dirt road. Her legs trembled, but other than that she appeared to be in one piece. She moved her arms and legs. No broken bones.

That was close.

"You worry too much," she said. "Jennings is dead, and I feel great."

She cut off the road to the left, took off her heels to make it easier to walk on the uneven ground as she moved past trees and prickly bushes. When she got to the area where the trees ended and a field of grass began, she took off her wig and the long skirt, rolled them up tightly, and put them in her bag. She pulled out her compact mirror, made sure her hair and makeup looked all right, and then she hurried across the field, unseen. With her heels back on her feet, she knew she only had to walk two more blocks. Then she would call a taxi and go home and enjoy a long hot soak in her bathtub.

CHAPTER 26

Kitally sat in the car outside Chalkor's house for more than two hours, waiting for him to make an appearance, but he was a no-show. Kitally turned the key and decided to go check out the neighborhood where the woman's pug had gone missing.

It was a nice neighborhood in Midtown. Trees lined both sides of the street. After sitting in the car for forty-five minutes, she decided to stretch her legs and take a walk around the area. Two blocks away, she spotted a sign stapled to a telephone pole. The sign offered a reward for a missing dog. She pulled out her cell and called the number.

"Hello," a male voice said.

"Hi, I'm looking at a sign offering a reward for a dog and I was wondering—"

"Don't tell me you found my dog, too," he said, none too happily.

"No. I happen to be missing a dog myself and I thought I'd call and see if you found your dog."

"Oh . . . sorry. Where are you right now?" he asked.

"Why?"

"I thought I took all the signs down already."

Kitally looked at the nearest street sign and said, "I'm on the corner of Sky View and Granite."

"No shit?"

Kitally rolled her eyes.

"Stay right there," he said before he hung up the phone.

Kitally had no intention of doing any such thing, but as she started to walk away someone called out, "Hey, you!"

She turned around and saw a ripped-looking guy in his early thirties jogging her way. When he caught up to her, he wiped his hand on his pants and then held it out to her.

They shook hands.

"So," Kitally said, "did you find your dog?"

"Yep, that's what I wanted to tell you." He took the sign down and waved it in the air. "I also wanted to get this so I don't get any more annoying phone calls." He smiled sheepishly. "Not that you were annoying me or anything."

"Right."

"I got a call within twenty-four hours of putting up just a couple of signs offering a reward." He gave his head an angry shake. "The bastard wanted five hundred dollars instead of a hundred, though. Said he had to miss work taking care of the dog. Then there was the expense of feeding him and putting an ad in the paper."

"That sounds like a rip-off."

"Tell me about it. I would have let the guy keep the dog if my girlfriend hadn't gotten all weepy about it."

"I'm looking for a missing dog, too. Do you think offering a reward helped?"

"Definitely. My dog was missing for two weeks. I put signs everywhere, and I didn't hear one peep. Not until I offered the reward."

"Well, I'm glad you have your dog back." Kitally started to walk away, then turned back. "How do you think the dog got lost to begin with?"

"Faulty lock on our gate is all we could figure. I just replaced it."

"Do you think the dog could have been taken from your yard?"

He took a moment to think that over, then flushed and slapped the sign against his thigh. "Motherfucker. Why didn't I see it before now? I gave that asshole five hundred bucks! Jesus Christ."

Kitally lifted a brow. "I wonder how many dogs in the neighborhood are missing?"

"I have no idea. But I knew there was something off about that guy. I should have known he'd scammed me." The guy was almost panting, he was so angry. "If I ever see him around here, I'm going to kick his ass."

"I guess that means he didn't give you his name?"

"Are you kidding me? That guy didn't even have a receipt for the items he said he paid for. I don't even think he fed the damn dog."

"Did you see the car he was driving?"

"No car. The smug asshole just walked right up to the door with my dog on a leash. He kept the leash and handed over the dog, but not until I paid him."

"Did you pay with a check?"

"He called the number he got from my sign. Said he would only take cash." He raked his fingers through his hair. "God, what an idiot I was. If my girlfriend hadn't been freaking out over the stupid dog, I might have been thinking straight."

Kitally handed him her card and a pen. "Chill a little and just give me your name and number, and then if I find the guy, I'll give you a call."

"Sure. Man, I just can't believe I was taken like that."

"Don't be so hard on yourself. People get attached to their dogs and will do almost anything for them. I'm sure your girlfriend appreciates you getting her dog back for her."

"Yeah, sure, I guess. I should have grabbed that guy by the collar, taken the damn dog, and told him to take me to court." He finished writing his name and number and handed Kitally her card back. "What are you, some sort of a pet detective?"

She laughed. "Sure, for today, anyway."

"If you find him, you'll really give me a call?"

"Definitely. You don't live far at all from the woman I'm working for. But if you're at work, I don't know . . ."

"Won't be a problem. I work from home. I'm a web coder."

"Really?" This guy had to be the most muscle-bound web coder she'd ever met.

He nodded. "The name's David Downing." He held out his hand.

"Kitally," she said as they shook hands, hoping he wouldn't crush any bones. "If I can get my hands on him, I'll call you."

CHAPTER 27

Lizzy sat in her office on J Street. No matter how hard she tried, she couldn't get Shelby Geitner out of her mind.

Lizzy had thought she could stay out of it, let Detective Chase do his job, but there was no way she could sit on the sidelines and do nothing. She pulled out her notebook and scribbled down the names of the girls Shelby seemed to hang around with in class. She'd pay each and every one of them a visit. She grabbed her address book and flipped through her contacts, writing down more names as she went, then used her resources, which included everything from the phone book to one of many free and paid public access sites on the Internet. It wasn't long before she had a dozen people she wanted to talk to. Before she could grab her purse and take off, the office phone rang. It was her real estate agent, Pat.

"Lizzy. I've been trying to reach you for days."

"I was just heading out. What's going on?"

"I was at your house today and—"

"I don't want anyone going inside that house."

"But I thought—"

"You thought wrong," Lizzy said, cutting her off. "I don't want anyone in the house."

"But his sister said—"

Lizzy couldn't believe what she was hearing. "Lynn? Jared's sister called you?"

"Yes. She made it sound like she was in charge."

"She's not. The house is in mine and Jared's name."

"I don't mean to be insensitive, but there are practical considerations that I know you're in no condition to—that you're far too busy to deal with right now. I want to help. There's a wonderful couple I know who clean out houses for busy people like you. They'll pack everything up nice and neat, label all of the boxes and—"

"I don't want anyone in my house. Do you hear me?"

Silence.

Lizzy swallowed the lump in her throat. "I'll call you if there's any change."

"Are you OK, Lizzy?"

Lizzy's shoulders dropped. She was tired of people asking her the same question every five minutes. No, she was not OK. She was a fucking zombie, and that was on her best days. If someone didn't like it, they could go to hell. She was doing her best.

"Are you still there?"

"I'm here," Lizzy said. "I'll call you if there's any change," she repeated, holding back from calling the woman a scavenger.

"OK. Sorry to bother you."

Lizzy hung up the phone, more than annoyed when it rang again. "Hello," she snapped.

"Is this Lizzy Gardner?"

"This is her."

"Wonderful. I've been watching you."

"What a surprise," Lizzy said. She considered hanging up, figuring it was just another prank caller, but something in the woman's voice made her hang on another moment and see what the woman wanted.

149

"I was hoping we could chat."

"Mind telling me who I'm talking to?"

"I'm the one you're looking for."

"That's great, because it's so much easier if the people I'm looking for just call me up and tell me where they are. I'm listening."

"I can't give you my name, of course, but overall I believe the two of us are a lot alike."

"Well, lucky you," Lizzy said. *Why does every asshole in the world think they know me? And why the hell am I still listening to this crackpot?*

"Like you, I had some rough spots when I was younger. Recently, though, I realized things had to change, and it was time to punish some people for the things they did to me."

Hmm. "You think that's what I'm doing?"

"I've done some research on you, and I think you're trying to rid the world of one bad guy at a time."

"Interesting, but I have to disagree. I'm not trying to rid the world of anything. I try to help kids learn to defend themselves and I also help people with whatever it is they need."

"Fine. You're helping people," the caller said, clearly annoyed. "I'm calling you because I have a proposition to make."

"I'm still listening." *Barely.*

"Since we're on the same side," the woman began, "I thought I would call you and ask you to lay off. No talking to the police. Just keep this between you and me."

Lizzy rubbed her forehead, again thinking about hanging up. She didn't have time for bullshit. "Keep *what* between you and me?"

"I know you talked to Melony Reed and Dean Newman's girlfriend. Did Melony hire you to investigate something?"

Lizzy straightened in her chair. Now they were getting somewhere. "That's privileged information."

"Melony's dead. I don't think she would care if you told me."

"Do you know Melony Reed and Dean Newman?" Lizzy asked.

"Perhaps."

"Do you know where Dean Newman is?"

"If I did, why would I tell you?"

"Because you just said we were on the same side."

"First I have to be sure I can trust you."

"You can trust me, but how do I know if I can believe anything you're telling me? How do I know you're not just another crazy who likes to call the police or investigators like me for attention?"

"I'll tell you this much . . . you're never going to catch me."

For a moment, Lizzy said nothing as she stared out the window. But then she took the bait and asked, "Work together how?"

"You need to stay out of my business. Let me do my thing, and trust me when I say certain people deserve whatever punishment I dish out."

Across the street, standing near the coffee shop, was a man. Tall and broad-shouldered, and he wasn't drinking coffee. He wasn't doing much of anything, for that matter. Just looking toward Lizzy's office, staring, watching.

The hairs at the back of Lizzy's neck stood on end. The woman was talking again, but Lizzy wasn't paying any attention. "Could you hold on just for one moment?"

Lizzy didn't wait for an answer. She set the phone on her desk, grabbed her cell phone, and began to take pictures of the man. She was able to zoom in, but the glass window and cloudy day didn't make for a perfect shot. On her feet now, she pretended to sort through a few papers as she slowly rounded her desk; then she grabbed the door, opened it, and sprinted for the coffee shop.

The man took off.

Lizzy took chase. Already up to speed, she might be able to catch up to him. He wore jeans and a bluish-brown plaid shirt. She hadn't been able to see his face since he also wore dark shades and a baseball hat. He was a big guy, though. Same large build as Detective Chase. He knocked a woman to the side and took off down an alleyway between two buildings. Lizzy cut into the alleyway just as he made a sharp right out of view at midblock.

Her breathing was growing labored. She hadn't taken her morning run in a while. OK, quite a while. She was out of shape. By the time she cut down the crossing alleyway, he was gone.

She stood there panting, hands on hips. After she caught her breath, she walked along the alley to the parking lot at its end.

Nothing but a few delivery trucks. Behind the solid wood fencing to her right were houses. She listened for any sign that might tell her he'd gone that way: barking dogs, people talking, footsteps. Nothing. It was cold out, and her breath came out in frosty puffs as she walked toward the delivery trucks. The back doors of the first two were thrown wide-open. Boxes were stacked high. She rubbed warmth into her arms as she walked along to the next truck. Its doors were more than three-quarters closed. She peered inside, couldn't see a thing. She grabbed the handle and was about to pull the metal door open.

"Hey, what are you doing?"

Damn. She stepped back and faced the uniformed driver approaching her with a box in his hands. Watching them both was another man, standing in the back doorway of the business the driver had apparently just left. Great: an audience. She didn't have time for a scene.

"Just looking for someone."

"Inside the back of my truck?"

"Well, yeah."

Shaking his head, the driver grabbed hold of the handle and yanked it open.

A kick in the face was what he got for his efforts. He was on the ground, flat on his back, his nose a bloody mess, and then the man Lizzy had been chasing was vaulting over him and charging off across the parking lot.

"Call for help!" Lizzy shouted to the business owner looking out the back door before she was on the run again. She sprinted across the parking area, made a right back toward her office.

She darted across the street. Tires screeched. Somebody shouted at her.

He was gone.

After losing her guy, Lizzy went back to check on the driver. It wasn't long before two police cars pulled up, and then another dark sedan driven by none other than Detective Chase. Just what she needed. She watched him climb out of his car, not an easy feat considering his size.

"Gardner, why am I not surprised to see you here?"

"I don't know, Detective. You tell me. And why are you here? The guy has a broken nose for God's sake."

"I was in the area when the call came in." He sighed as he rubbed bloodshot eyes. His hair was a mess. For the next ten minutes, he questioned the driver. Then he made his way to Lizzy where she'd taken a seat on the pavement, her back resting against the side of a building.

"The guy with the broken nose said he was kicked in the face by a seven-foot-tall Caucasian NFL linebacker."

Not interested in talking to the detective's knees, Lizzy pushed herself to her feet. "Not seven feet. In fact, he's not as tall as you," she said, "but he's Caucasian and definitely as big as a linebacker."

He stifled a yawn as he made notes.

"Didn't get enough sleep last night?"

"I can't remember the last time I got enough sleep."

"Do you need anything else, Detective, or am I free to go?"

"What's going on, Gardner?"

"What do you mean?"

He gave her a stern look that was meant to intimidate. "Who was this guy? Why were you chasing him?"

"If you didn't already know, I tend to attract weirdos like honey attracts bees."

"So you've seen him before today?"

She nodded. "He's been following me around for a while."

"Why didn't you tell me?"

She cocked a brow. "Tell *you*? Why would I tell you?"

"Fine," he said, "maybe I deserve that, but believe it or not, I care about keeping the citizens of Sacramento safe."

"Good to know."

"Has he broken into your home?"

"Not that I'm aware of. So far he seems to be a lurker. Today was the first time I saw him in the middle of the day. Usually it's after the sun goes down."

"The delivery man over there said the guy had on dark glasses and a cap."

She nodded. "White cap. Dirty."

Awkward silence filled the space between them. It took her a second to get it. Detective Chase thought she knew more than she was telling him. She plunked a hand on her hip. "If I had any idea who this guy was, I'd tell you."

"You're sure about that?"

"Why wouldn't I?"

"Rumor has it that you're losing it, maybe even have some sort of death wish."

"Listen, Detective, I don't know who your informants are, but nothing has changed. I want to keep the people of Sacramento safe, too. And before you go around accusing people of such things as *losing it*, you might want to get a couple of hours of sleep. You look like shit."

Five minutes later, tired and clearly off her game, Lizzy walked back into her office. She lifted the phone to her ear, then set it back in its cradle. Until that moment, she'd forgotten all about the caller, the woman who could very well be responsible for at least five deaths, maybe more.

She leaned over to pick up a piece of paper that had fallen on the floor. That's when she noticed a few other things out of place. Her pencil holder had been knocked over. The bottom drawer of the filing cabinet was open. Other drawers were open, too. Her purse was still there. Nothing appeared to be missing.

Frustration coursed through her veins. Her heart raced. While she was talking to the detective, her stalker had been in her office going through her things.

The detective had been right about one thing: she was losing it.

"You're oh for a thousand," Lizzy told herself. "Keep up the good work."

It wasn't until she was getting ready to leave that she found a folded piece of paper inside her coat pocket. Chills swept over her as she read the note:

What wood my life have been like without you in it?
I can't imagine. Love, Jared

CHAPTER 28

Lizzy and Hayley sat in the family room, both on their laptops. Lizzy tried to distract herself from the note she'd found earlier, but it wasn't easy. Who was this man who was so damned determined to track her every move? What did the note mean? It definitely wasn't Jared's handwriting. Besides, Jared could spell. The guy wanted to throw Jared into the mix, it seemed. Just another asshole trying to screw with her. *OK, it's on. Bring it.*

She wasn't ready to share the note with anyone, so she concentrated on the Ambassador Club list that Melony Reed had given her: Stephen White had died from an explosion after the barbecue blew up—gunpowder and nitroglycerine. According to the reports she'd read, three others had died of possible heart attacks: Debi Murray before her car went off the road, Rachel Elliott before falling on punji sticks, and then Gavin Murdock at a family barbecue. It wasn't often that a thirty-year-old person, let alone three, dropped dead from heart failure. Lizzy had called the coroner's office, and as far as they could tell, no autopsy or toxicology reports were ordered for any of them. The families of these victims had accepted the causes of death and that was that. Lizzy intended to talk to family members to see if lab testing had been ordered. Melony had insisted that Rachel was healthier than

156

most. Lizzy made a note to call the family doctor and see if she could learn more about Rachel's death. Accidents caused by punji sticks and falling on knives in the dishwasher were too far out there. It didn't add up.

The front door opened and closed. "I'm starved," Kitally said, "and I'm going crazy. I've been sitting in my car every day for weeks. I feel like a caged animal."

"Did you get more pictures of Mr. Chalkor?" Hayley asked without looking up from her computer. "The insurance company called today. They're getting antsy."

Kitally plunked her bag on the dining room table. "Mr. Chalkor is onto me. He called me out the other day when I followed him to a park, and now he hasn't come out of his house in days. I've been parking in new spots every day, but I think maybe I'll have to drive a different car."

"If you don't get pictures by the end of the week, we might need to change tactics."

"Who made these cookies?" Kitally asked from the kitchen.

"Your neighbor brought those about an hour ago," Hayley said. "She told me that she hadn't brought you cookies in a very long time."

"Really?" Kitally asked. "What neighbor?"

"A perky brunette with a seventies hairdo and vintage eyeglasses. I thought she seemed a bit off, but who am I to judge fashion?"

"True that," Kitally said. "But that's really strange, though. I don't remember anyone ever bringing me cookies before." Kitally went to the cupboard to get a glass.

An uneasy tingling rippled through Lizzy as she mulled over each of the victims' causes of death once again. Three of the deaths were being attributed to heart attacks. Were these people being poisoned in some way? If so, the killer might know more than a little about toxic chemicals and/or poisons. Lizzy suddenly recalled the woman who had called her today at the office. God, how had she forgotten about her? She'd sounded annoyed when she thought Lizzy wasn't taking her seriously enough. She'd wanted to proposition Lizzy—said they were on the same team.

Lizzy jumped from her chair and ran to the kitchen, bumping into a table on her way.

Kitally had poured herself a glass of milk. A cookie was inches from her lips.

Lizzy slapped the cookie out of Kitally's hand, sending it flying across the room. The cookie hit the pantry door and broke into pieces.

"What are you doing?" Kitally asked.

"Don't touch those cookies."

"Lizzy," Hayley said. "What's going on?"

"Somebody is trying to kill us," Lizzy announced. "All of us."

"Who?"

"A woman—a crazy bitch."

Lizzy took the plate of cookies and tossed them into the garbage. She was about to hit the trash compactor button but stopped herself. "Don't be a dumbass, Lizzy!"

Kitally looked at Hayley, eyes wide.

Lizzy started opening drawers and pulled out a pair of metal tongs that she then used to reach into the trash and pull out more than one cookie. She slid them into a plastic Ziploc bag. "I really do need to get my act together."

Hayley exhaled. "Lizzy, you're talking to yourself."

Lizzy shrugged. "Got a problem with that?"

"Yeah, I sort of do. Why don't you tell us what's going on. You're talking crazy talk."

Lizzy held up the bag. "I'm going to have these tested. Is that all right with you?"

Nobody said a word.

"Wash your hands," Lizzy told Kitally. "Scrub them good." She turned to Hayley. "I'm taking these to the lab first thing in the morning."

"Could you stop for one moment and tell us exactly what's going on?"

"I thought I just did."

"You're mumbling—talking to yourself. You need to slow down and take a minute to gather your thoughts."

Lizzy knew Hayley was right. She took a steadying breath. She needed to settle down. "Let's have a seat in the living room," she said, "and I'll answer all of your questions."

Lizzy started from the beginning. She told them all about her meeting with Melony Reed and how days later the woman was dead, a freak accident in her kitchen. Next, she showed them the lists of names Melony had given her: the list of Ambassador Club members who were dropping like flies, and the list of all the people Melony thought had gotten the worst of the Ambassador Club's abuse, the ones she thought might be capable of revenge. Lizzy also recounted her visit with Dean Newman's girlfriend.

"How many members of the Ambassador Club are still alive?" Hayley asked.

"According to Melony, there were a total of thirteen members. Two live out of the country, Louise Penderfor and Claire Moss, so I crossed them off the list. That leaves four, not including Dean Newman, who could still be alive."

"How long has this Newman dude been missing?"

"Three or four days, I believe."

Hayley looked over the list. "So you believe the same woman who killed these people is also trying to kill us?"

"Yes."

"Why would she want to kill us?" Kitally cut in. "*We* didn't bully her."

"When I was at the office today," Lizzy said, "a woman called—said she wanted to make some sort of deal. She knew I had paid Melony Reed and Dean Newman's girlfriend a visit. At first I thought it was just another prank caller. I asked her—or maybe I accused her, I can't remember—of being just another crazy out there who wanted some attention."

"Then what?" Kitally asked.

"As I waited for her to make her case, I glanced out the window, saw the same man who we all saw in this very yard standing outside the coffee shop across the street. I ran after him."

"What about the caller?"

"I dropped the phone and took off. Of course, by the time I returned, she'd hung up. I'm pretty sure I pissed her off pretty good."

"Poison cookies," Kitally said. "Yeah, I'd say you might have hit a nerve."

Hayley stretched her neck as though working kinks out of it, clearly uncomfortable with Lizzy going after the big guy. Again.

"I'm afraid to ask," Kitally said. "Did you catch up to the man you went after?"

"Yeah, I did. Twice. The second time, he kicked a man in the nose and took off, leaving me in the dust."

"Did you get a look at him?"

"No, I mean yes. I got some crappy pictures of him. He's tall, broad-shouldered. He wore jeans, an ugly plaid shirt, dark glasses, and a hat."

"Bummer."

"If those cookies really do turn out to be poisonous," Kitally said, thinking out loud, "that would mean this female killer of yours thinks you're getting too close for comfort. Since you weren't willing to listen to her, she decided you had to go, too."

Lizzy nodded.

"If we assume Dean Newman is a goner," Hayley added, "that would mean there are four people left on her list—Mindy Graft, Aubrey Singleton, Chelsea Webster, and Gary Perdue." Hayley held up both lists. "On the other list Melony gave you—the list of people Melony believed could be seeking revenge—we have ten possibilities. Where are you going to put your efforts? Warning the four people left on the Ambassador Club list, or going after the person who may be responsible?"

"We have to warn the four people who could be in danger," Lizzy said.

"I think we need more help," Kitally said.

"From who?" Hayley asked. "The police?"

"I've already talked to Detective Chase," Lizzy said. "He was quick to believe the deaths were all accidental. I can't really blame him, since not one family of the deceased has yet to question the cause of death."

"It's up to a victim's family to ask for an investigation?" Kitally asked.

Lizzy shrugged. "Often the case. If nobody raises a stink, the cops tend to naturally head off for the next crime they *know* is a crime."

Kitally shook her head. "These people must have been real assholes if their families didn't care enough to at least check it out."

Hayley nodded. "It's not easy to get a family to agree to an autopsy, either. They're already grieving from loss and then there are costs involved and a long wait for the results, which could delay the funeral arrangements."

Kitally shook her head. "This woman is literally getting away with murder."

"If she's using poison to make it appear as if these people are dying of heart attacks," Hayley went on, "that would mean that the killer probably has some degree of knowledge in that field."

"True," Kitally said. "The killer could be using cyanide, rat poison, or antifreeze. Even a large dose of potassium would do the trick. Maybe we could narrow the list of ten by figuring out who has a background in medicine or chemistry."

"I would like the two of you to concentrate on warning the last four people," Lizzy said. "Not only is this woman dangerous; she's working fast. She's not afraid to take risks, which is why I want you two to stick together. I'll concentrate on whittling down the list of suspects."

"Sounds good," Kitally said as she stood, then looked vacantly around the kitchen. "I really am hungry." She turned to Hayley. "Did the neighbor leave anything else for us to eat?"

"Just the cookies," Hayley said. "Although I wouldn't touch that casserole I saw in the refrigerator."

"Don't listen to her," Lizzy said. "It's delicious."

"What is it?"

"Tofu casserole."

Hayley shrugged. "You've been warned."

"Are you saying I would be better off trying one of those cookies?"

"Absolutely."

"This is serious business," Lizzy reminded them.

"I'm sorry," Kitally said. "You're right."

Hayley looked at Kitally. "What did I tell you about always saying you're sorry?"

"I can't help it," she said. "Sorry."

"What's wrong with her saying she's sorry?"

"It's demeaning," Hayley told them. "Do you ever hear men apologize after a waiter screws up their order? No. Kitally needs to save the *I'm sorry*s for when it really matters. If someone knocks into her, *she* apologizes."

"A lot of women do that," Lizzy said with another shrug. "It's a nurturing thing."

"I don't care about other women. I care about Kitally."

"Well, that's nice of you to—"

"You have an auto-apology problem," Hayley interrupted Kitally. "So knock it off."

Kitally almost apologized again but stopped herself.

"I don't think it's that big of a deal," Lizzy said.

"Apologizing for things that aren't your fault is degrading and shows low self-esteem. It's stupid."

Lizzy shook her head. "I think you're fine, Kitally, really."

"That's because Lizzy doesn't know which way is up right now. Her head isn't screwed on right."

Lizzy stiffened. "Who are you suddenly—the fucking Queen of Know-It-All?"

Kitally put two fingers to her mouth and sliced the room with an ear-piercing whistle. "I'm sorry," she said, "but somebody needed to shut you two up. You're both insane. It's late. I'm hungry. And I think we should call it a night."

CHAPTER 29

It felt like only yesterday that Lizzy had last sat across from Linda Gates and tried to explain how she was feeling. How many different ways could she describe the empty, dank void inside her?

"I got an emotion for you. I was angry yesterday," Lizzy said, filling the silence. "In fact, I can't remember the last time I felt so livid."

"That's a good sign."

"I should have known you would be happy to hear that I was fuming mad."

Talk about lack of emotion. Lizzy might as well be talking to a fucking wall.

"What were you angry about?" Linda asked.

"Shelby Geitner."

"Is that the girl you told me about on the phone the other day? The girl who's missing?"

Lizzy nodded.

"From what you've told me over the past month, you have quite a few cases you're working on, lots of things to be angry about. So why this particular missing person case?"

"It's not *my* case—it's being investigated by authorities—but Shelby has been coming to my defense class for at least five years

164

now. It's hard for me to believe that someone would have been able to hide in her car without her noticing."

"And that makes you angry."

"Of course it does. I taught her well. What is this world coming to when you can't even be aware of the dangers around you and stay safe? Boyfriends and family members are turning on the people closest to them. It's sickening."

"Lizzy, most people don't live in constant fear, waiting for someone to attack them."

"Well, anyone associated with me or standing anywhere near me . . . anyone who knows me, for that matter, probably needs to be aware that they could be attacked at any moment for doing absolutely nothing. It's a fucking zoo out there."

"So you think whoever took Shelby was someone she knew?"

Lizzy thought about it. "Yes. I do."

"It's good to hear a little passion come back into your voice."

"I don't know what you're hearing in my tone, but whatever it is, it's got nothing to do with passion. I'm angry, though."

"So you've said."

"So I've said," Lizzy repeated, wondering why Linda seemed to be purposely prodding her. "I'm angry enough to start taking matters into my own hands." Lizzy came to her feet and began to pace the room. "I'm starting to think Hayley's had the right idea all along."

"How so?"

"She knows the difference between right and wrong. When it comes to solving a case or proving someone's guilt, she'll do whatever it takes. If that means breaking and entering, or using physical force, she'll do it without thinking twice."

"If I remember correctly, the tactics you've used to solve cases in the past haven't always been between the lines of the law."

"True, but I always thought long and hard about each and every step I took. There were many times I could have broken into a home in search of evidence I needed to close a case, but I didn't."

"And now you would?"

"In a heartbeat."

"Why?"

"Because time isn't on my side."

"Why do you say that?"

"I've got every lunatic in Sacramento, maybe the entire country, on my tail, watching my every move. Now I even have one calling me up to tell me we're all on the same side. I think that's reason enough."

"If you decide to ignore the law, what do you think Jared would say to that?"

"Are you serious?"

Linda nodded.

Lizzy stabbed the back of the couch with a finger. "I come here for one fucking hour every week and you always want to bring the conversation back to Jared. I'm the one you need to worry about, not Jared. I'm the one who's paying your ridiculously high hourly rates and I don't even know why. What good are you doing me, Linda, tell me that?"

"That's a good question, one that would be worth your taking some time to think about. If you come to the conclusion that I'm not helping you, then—"

"Then what? I should just stop coming? After all these years, you would just tell me we're finished—just toss it off, like some kind of afterthought?"

"I'm not telling you to stop coming, Lizzy. I'm just reminding you that we all have choices. The same thing goes for using physical force and deciding right from wrong. Every day we're inundated with choices—you, me, Hayley. It's the same for all of us."

"Well, thank you for that little sermon, Dr. Gates. I'll go home and think about everything you've said today." Lizzy put her hands out, palms flat up, and pretended to weigh her options. "I'll even ask Jared what he has to say before I make any important decisions."

"Lizzy, why don't you have a seat?"

Lizzy grabbed her jacket and went to the door, her other hand gripping the knob. She took a breath and looked over her shoulder at Linda. "I'll see you next week, OK?"

Linda nodded. "I'll be here."

CHAPTER 30

"Please let me go. I'm freezing. We'll both die out here in the woods. I'm scared." The girl's teeth chattered, loud enough for him to cover his ears to drown out the noise. He should have killed her the first day he'd brought her up the mountain. Shelby Geitner talked too much, was even demanding at times—telling him to get her more blankets and another sweater. Always something.

Frank Lyle added wood to the fire. It was a small fire, but it would heat up the soup he'd stolen and it would keep his hands warm.

"You know you're going to go to prison for kidnapping, don't you?"

"I've been locked up before. It's not so bad. Three meals a day, hot showers, television, a library."

"What were you in prison for?"

He didn't answer her.

"Do you read?" she asked.

"None of your business."

"If you could bring me a book to read, I wouldn't be so bored during the day."

"You won't have to worry about being bored for too much longer."

"Why? Are you going to kill me?"

"Not yet."

"Why not now?"

He grunted.

"Why are you doing this?"

"No more questions." He grabbed a cup, poured some soup into it, and brought it to where the girl was bound to an oak tree. He began to spoon-feed her. She was hungry. Feeding her was like feeding a baby bird. She opened her mouth before he even had a chance to ready the spoon.

He saw a spider crawling next to her and didn't hesitate to squash it with the heel of his boot.

He wasn't Spiderman. Unlike Spiderman, he didn't give a shit if they were called arthropods or arachnids. Spiderman considered the eight-legged things to be his friends. Frank didn't want any friends, creatures or otherwise. He wasn't a wannabe. He had plans of his own. He was going to make a name for himself.

Eventually he would have to kill Shelby Geitner—he might even rape and torture her before killing her—but not tonight, and probably not tomorrow, either. Not until he found an empty cabin or maybe a shed, some place where he could keep his prey. Then he would focus on Lizzy Gardner—find a way to lure her there, into his own private hell, make her watch him do to Shelby what he did best. When the moment was right, he would do the world a favor and kill Lizzy, too.

CHAPTER 31

The Geitner family lived in the Boulevard Park area in the heart of Sacramento, just a few blocks from downtown. It was known as the historic residential area, convenient due to the close proximity of restaurants and shops.

Lizzy knocked and then waited for someone to come to the door. She had called ahead of time to make sure Shelby's parents would be willing to talk to her.

Mr. Geitner came to the door. Pleasantries were exchanged before he led Lizzy inside. They passed by a grand foyer with a formal staircase. Shelby's mother, Denise Geitner, awaited them in the main sitting room. She sat quietly in one of the cushioned chairs surrounding the stone fireplace.

"Thanks for having me," Lizzy said before taking a seat across from Mrs. Geitner.

"The more people looking for our Shelby, the better," Mr. Geitner said.

They had known each other for years, but Denise barely acknowledged her. It was clear the woman was holding something in, maybe resentment or blame. Lizzy wasn't sure. "I am so sorry," Lizzy began.

"Sorry for what?" Denise asked. "Is there something you know?"

"Let her finish," Mr. Geitner cut in.

Lizzy tried again. "I can't imagine what you two are going through—"

"But you know exactly what Shelby is going through," Denise said. "Is he torturing her? Raping her? Is she tied up? Where is my daughter? What is he doing to her?"

"She's here to help us, Denise. Give Lizzy a chance."

"I don't understand what you think you can do, Lizzy. The entire police force is working on finding Shelby."

Lizzy didn't let the woman's tone rile her. She'd been dealing with distraught parents for over a decade. Denise was panicking. Probably hadn't gotten much sleep. She wanted to blame someone . . . anyone.

Lizzy just needed to stay calm, find out what she could if she was going to be able to help Shelby. "I was wondering if you could tell me what Shelby's mood was in the days before she disappeared."

Mr. Geitner sighed. "Detectives asked the same question. Neither of us noticed any changes in Shelby. She's a happy, healthy teenager. She has lots of friends. We didn't notice any changes in her demeanor."

"I did notice something different about Shelby," Denise said, her voice a whisper. "Shelby seemed skittish, always looking over her shoulder, as if someone were watching her."

Lizzy felt a chill settle over her.

"You didn't mention any of this to the detective when he questioned you," Mr. Geitner cut in, clearly out of sorts. "I thought you said she'd been the same as always—doing her homework, helping with chores . . ."

"I haven't been sleeping, of course," Denise went on, ignoring her husband and speaking directly to Lizzy. "Last night it hit me. But even before that, I think I knew something was off with my daughter, but I wasn't able to put my finger on exactly what it was until last night. I think Shelby knew she was being watched."

Mr. Geitner frowned. "Watched by who? She would have told us if she was worried about a stalker."

"I don't think she knew for sure," Denise said, her voice growing stronger. "I think her reactions were instinctive."

"How long did you notice this behavior?" Lizzy asked.

"A few days at least. A week at the most."

Mr. Geitner grew red in the face. "And you didn't think to tell me?"

"Bill, I'm saying it now. What do you want from me? None of this came together for me until just last night. Why don't you stop harassing me and go out there and find your daughter?"

"I've been out on the streets, going door to door every day and night. I'm doing everything I can. What have you been doing? You didn't even want to talk to Lizzy."

"Please," Lizzy said, not wanting to get in the middle of their argument, but feeling as if she had no choice. "These are stressful times. Your lives have been turned upside down. Don't let this come between you. You have other children who need you. The two of you need to stick together . . . for everyone involved."

"Lizzy is right," Bill said.

For the first time since she'd walked into the house, Denise looked into Lizzy's eyes. "Find her. And hurry."

CHAPTER 32

It was hard to believe it was already February. The sun was out, and the warmth felt good against her back as Jenny walked across the parking lot toward her car. The average temperature for the month of February was usually between 57 and 62 degrees. Today the temperature had to be somewhere in the seventies. Sweat trickled down her spine.

"Jenny! Hold up!"

She turned around, surprised to see Dwayne Roth running her way. Had he seen her take the vials out of the lab? No, that couldn't be. She'd made certain nobody was around, even took the extra precaution of getting to work early, when the building was practically deserted. Maybe someone else within the company was onto her and he wanted to warn her.

"Man, oh, man," he said when he caught up to her, bending over to catch his breath. "I've been trying to talk to you for days now. You left early yesterday—"

"I came in early, that's why."

"Oh, no," he said, putting his hands up as if in self-defense. "I'm not accusing you of cheating on your hours. I would never do that. I am doing a good job of making a fool out of myself, though, aren't I?"

She didn't know what to say to that, so she simply stood there, waiting to see what it was exactly that he wanted.

"Let me start over." He stood tall, straightened his tie, fixed his hair—making a big show of setting the moment, but for what?

Dwayne was an odd duck, in a good way, if that was possible. He was one of the few men who bothered dressing up for work.

"I was hoping you would go to a movie with me."

The anxiety that had been building since first seeing him sprint toward her disappeared completely. "That's what this is all about? You're asking me on a date?"

"Yes."

She looked at him again, this time taking note of his pale skin and curly, almost wiry, brown hair. He was much taller than Brandon had been. She had to tilt her head and crook her neck in order to look into his eyes. He was cute in somewhat the same way the singer Josh Groban was. Not that Dwayne was that good-looking, but he was definitely attractive in his own quirky way.

Jenny had never been asked on a date before.

The only reason she'd ended up with Brandon was because she'd met him on the plane during a long delay when all the passengers were stuck in their seats and had nowhere else to go. He had been so charming, and she'd been absolutely gobsmacked that a ridiculously handsome man such as Brandon was paying her any attention at all, which is why she'd said yes when he'd asked if he could stay at her place during his two-day layover. During the night, he'd crawled into bed with her and that was that. He was the first man to make love to her without using force. The feelings she'd felt for Brandon had been instantaneous. He'd wanted her and he'd told her she was beautiful.

And you believed the idiot. A complete stranger. Don't forget that. You can't afford to make friends right now. Not when you're so close to finishing what you've started.

"I'm sorry," Dwayne said, mistaking her hesitation as disinterest. "I know this might seem sudden, but it's not. I noticed you months ago when you first came to work for Ecco. It just took me this long because, well, look at me."

She did look at him—again—but this time she let her gaze drift a little south and then north.

"I'm not exactly God's gift to women."

He's a twit. Dwayne Roth wants what every other man wants—to get inside your pants. Turn around, get in your car, and drive away.

"I guess you did kind of catch me off guard," she told him.

He rubbed the back of his neck. "I'm sorry. It's clear I've made you uncomfortable. I never intended to jeopardize our friendship by asking you out. Maybe we should pretend this never happened."

"No," Jenny blurted. "I would love to go to a movie with you."

"Really?"

"Definitely. When were you thinking?"

The hopeful and excited look on his face was endearing.

Are you kidding me! Wake up and smell the oxytocin.

"How about Saturday afternoon?"

Today was Friday. "Tomorrow?"

No way! You have a kill list to finish off.

"Too soon?" he asked.

She shook her head. "No, not at all. Saturday is fine."

You're a fool.

"I'll pick you up at six for dinner. Do you like Mexican food?"

"That sounds perfect. Do you know where I live?"

Don't do it. Don't tell him where you live.

"Having your address would be helpful if I'm going to pick you up." He patted his pockets. "No pen or paper. I ran out of my office so fast, I didn't bring my cell phone, either."

Meet him at the theater. Don't give him your address.

She reached into her purse, shuffled around until she found a slip of paper to write her address and telephone number on. Then she handed it to him.

"You've made my day, Jenny Pickett. I'll see you tomorrow."

"I'll be waiting."

CHAPTER 33

Hayley crouched low, kept hidden beneath a wall of brush. The beams of his headlights shot past the top of her head as he pulled his car into the parking lot of the apartment complex.

For over a month now she'd been watching three different men, all rapists, all let out on parole much too soon. This guy, Paul, was the oldest and the most dangerous. He lured young girls in with his quick wit and charming good looks. He was like a bright beacon of light on cold, windy nights like tonight. He went after young girls who were homeless or had run away from their troubled homes, and then *ZAP*; they didn't know what hit them until it was too late.

According to RAINN—the Rape, Abuse & Incest National Network—54 percent of rapes were never reported. Only three out of every one hundred rapists spent time in prison. The odds were almost always in the rapist's favor.

Once Hayley was sure he went to his apartment alone, she would go home and come back another night. It was almost one in the morning. Usually Paul returned home closer to midnight.

She watched him climb out of his car.

Hayley couldn't see anyone else inside the vehicle. She hadn't realized she'd been holding her breath until she exhaled and released some tension. She watched him walk to his apartment on the bottom floor, unlock the door, and head inside. The kitchen light went on.

Hayley stood, stretched her legs. She was about to head off when the guy walked outside again and headed back for the car.

What the hell?

Only half-hidden now, she held still, didn't move a muscle. It was dark enough that he wouldn't see her unless he allowed enough time for his eyes to adjust to the dark. The few outside lights surrounding the apartment building had either gone out eons ago or someone had broken the bulb for the hell of it. It was a building filled with degenerates. Even if neighbors took the time to look out their windows to see what Almost Dead was up to, they wouldn't give a shit. He had nothing to worry about, which was why he remained focused on the task at hand. Just another night for the guy . . .

He opened the back door and scooped up a young girl who had passed out in the backseat. Then he turned, used his foot to shut the car door, and headed back into his apartment.

Fuck.

Although she watched these losers for this very reason, she really wasn't in the mood for an altercation. It wasn't that she minded kicking his ass—quite the opposite. If anything, she was afraid of what she might do to the guy. If his probation officer could watch some of the worst offenders just a little bit closer, she wouldn't be here now, taking care of business.

She pulled out her baton, extended it fully, practiced a few moves, and then put it away. She checked the sheaths at her ankles. Knives were in place. She craved a smoke, but there was no time for that. As she walked toward his apartment, she wondered for a moment if he had any idea, any inkling at all, that he was almost dead.

CHAPTER 34

The lady with the missing pug—Jacque Victoria Mason—was a pain in the ass. While Tommy worked on installing a video camera in the entryway, Kitally tried to keep Jacque Mason busy. The woman preferred to be addressed by her full name, but that was too bad.

She was a talker. She was also nervous and fidgety and couldn't hold still for more than a few minutes at a time. Her pug, Gracie, had been missing for almost a week now, but the good news was that less than forty-five minutes ago, Jacque had gotten a call from a man who said he just saw her sign and he happened to have her dog.

That didn't give Kitally much time to prepare. She should have waited until after Tommy installed the camera before she hung up the reward signs.

Too late now. You live and you learn.

"Where is he? Why hasn't he brought back my Gracie?" the woman asked for the third time in five minutes.

"I'm sure he's on his way," Kitally said.

No sooner had the phone rang than Jacque took off, running as fast as her eighty-year-old legs would take her, which was impressive considering she used a cane and walked with a limp. None of that stopped the elderly woman from picking up the phone before it could ring a second time.

"Oh, hello, dear. I was hoping it was Gracie's dognapper calling again. Yes, I'll let you know as soon as Gracie is back home." She hung up. Her shoulders sagged.

Kitally and Tommy exchanged pitiful looks.

"That should do it," Tommy said as he stepped down from the stool. "The camera also has a voice recorder," he told Jacque.

He was about to open the door, but Kitally stopped him. "Duck!" she told him. "I see someone coming now."

Jacque lunged for the doorknob.

"Don't open the door," Kitally said. "We need him to come all the way up to the door."

Tommy placed his hands on Jacque's frail shoulders. "Try to hold the door as wide-open as possible to make sure we get a good shot of the guy."

Jacque looked at the landscape painting in the entryway. "Are you sure this is going to work? I can't see the camera."

"That's the idea," Kitally told her. "The camera is tiny for a reason. We don't want this guy to know we're onto him. Tommy, is everything ready?"

"We're good to go," he said.

"There isn't enough time for us to hide outside," Kitally explained. "Is there a back room where we can hide?"

Jacque led them to the hallway and then pointed to the back room to the left.

A knock on the door caused her to jump.

"Stay calm and everything will be fine," Kitally told her.

"Don't forget to open the door wide," Tommy said as she walked off.

Tommy had downloaded an application that made it possible to watch the scene from his phone. They watched Jacque put her cane to the side so she could open the door. She opened it wide and left it that way.

"She's doing good so far," Tommy whispered.

"Gracie," Jacque cried as she reached for her dog.

The pug tried to wiggle out of the man's arms, but he wouldn't let Gracie go.

"Give her the dog," Kitally said under her breath. "Why isn't he giving the old lady her dog?"

"Shh, let's just watch."

"Where's my money?"

Jacque handed the man one hundred dollars, just as they had rehearsed.

He grabbed it and stuffed the bills into his front pocket, but he still wouldn't hand over the dog. "I want you to know that I had to take a day off work so that I could take your dog to the vet. It cost me five hundred dollars. I also had to feed him. I'd appreciate it if you would reimburse me for all costs."

"That's a lot of money."

"Sorry, lady. No money, no dog."

"Do you have receipts?"

He used his free hand to pat his back pockets. "Nope, didn't think to bring them."

"Oh, my, let me get my purse. I'll write you a check."

Before Jacque could walk off, he stopped her. "I'm having problems with my bank. Cash would be better."

"Let me see what I can do." Jacque hurried back to the room where Tommy and Kitally were hiding. "He wants more money."

"What are you going to do?" Kitally asked.

"I'm going to have to pull some cash out of my hiding place. You two go into the bathroom for a moment."

As soon as she was done rummaging through her closet, she gave them permission to come out of the bathroom.

Kitally stuck her head out the door and watched Jacque make her way back to the front door. "The poor woman is being taken. What if nobody is able to ID the guy from the video? We can't let him get away with—where are you going?"

Tommy was at the door. "I'll slip out back and circle around, follow him when he leaves."

"I'll keep your phone," Kitally said, "so I can keep an eye on Jacque."

A few seconds after Tommy disappeared, Kitally got an idea. She grabbed her phone, found the number of the guy who lived in the neighborhood, the guy who wanted to know if Kitally ever found the dognapper.

She held one phone to her ear while she watched Jacque in real time on Tommy's phone. Jacque handed over another four hundred dollars, but the dognapper still wasn't satisfied.

David Downing answered on the third ring. Kitally quickly explained what was going on. "If you want to talk to this guy, he's at 411 Ashley Court, just down the block from the telephone pole—"

"Hell yeah! I'm just around the freaking corner! I'm there." He clicked off.

"I meant five hundred additional dollars," Kitally heard the man say to Jacque as he shoved another wad of cash into his pocket.

"That's highway robbery, young man. You should be ashamed of yourself."

"Listen, lady, give me all the money you have, or you're never going to see your dog again." He squeezed the pug hard. The dog yipped.

When she reached for her dog, he took a backward step. "How many times do I gotta tell you? No money. No dog. Do you have Alzheimer's or somethin'?"

Jacque grabbed her cane, stepped outside, and whacked him hard across the knees.

He cursed but held tight to the dog.

She hit him again, this time in the shoulder and then below the belt, careful not to hurt Gracie.

The dognapper dropped to his knees.

Gracie wriggled out of her captor's arms and ran inside the house. Jacque stepped inside just as Kitally ran past her—but Kitally was too late.

The dognapper was limping away and never saw what hit him until he was on the ground.

David Downing was fast, and he was on top of him. It got ugly in a hurry. Kitally and Tommy didn't really get to enjoy the moment before they had to wade in and drag the guy off him. No sense in giving the cops two arrests to make.

When they had David under control, Kitally handed Tommy his phone and had just pulled out hers to call the police when she heard Jacque already on the line with them just inside the house.

Only then, with the dognapper moaning at their feet, were Kitally and Tommy able to relax enough to share a grin and a high five.

"Another case solved," Kitally said.

Tommy laughed. "You really do have a knack for this investigative business, don't you?"

"I don't know about that," Kitally said, unable to get the smile off her face. "But I actually look forward to waking up each day." Just inside the door, Jacque's fat little pug was happily leaning up against her leg as she finished her call with the police. "That's job satisfaction, right there. Jacque Mason has her dog back."

"Twenty minutes ago, you thought she was a pain in the ass."

"I still think Jacque Victoria Mason *is* a pain in the ass. But she has her dog back, and that's all that matters. God, I love it."

"Love what?"

"The whole thing. The thrill of cracking a case—following clues, searching for the truth. It's a high that can't be beat."

"It's also dangerous. Lizzy and Jared are proof of that."

She heard sirens in the distance. "Sadly, I think that's part of the appeal."

"All you girls are so different and yet so much alike at the same time."

"Yeah, we're sort of a crazy family now."

"I guess you are. You're all living together. How's that working out?"

"It's horrible," she said with a laugh. "You know, people trying to poison us, stalkers in the backyard—your average family. We each have our own bathroom, so it works."

"I'm glad."

"In case you didn't know, you're part of the family, too."

Before Tommy could respond, the police car pulled up, red lights swirling.

CHAPTER 35

As Jenny walked down the narrow hallway to her office, she didn't bother straightening the picture frames. She sat at her desk and pulled out the list.

~~Brandon Louis – stabbed~~
~~Terri Kramer—Food poisoning~~
~~Stephen White—Explosion~~
~~Debi Murray—Car accident/brakes~~
~~Gavin Murdock—Heart attack/antifreeze~~
~~Rachel Elliott—Running accident~~
~~Melony Reed—Kitchen accident~~
~~Ron Jennings—Car accident~~
~~Louise Penderfor—Moved~~
Mindy Graft
Aubrey Singleton
~~Claire Moss—Moved~~
Chelsea Webster
~~Dean Newman—Suicide~~
Gary Perdue

Four more people to take care of. How am I going to get rid of them?

A fall down the stairway. Poison. Drowning. Electrical mishap. Contaminated well water. Suffocation. Choking. Carbon monoxide poisoning.

OK, OK. That's enough. Her mind was muddled. She couldn't stop thinking about Dwayne. Tomorrow night she would be going on her first real date—dinner and a movie. She'd never been to a movie with a man. What would she wear? What would they talk about?

Try doing a search on the guy, why don't you? Something you should have done when you met Brandon.

Not a bad idea. She typed *Dwayne Roth* into her search engine and hit the Return key. A picture of him, and in a minute she had enough for a short bio. He attended McClatchy High School and then went on to receive top honors at UCLA. Like her, he was a senior research chemist. He didn't have a Facebook page. She couldn't find anything about family or friends, but so far, so good. They had a lot in common—grew up in the same area, worked in the same field. She hit the Back button and ended up on the website for Lizzy Gardner Investigations.

Lizzy Gardner. What was she trying to prove?

She'd tried to talk to the woman, but she wouldn't listen. She wondered if the cookies she'd delivered had proved useful. She didn't dare risk a drive-by, so she decided to make a quick call and see who picked up.

The phone rang three times before she heard, "Lizzy Gardner Investigations. Can I help you?"

"Yes. I would like to speak with Lizzy Gardner, please."

"Can I tell her who's calling?"

The person who had answered sounded calm, even relaxed. Maybe they weren't ready for word to get out that Lizzy and her friends were in the hospital or, better yet, dead. Jenny exhaled and said, "Tell her it's a friend calling about the Melony Reed case."

"Just a moment."

A little charade, pretending Lizzy was in any condition to take the call. Maybe they were trying to trace it. Let them try. Jenny brushed her fingers over her list. Impatient, she scribbled Lizzy's name on the bottom and prepared to draw a line through it.

"This is Lizzy Gardner. How can I help you?"

It couldn't be.

"Who is this?"

Silence.

"I sent one of the cookies to the lab," Lizzy said. "I should have the results in a few weeks."

"How did you know?"

"Just a hunch."

"Very shrewd of you."

"It's obvious you have a knack for toxicology."

"Obvious? How so?"

"People from your high school are suddenly dying from heart attacks at a young age and punji sticks dipped in a toxic substance."

"I don't believe that has been substantiated."

"Maybe not, but that's the reason I didn't think it was a good idea to eat homemade cookies baked by a stranger and delivered by a neighbor nobody has met before."

"*Somebody* must have eaten a cookie. They were delicious."

"I'm sure they were divine, but we try to stay away from food that has been contaminated," Lizzy said. "Oh, and I'm sorry I had to leave you hanging on the phone the other day. This dark shadow of a man has been watching me, and I felt the urge to give chase."

"Is that so?"

"Sadly, it's the truth."

"You didn't catch him?"

"Not yet."

"You *are* popular with the more malevolent crowd, aren't you?"

"So it seems."

"What's so special about you, I wonder?"

"Hmm, I don't know if *special* would be the word I would use," Lizzy said. "*Luckless* maybe? *Unfortunate* perhaps?"

"You're an interesting individual."

Lizzy didn't respond. For a few seconds neither said a word, and Jenny sensed that they were both perfectly comfortable in the shared silence.

"There are four more people on your list," Lizzy finally said.

"You *have* done your homework."

"I think you should turn yourself in."

"I did nothing wrong," Jenny answered, feeling a tight pull in her chest. "I was abused every day for four years. All I wanted was to be left alone. I did everything I could to be invisible to those people, but nothing I did mattered. They had it out for me. I was pushed and shoved, pinched and pulled. I was blindfolded, taken for a ride, and left alone, miles away from my home, in the dead of night. And that was just the beginning. I was also raped and then held down for his friends. I was humiliated, battered, insulted in every way possible. Each and every one of those animals deserves the death penalty."

"There is a criminal justice system in place to impose penalties for those who break the law."

"Don't make me laugh. You know as well as I do that sometimes people need to take the law into their own hands if they want any justice in this world. I went to the principal. I talked to my teachers. They did nothing. Nobody cared."

"So why now?"

"Why not?"

"After all these years," Lizzy said, "something must have triggered your deep-seated resentment."

"Oh, listen to you," Jenny said. "Well, I know some things, too. Like that you've been seeing a therapist for years. Sounds like she's rubbed off on you."

"Want me to give you her phone number? I'm sure she could help you."

"No, thanks," Jenny said. "The *trigger*, as you called it, was a man—the proverbial straw that broke the camel's back."

"Is he still alive?"

"I have no idea," she lied. "He was a pig. Who cares?"

"I'm going to warn the four people still left on your list that they're in danger."

"I wish you wouldn't."

"I don't have a choice."

"We all have choices."

"And that includes you," Lizzy said.

"I've made mine."

"Are you talking to me from your home phone?"

"Afraid not," Jenny answered. "I purchased some of those throwaways. Convenient, really."

"I would say so. I guess I won't be able to call you when I need someone to talk to?"

Jenny laughed. "I'll call you again, but it looks like I have a lot of work ahead of me now that I have a deadline."

"Who's next on your list?" Lizzy asked.

"You sound suddenly anxious. Does it bother you to know that you might have just shortened their lives by a few days?"

"Don't do this. I know they were wrong in what they did to you. But what you're doing isn't right."

"I'm glad we had this talk, Lizzy."

"Please don't hurt anyone—"

You never should have called her. She's not going to give up. Lizzy Gardner always gets her man.

Yeah, that's the problem. She's dealing with a woman this time. Not just any woman, either. You're forgetting who I am—I'm Jenny Pickett.

CHAPTER 36

It was still early when Lizzy wandered into the kitchen.

Once again Kitally was cooking at the stove.

"Hey, there," Kitally said, sounding much too chipper.

Lizzy's greeting came out sounding a lot like a grunt. She found a mug and poured herself a cup of coffee. "Have you ever considered opening a bed-and-breakfast?"

Kitally snorted. "In Carmichael?"

"I was thinking Napa or La Jolla."

"Nope, never crossed my mind."

"You're one of those people who've never met a stranger. You like to cook, and you're a morning person. It makes perfect sense."

"I'm really not sure what I want to do when I grow up. Right now I'm just happy to be doing what I'm doing. Catching that dognapper was very satisfying. And the *Sac Bee* called me. They want to interview me."

"You're going to be Sacramento's sweetheart," Lizzy said.

"What would you like in your omelet?"

"I'll take whatever you've got," Lizzy said as she took a seat at the table. "Hayley's door was open, and she's not in her room. Any idea where she might have gone?"

Before Kitally could answer, the front door opened and closed. Hayley gave a slight nod of her chin as she walked by.

Lizzy got up and followed her halfway down the hallway. "Is that blood on your arm?"

"I don't know. I don't think so."

"Where have you been?"

Hayley turned around.

They were face-to-face, only inches apart.

The girl smelled like cigarettes and bad news.

"We've talked about this before, Lizzy. No mothering me. You do your thing and I'll do mine."

Lizzy didn't know what to say to that. Kitally kept telling Lizzy that the three of them were in this together, they were all a team, but were they really? They were each living in their own little worlds within the same house. Insanity was what it was.

Hayley's hair was mussed. She looked exhausted, her eyelids at half-mast.

"I'm going to take a shower. I'll be down in a little bit." With that, Hayley walked off.

Lizzy trudged back to her chair at the kitchen table. "That girl is not taking care of herself."

"Two peas in a pod," Kitally said as she slid a plate in front of Lizzy, complete with a sprig of parsley.

"What do you mean by that?" Lizzy asked.

"Just what I said. You two are a lot alike. Neither of you take care of yourselves. You don't get enough sleep, don't eat the right things, both on automatic pilot."

"That's not true."

Kitally blew out some air. "When was the last time you laughed?"

"Just the other day, when someone told me a joke."

"Tell me the joke."

"A magician was driving down the road." Lizzy paused for effect. "Then he turned into a driveway."

Kitally pulled the pan from the heat. "That's not even funny. I know you didn't laugh at that one."

Lizzy shrugged. "Trust me—I can tell a joke. And I don't come home at five in the morning with blood on my arm."

"Are you sure it was blood?"

"Almost positive. She's up to her old tricks."

"What did I miss?" Kitally asked. "What does that mean?"

"Before you came along, Hayley used to stay out at all hours. It was in the paper, and there was even a blurry video on You-Tube showing a young woman taking out a couple of punks in the middle of the night."

"You think she's doing that again?" Kitally asked.

"Doing it still, not again."

"What's she think she's doing?"

"Taking care of business. Doing the same thing the woman who keeps calling me is doing."

"The woman who delivered poisonous cookies?"

Lizzy nodded.

"So you think Hayley might have her own personal kill list?"

"No, I don't think Hayley would go that far, but I do know that not too long after I saw the video, Hayley was taken into custody for cutting off a man's penis."

They were quiet for a second after that. Then Kitally said, "Well, I agree. I don't think Hayley would kill anyone—"

"Of course she wouldn't."

Kitally sighed. "I wasn't finished. I don't think Hayley would kill anyone who didn't deserve it."

Lizzy closed her eyes. *Just breathe*, she reminded herself.

"Don't worry, Lizzy," Kitally said. "I would never take a life unless it was in self-defense."

Lizzy had no response to that.

"But I guess I wouldn't mind finding other ways to make some of these people pay for their actions."

"Let's change the subject," Lizzy said. "It's much too early in the morning to have this conversation."

Kitally carried another plate to the table and took a seat across from Lizzy. "All right. On a cheerier note, I was able to reach three of the four people on the kill list: Chelsea Webster, Mindy Graft, and Aubrey Singleton. All three of them sounded concerned and yet doubtful at the same time."

"Well, all we can do is warn these people," Lizzy said. "Tell them we believe it's a woman and that she's used a variety of ways to kill and make it look like an accident."

"That's exactly what I did. I read off the list of people who've died. I told them everything I knew, told them not to eat anything they didn't cook themselves. The rest is up to them." Kitally sighed. "As long as they're aware of their surroundings, stay alert, and keep their doors and windows locked, they should have a fighting chance, right?"

Lizzy shrugged. The fact was, no matter how careful they were—how careful *any* of them were, every last one of them was vulnerable as hell. She thought of Shelby Geitner. There was no way Shelby hadn't been careful, and it hadn't mattered. She'd still been taken. Lizzy closed her eyes and curled around the painful ball of impotent rage that seemed to be growing inside her, day by day.

"Hayley suggested we keep an eye on some of these people," Kitally said. "Maybe we can catch this woman in the act."

Lizzy forced herself to open her eyes, take a breath. "As long as the two of you work together, I'm not opposed to that idea."

CHAPTER 37

Kitally followed the light-blue Toyota Yaris into the parking lot of a discount market, parked in the next lane where they would have a clear shot of the car, and shut off the engine.

Hayley sat in the passenger seat and breathed in that new car smell everyone always got all worked up about. She didn't understand the appeal. It just smelled like rubber and leather.

"Mindy Graft was just warned that someone might be after her," Kitally said. "Someone armed and dangerous, and she didn't even bother to lock her car."

They watched the woman stroll toward the store.

Hayley shrugged. "I don't think any of these people are taking the threat on their life too seriously."

"I wasn't able to reach Gary Perdue. We should drive by his place later if we have time."

"Where does he live?"

"Auburn."

"Let's watch Mindy's car until she comes back. Make sure the woman calling Lizzy isn't watching her, too."

Hayley looked around the parking lot until her gaze settled on a black Land Rover. A woman was sitting in the driver's seat. Hayley was about to go check the license plate number when the woman got out, opened the back of the car, and pulled out a stroller. "Lizzy said the woman should be in her early thirties and single. Isn't that right?"

"That's correct."

Hayley forgot about the woman with the baby and continued her search through a sea of cars. Nothing unusual.

"So, what do you do late at night when you're out walking the streets of Sacramento?" Kitally asked.

"Just keeping an eye on a few people."

"What sort of people?"

"Bad people. Evil people. Just making sure they're staying out of trouble."

"What happens if they're not staying out of trouble—if they do something you don't like?"

"I give them a few warnings—let them know they're being watched."

"You can't watch every loser in town."

"No, I can't. That's why I keep the number to a minimum. And I have rules."

"Wow, you're really serious about this, aren't you?"

Hayley pushed a strand of hair out of her face and kept her focus on the parking lot.

"What sort of rules?"

"I wouldn't bother teaching them a lesson unless I was sure they couldn't be rehabilitated any other way."

"How could you possibly know?"

"I just know."

"You sound like a vigilante."

"I guess if you have to label it—"

A siren broke into their exchange, growing louder as an ambulance with flashing warning lights pulled in front of the store.

"What the hell?" Hayley got out of the car and started jogging that way with Kitally on her heels.

The back of the ambulance flew open. Two men in white grabbed a stretcher and headed inside the store.

Hayley tried to follow them inside but was stopped by store security.

It wasn't long before a woman was brought out on the stretcher. There was an oxygen mask on her face and a tube in her arm.

"Mindy Graft?" Kitally asked.

"No."

Hayley heard panic in a medic's voice as he called for backup.

A police car pulled up next to the ambulance, leaving enough room for the medics to do what needed to be done.

Countless sirens sounded in the distance. A fire truck pulled into the parking lot, followed by two more emergency vehicles.

People were coming out of the store now. Many of them were talking on their cell phones; some were crying, others running for their cars.

"What the hell happened in there?" Kitally asked nobody in particular.

A police officer used a bullhorn to tell people to back away from the front of the store. If they weren't waiting for someone inside, they were to leave the vicinity immediately. Nobody would be allowed inside.

Not too far away, a man was talking loudly, recounting to a police officer everything he'd seen. Before he'd entered the store, there was a woman standing near the entrance passing out brownie samples. She said she was opening a bakery and was doing a little test marketing. He hadn't eaten all morning, so he tried to get one, but someone else snatched the last one before he could get a bit of brownie for himself. He said that the woman who was brought out on the stretcher was one of the people who he'd seen eat a sample. When the officer asked for a description, the man said she was a white lady with red curly hair. She wore plastic gloves, which he thought made sense since she was dealing with food. He couldn't see her eyes because she had on a pair of dark oversized sunglasses. She wore a long dress and was heavyset.

"That's Mindy Graft," Kitally said in a low voice when another stretcher was wheeled out. There was a white sheet pulled over her face.

"How do you know that's her?"

"The boots. Look at her feet."

"You noticed her shoes when she left her car?"

"Of course. Valentino with the bow over the knee boots. I've been eyeing those for a while now."

Hayley had no words, so she started walking for the car.

"Where are you going?"

"There's nothing more we can do for Mindy Graft. We better pay that Auburn man a visit and pray we get there in time."

Lizzy's footfalls echoed as she made her way past the nurse's station toward Jared's room. She could feel a half-dozen pairs of eyes boring into the back of her head. She pivoted about. "What are you all looking at?"

One nurse looked away; another grabbed a clipboard and took off in the other direction. The chirpy nurse, the one who always told her how good Jared looked, walked her way, cupped her hand around Lizzy's elbow, and ushered her into an alcove where they could talk in private. She said, "I wanted to let you know that Jared's family is here."

"Jared's father?"

"There's three of them in his room right now—his mother, father, and his sister."

Was she being ambushed? "Do you know if a decision has been made as far as the directive goes?"

The nurse shook her head. "I'm not sure. I do know that whenever a family member petitions the court to be named guardian, these things sometimes take time. And being that Mr. Shayne is a former judge does not help matters. Until the court makes a ruling, your hands and ours are tied."

Lizzy took in a breath as she tried to decide whether to leave for now and come back later. The nurse must have read her mind because she said, "Mr. Shayne told me he planned to wait until you arrived."

"How long have they been here?"

"Over an hour."

Lizzy thanked her and said, "If Dr. Calloway is around, could you ask him to join us?"

"I'll page him," the nurse said before heading off.

Lizzy walked down the corridor to Jared's room. His family hadn't bothered to call or visit in years, but now that Jared was on his deathbed, they wouldn't leave him alone. This was crazy. Lizzy refused to back down. It was time to hear what Dr. Calloway had to say and hopefully set them all straight.

Jared's father stood near the window looking out, while his sister and mother sat near his bedside, talking to one another in low voices. Both women looked up when she entered the room.

"Hi," Lizzy said. "You wanted to talk to me?"

Michael R. Shayne, a tall, distinguished man with silver hair, turned to face her. His piercing blue eyes narrowed. "We were hoping that if we all met face-to-face, you might come to your senses."

"Come to *my* senses?"

"Yes. As Jared's father, I have the right to make any and all decisions regarding my only son."

"I would be fine with that," Lizzy stated firmly and calmly, "if that's what Jared had wanted."

It never took much to get a rise out of the man, and today wasn't proving to be any different. His face turned red. "There's no way that directive will hold up in court."

It was plain to see that he was grasping for straws. "Why do you say that?"

"For starters, you're not exactly a stable and competent being." Lizzy lifted her brows. "But you are?" Lizzy recalled the night when Jared was called home because his father was waving a gun around, threatening his mother's life. "I don't think you want to bring this to court, Mr. Shayne."

He pointed a finger Lizzy's way. "Your witnesses aren't exactly model citizens."

More grasping. And it took everything Lizzy had to impede her mounting resentment. "Jessica Pleiss is currently training to be an FBI agent," she told him. "And Hayley Hansen has proven herself time and time again to be a caring and thoughtful human being. They are both over eighteen and well-thought-of witnesses, handpicked by your son."

Lynn looked at Lizzy with pleading eyes, as if she thought there was a chance, however slim, that Lizzy would sign over a release naming Mr. Shayne as Jared's new health-care proxy and then simply walk away forever. It was the same as it had been in high school when Lizzy had first started dating Jared—Lynn would do anything to avoid conflict with her overbearing father.

Before Lizzy could say another word, Dr. Calloway knocked on the open door and came inside. "Is this a bad time?"

"No. It's perfect timing," Lizzy told him.

Quick introductions were made before Dr. Calloway asked everyone to take a seat. Of course, Mr. Shayne insisted on standing. He liked to tower over people when they talked to him. "There is always discomfort when it comes to determining when continued care is futile," the doctor said. "The situation we find ourselves in concerning our patient is always difficult. Sometimes medicine has nothing more to offer, and I'm afraid that's where we are today."

"So this is it?" Lizzy asked. "That's your official determination?"

"Yes, I'm afraid so."

"Well, I think we need a second opinion," Michael insisted.

"That's fine," Dr. Calloway said, "but I am afraid Lizzy has the legal authority here."

Michael was about to protest before Dr. Calloway cut him off. "And you do realize that your son gave Lizzy power of attorney stating that in the event he was ever diagnosed as being in a vegetative state, his directive is clear: withhold all treatment."

"Clearly, my son wasn't thinking straight when he signed that worthless piece of paper. Otherwise he would have chosen life over death."

"Jared is not breathing on his own," Dr. Calloway stated calmly.

Michael finally looked at Jared.

"His kidneys are shutting down," Dr. Calloway continued, his tone respectful and professional. "The only thing keeping your son alive is the ventilator and feeding tube."

"This isn't about me or you," Lizzy said to Michael. "It's about doing what's best for Jared." She forced herself to take a deep breath. "I love Jared. I don't know how I will go on without him, and if you decide to drop your petition, I'll let him go because I love him."

Silence.

And then Jared's mother stood and turned toward Michael. "She's right. We must honor Jared's wishes. If you love him like you say you do, you'll let Lizzy handle this. You've got to let him go."

Mr. Shayne's entire body seemed to tremble. He looked from the doctor to Lizzy, his eyes no longer blazing with anger but with a sudden bleak understanding. And then, with sadness weighing down his shoulders, he left the room.

Thirty minutes later, Lizzy sat alone by Jared's side, exhausted as she watched him. She felt no victory in having seen clarity come to his father's face or with knowing his mother was on her side, since there was no good side in this fight. They all loved the same man, wanted only the best for him.

Her gaze drifted to the flowers by the bed. She took the tiny envelope and opened it.

> *I kood have killed him, put a pillow over his nose and mouth. So easy. But I want to watch you sufer instead.*

She closed her eyes, swallowed, read the note again. Shooting to her feet, she looked around the room, from right to left, for any further signs that a madman might have been inside this room.

A nurse came by, and Lizzy called out to her and asked her who left the flowers for Jared.

"He came by this morning to drop the flowers off. A tall man, said the two of them went way back."

"Did he sign in?" Lizzy didn't wait for an answer. She headed back to the nurses' station to see for herself. The nurse followed her, even passed her by. She tried to grab the sign-in sheet before Lizzy could get her hands on it. "He signed in an hour ago. His name is Samuel Jones."

Lizzy pulled out her cell phone and took a picture of the sign-in sheet.

"What are you doing?"

Lizzy ignored her.

The nurse grabbed the clipboard. Lizzy didn't care. She had what she wanted. She walked back to Jared's room, took pictures of the card and the flowers, then tucked the card into her purse.

Outside, she walked quickly to the parking garage. It irked her to know that she might have driven past the man who was doing his best to make her life a living hell.

The lighting in the garage was minimal.

She watched a car pull in, take a ticket, and move on. As she made her way to the elevators, her gaze roamed over every alcove and dark space between cars. She felt for her shoulder holster, made sure her gun was in place. She fingered the pepper spray on her key chain as she approached the elevator doors, pushed the button, and waited.

A ding sounded.

The door opened.

After she stepped inside, she realized she'd been holding her breath. As she exhaled, a hand reached in and stopped the elevator doors from closing.

The second she saw his face, she aimed the nozzle at his eyes and sprayed.

He cursed as he bent over, rubbing his face with the sleeve of his left arm as he reached out with the other. She darted past him, out of the elevator, and ran for the exit.

CHAPTER 38

Jenny stayed inside her car until she heard the garage door clank shut. Then she climbed out and hurried inside the house.

Once she was in her bedroom, she flung off her sunglasses. The curly red wig came off next. Her heart raced as she wrapped the wig in tissue paper and then placed it with the others inside the bottom drawer.

That was a close one.

"You worry too much."

She pulled off the ugly dress she'd worn and then removed twenty pounds of padding underneath. It felt good to remove all that extra weight.

There were probably security cameras all over the place.

"It doesn't matter. I parked far enough away. Nobody would have paid me any mind at that point. And this won't be the first time I was caught on video. Nobody will recognize me."

What about the tray you dropped in the garbage?

"It was disposable, and I wore plastic gloves."

You're going to get caught for sure this time.

She slipped into a terry cloth robe and tied the sash around her waist. "I'm tired of your constant jabbering. I'm not going to listen to you."

You haven't scrubbed the kitchen sink in days. Those tiny organisms are on everything. I saw them with my own eyes. They cause disease.

"Shut up! Shut up! Shut up! I'm done listening to your endless tirades. You need to back off. I mean it."

Silence. Finally.

She used baby oil to take off a layer of thick makeup, then turned on the bathwater before making her way to the living room and turning on the television. It was the same on every local new station: five people dead, one in critical condition. She wasn't worried. She'd seen Mindy Graft eat the brownie in two quick bites. She wouldn't be dead, none of them would be, if they mixed things up every once in a while. They all trundled around along their little tracks. Same routine, day in and day out. Mindy Graft hit the grocery store every Saturday, rain or shine. And today had been no different.

Jenny hadn't meant to, or at least hadn't wanted to, kill innocent people who were not on her list, but she'd known in this case that it couldn't be helped. After watching Mindy pull up to the store and park her car, Jenny had grabbed the tray of brownies and hurried to the entrance. Even after she had Mindy in her sights, she'd waited, not uncovering her tray until Mindy was within ten feet of her. Within the blink of an eye, the people walking into the store had become scavengers. Jenny had been forced to shoo away a couple of people just to save a brownie for Mindy. It was as if they'd never eaten before.

Leaving the television on, she made her way to the bathroom and turned off the water. Then she went to her office and pulled out the kill list. Using a fine-tip marker, she drew a line through Mindy Graft's name.

She wanted to call Lizzy, find out if Mindy had been warned before she took a brownie from a stranger. But Jenny didn't have time for unnecessary chitchat at the moment—she was going on a date with Dwayne Roth. He'd told her that he'd noticed her from the start, since she'd first started working at Ecco Chemicals.

With a smile on her face, she headed back for the tub, slipped out of her robe, and climbed into the hot water, letting her mind drift to thoughts of sun-kissed beaches; blue, cloudless skies; and Dwayne.

CHAPTER 39

After being taken by surprise in the parking garage, Lizzy had spent two hours filling out police reports. The man she'd sprayed was nowhere to be found.

She never should have left the scene.

For the first time in her adult life, she'd panicked and ran.

There was absolutely no excuse. She'd been carrying a gun—had him right where she wanted him.

And what did she do? She ran.

So disturbed by her actions, or lack thereof, she found it next to impossible to concentrate. And she *had* to concentrate. At the moment, Lizzy sat across a kitchen table from Shelby Geitner's boyfriend, Ben, while his mother hovered over them with her arms crossed, her mouth a tight line.

Ben was a cute kid. He had recently turned eighteen. He wore jeans and a dark-blue T-shirt. His blond hair was cut short, except for the bangs that fell across his forehead and covered his right eye when he wasn't pushing the hair out of his face.

"How did Shelby seem to you the last time you saw her?" Lizzy asked the boy.

"I'm not sure what you mean."

Ben seemed nervous. He twiddled his thumbs and had a difficult time keeping eye contact. What was he hiding?

"Over the course of the past few weeks," Lizzy tried again, "did Shelby act different in any way? For instance, was she overwhelmed by schoolwork or preoccupied with teenage drama of any kind?"

"She does have a good friend," Ben said, "who was afraid she might be pregnant. I know Shelby worried about her, but—"

"Ms. Gardner, I really don't see how talking to my son is going to help you find Shelby."

Lizzy looked at the boy's mother, peered into her eyes. "If your son was missing, wouldn't you want me to talk to everybody he'd been in contact with, including his close friends?"

The woman managed a barely discernible huff, but she backed off.

Lizzy turned back to Ben. "Mrs. Geitner remembers Shelby looking over her shoulder a lot, as if she thought somebody might be following her. Did Shelby seem nervous or skittish to you?"

Ben straightened slightly, and for the first time he looked right at her. "You know, Mrs. Geitner is right. Shelby didn't even want to go to a movie because she said she had a bad feeling about going out at night. I asked her why, but she shrugged it off, said she really wasn't sure. I laughed and told her she'd been watching too many scary movies. But I could tell she was feeling weird. Something was going on, but I didn't take it seriously."

Lizzy's cell rang and she excused herself to take the call. It was Hayley. "What is it?"

"Mindy Graft is dead."

Impossible. "How? When?"

"Not more than twenty minutes ago," Hayley said. "We watched her house all morning, then followed her to the grocery store. She didn't lock her car. I kept a lookout, watching the parking lot, but nobody stood out. About ten minutes after she went inside, there were sirens and emergency vehicles all over the place. Five people are dead. One person is hanging on, but it's not Mindy."

"Do you know what happened?"

"We overheard a man telling one of the officers at the scene that a woman was handing out free brownie samples. He said she ran out of samples fast. Described her as a white woman, overweight, curly red hair, wearing sunglasses and a long dress. The witness was adamant about what he'd seen, even recognized the first woman who was brought out on a stretcher as one of the people to eat a brownie."

"Have you talked to the other three people on the list?"

"Two of the three have been warned—just like Mindy. We haven't been able to get a hold of Gary Perdue. We're on our way to his house in Auburn to see if we can locate him."

"Be careful."

"We'll call you if we find anything."

Lizzy hung up the phone. She needed to see Detective Chase sooner rather than later. She quickly thanked Ben and his mother for answering her questions. The woman must have felt badly about her initial reluctance to help out because she gave Lizzy a piece of paper with her number on it and told her to call if she had any further questions.

Before Lizzy got to her car, Ben called her name as he ran out of the house and caught up to her. "There's one other thing I wanted to tell you, but not in front of my mother." He looked over his shoulder toward the house.

They could both see his mom looking out the window, her shoulders stiff.

"Go on," Lizzy said.

"Two days before Shelby disappeared, we had sex for the first time."

Lizzy waited patiently for him to continue.

"We've been dating for three years," he went on, "but Shelby told me more than once that it was important to her that we wait. Recently, though, I . . . I put a lot of pressure on her." He swallowed, looked away. "I told her I wasn't sure how much longer I could hold off. Now I'm afraid I might be the reason she's gone. I think I scared her off."

Lizzy touched his arm. "I appreciate you telling me, Ben, but just between you and me, I don't think you scared her off. Last time I saw her, in fact, she told me all about you. She seemed happy about the relationship."

The boy visibly relaxed. "Thanks. That's a relief. I miss her, and I would do anything to get her back. Is there anything I can do to help?"

"Keep talking to Shelby's friends, anyone who knew her. Ask them questions, lots of questions. Sometimes that's all it takes to jar something loose. Somebody might not realize that what they saw or heard is a gold nugget of information that could help us find her."

"I'll do that."

"You have my number. Call me if you learn anything new, anything at all."

He nodded.

Lizzy got into her car and drove off.

Before she got more than a couple of blocks, she was overtaken by a painful tightening in her gut.

She pulled over to the curb, her knuckles white on the wheel.

Shelby had been afraid to go to the movies.

Shelby had been looking over her shoulder and was suddenly afraid of her own shadow.

There was no doubt in Lizzy's mind—the answer to Shelby's disappearance had been right in front of her all along.

She could feel it—a burning sensation inside, a flash of insight. It was *him.*

Lizzy had been unforgivably stupid not to have seen it before now.

It was because of *her* that Shelby had been taken.

Lizzy closed her eyes, fought it for as long as she could, then loosed a scream of frustrated rage.

CHAPTER 40

Detective Chase was easy enough to locate. He lived in the Regency Park area in Sacramento. His house was a one-story, single-family home set on a corner lot and was painted a cheery yellow, which contrasted greatly with the man who opened the door.

Detective Chase looked different dressed in casual weekend clothes, but they didn't make him appear any less threatening. He stood inside the entryway, looking out at Lizzy with his usual deadpan expression. "So, this couldn't wait until Monday?"

"It's important."

"Of course it is." Reluctantly, he opened the door.

Lizzy stepped inside. The place had *mantuary* written all over it. The detective's man cave was complete with a putting green where the dining room table should be. Half of the living area was taken over by an eighty-inch flat-screen TV. She'd caught him in the middle of a basketball game. On the table in front of a worn leather couch was a grilled cheese sandwich and a glass of milk. Her stomach rumbled.

"Have a seat," he said, "and I'll make you a sandwich."

"Really? You're going to make me something to eat?"

He was already halfway to the kitchen. "I can't exactly eat with you watching me, can I?"

"You've got a point. I'll talk while you work."

He gathered everything he'd need to make another sandwich: grater, Jack and cheddar cheese, pickles, sourdough bread, and butter. The pan he'd used earlier sat on the stove. "What brings you to my doorstep on my day off, Gardner?"

"It's about Shelby Geitner."

"I thought we made a deal."

She tried to look surprised. "What deal? Are you talking about the four-questions-and-I'll-leave-you-alone thing?"

"That's exactly what I'm talking about."

"Forget about all that," she said with a wave of her hand. "I know who took Shelby."

He finally looked away from the frying pan and into her eyes. "Who would that be?"

"The same man who's been following me. He even visited Jared. Signed in under the name Samuel Jones. I've got two notes from the man. Maybe you could have some sort of handwriting analysis done."

He expelled a heavy sigh. "Are you talking about the linebacker from the other day?"

"That's right." She refused to let his blasé attitude affect her. "You can order the hospital to release the tapes from the security cameras. I know his exact time of arrival." She dug around inside her purse. "Here's one of the cards he left at the hospital. Wanted me to know he could have killed Jared but he wanted me to suffer instead."

He paused. "And this has something to do with Shelby?"

"Yes. This guy is trying to screw with me . . . following me, leaving notes, and that's why he decided to take Shelby."

He said nothing.

"So, you'll get the tapes?"

"That could take weeks."

The man was a bastard. "If you threw your weight at them like you throw it at people like me, we could find her."

Again. Nothing.

Lizzy pushed the hair out of her eyes and said, "It's *something*, isn't it? I've installed cameras on the property where I'm staying. If we could set up twenty-four-hour surveillance, there's a good chance someone will spot him, and we could follow him."

"There's that *we* again." He held up a hand, stopping her from saying anything more before he could finish. "Listen, I know you've been talking to Shelby's friends and family. As long as you don't get in the way of the investigation, I've decided to let it go, but we don't have the manpower to follow you around because of a hunch."

"It's not a hunch. He *has* Shelby."

He flipped the sandwich, turned down the burner, and then used the spatula to flatten the bread. Cheese oozed out from two slices of thick sourdough. He pulled out a cutting board and sliced a pickle into quarters. He then searched through the cupboard for another plate. The man obviously didn't have guests very often. When everything was ready to go, he took the plate and another glass of milk and headed for the family room.

"Come on," he said. "We're done in here."

When they made it back to the couch, he gestured for her to have a seat, which she did. "Are you sure you don't want this sandwich?" she asked. "It's bigger than yours and it's hot."

"No," he said. "I like my grilled cheese cold and my milk warm. I'm good."

She ate her sandwich, watched the game, and thought about Shelby. She wondered where the man was holding her hostage. She wouldn't allow herself to imagine that Shelby was no longer alive. Twice now she'd caught a glimpse of the man at close range.

She hadn't been able to make out the color of his hair or the shape of his eyes. Just like the detective said; he was a big white guy. "The man was wearing a plaid shirt," she blurted.

He picked up the remote and hit the Mute button. "What are you trying to say, Gardner?"

"Who wears a plaid shirt?"

"The question should be, who doesn't?"

Lizzy sighed. "It was filthy, worn. As if it was the only shirt he owned. Same with his jeans."

"So he's either a slob or he's homeless."

"Exactly."

"You told me he was cleanly shaved."

"Not a superclose shave, but he'd definitely taken a razor to his jaw. I'm telling you, we need to put all your manpower on this. Shelby is out there right now. Can you imagine what it's like to be taken by a stranger? Tied up somewhere, cold and hungry? I can't—"

"Lizzy," he said, stopping her short.

He never called her Lizzy. She stared at him, unblinking, waiting. "What?"

"What I'm going to tell you is confidential. I'm *only* telling you this because I'm concerned for your well-being, afraid you're going to drive yourself crazy going after a man who might not exist."

She tried to protest, but he stopped her with a raised hand. "Less than twenty-four hours ago, a close friend of Shelby's came forward with some pretty damning evidence." He paused. "It seems Shelby had been seeing another boy. An older boy who's not from around here."

"That's hard to believe, but even if it's true . . . yeah, so?"

"There's details I can't discuss. We haven't found the boy, but when we do, we hope to find Shelby, too."

Lizzy rubbed her forehead. This was insanity. They didn't know Shelby like she knew her. "She has a boyfriend of three years. That's ridiculous."

"Her parents are strict."

Lizzy raised her hands in frustration. "What does that mean? They're good people, great parents. They lay down the law, but I've never heard either one of them use a harsh tone toward their daughter. What does their parenting have to do with anything?"

"Shelby knew her parents wouldn't approve, so she hid this new relationship from them."

Lizzy came to her feet.

"There are emails Shelby sent to her friend that back up what the girl told us."

"OK," Lizzy said, "so if you think she ran off with this guy, why were there signs of a struggle in her car?"

"I didn't say anything about Shelby running off with the guy."

"You think he forced her to go with him?"

"I don't think he had to use force at all. Not in the beginning. Not until he got her far enough away from the school."

That would explain a lot, Lizzy thought, but she'd seen the way Shelby acted around Ben. Not only did Shelby obviously like Ben; she had recently had sex with the boy. Something about this story didn't add up. "Do you have a face or a name to put with this crazy story?"

"Not yet."

"So, you think *my guy*, as you called him a moment ago, is a phantom? A figment of my imagination?"

"After talking to witnesses, it's clear you were chasing a man who fits the description you gave."

"But—"

"But it could have been anyone, Lizzy. Like you've told me many times, your line of work brings you in close contact with a lot of nut jobs."

"The guy broke that driver's nose! He's not exactly harmless."

"Maybe you should do what you tell many of your clients to do?"

"What's that?"

"Hire a bodyguard."

"So that's it?"

"I'm sorry."

She headed for the door.

He got to his feet and followed a few steps behind.

"Thanks for the sandwich," she said before opening the door and then slamming it shut behind her.

She marched to her car, angry with Detective Chase, furious with herself, pissed off at the world.

Shelby could have fought off a boy her age, but there was no way she could've fought off a giant with the build of a lumberjack.

"Don't worry, Shelby," she said out loud. "I'm not going to give up on you."

After she climbed in behind the wheel of her car, she realized she hadn't even gotten a chance to talk to him about the calls she'd gotten from the woman who was taking out the Ambassador Club one member at a time.

She started the engine, but before she drove off she noticed a white Volkswagen Passat parked across the street. She killed the engine, climbed out of the car, walked straight over to the Volkswagen, and tapped on the driver's window.

There wasn't any point in talking to Detective Chase about the Ambassador Club murders since he wasn't taking her seriously, but she was pretty sure Murphy, or whatever his name was, would love to hear every detail.

She motioned for him to open his window. He did, and he didn't give any sign of embarrassment or concern that he'd been caught following her.

"Are you following me?"

He nodded.

"A little pushy, aren't you?" she asked.

"That's what they teach in school."

"Is that right?"

He nodded again.

"How old are you?"

"Twenty-nine."

"Just trying to catch a break?"

"Yeah, you could say that."

"Why don't you follow me to the coffee shop down the street and I'll give you a story that the public will love."

"A story about you? About your life?"

"Nope. A different story."

He had the gall to look at his watch.

"If you don't have time, I'll be happy to call Miste Newport at Channel 13. She's always hungry for a good story."

"I'm good with it," he said.

"Well, good. You're buying."

Derek Murphy, the rookie journalist, was getting on her nerves. Every time he opened his mouth, she thought of one of those he's-so-dumb jokes: he had to get naked to count to twenty-one, or it took him an hour and a half to watch *60 Minutes*.

His head angled to one side like a puppy dog. "You didn't answer my question."

She tried not to smile. "What was it?"

"Am I amusing you?"

"Not in the least."

"So you're telling me that all of these accidents aren't accidents at all?"

"That's right."

"Do you have any proof?"

"If I did, maybe Detective Chase would be taking this all a bit more seriously."

"So, this is all conjecture on your part . . . nothing more than speculation."

She moved her coffee cup to the side and leaned forward. "I've been talking for ten minutes straight and you haven't listened to a word I've said."

"This person who was bullied—the killer—what's her name?"

Lizzy's chin dropped to her chest. It was no use.

"This is all really interesting," he said, "but I think the public really wants to know about you and how you're doing."

"Wow. You really are something."

His face got all animated. "The public loves you. Think about all the business a story about you and what you've been through could stir up. People will be knocking at your door to find their long-lost loves."

" 'Cuz that's what I do—look for long-lost loves." She put the strap of her purse over her shoulder and began to scoot out of the booth.

"I'm sorry. Please. Can we start over?"

She didn't want to stay, but what she wanted was for the Ambassador Club story to get out to the public, let them stir up some trouble and get Detective Chase off his ass. She wanted the public to know what was going on, so she stayed where she was and said, "Want to know what the public would really love?"

He nodded.

He reminded her of one of those annoying bobbleheads. "The public would love to find out that you were stalking me after all I had been through, and then learn that I proceeded to kick your ass."

This time he flinched. It was about time.

"Listen, rookie. I don't have the name of the killer. If I did, do you think I would be wasting my time talking to you?"

He actually remained silent.

"I'm giving you a story, a real-life mystery. I'm handing it to you on a fucking silver platter and you're waffling. I'm not asking you to name names of those who have perished. But if you stop talking for one minute and really listen, you might see the whole picture."

He started to talk. Lizzy stopped him and said, "Pull out your notebook and pen. When I start talking, you better start taking notes or I'm out of here."

He did as she said.

"OK," she said, "Melony Reed, the leader of the Ambassador Club at Parkview High School in 2002, hired me because she was scared out of her mind. Four people in her club, a club filled with bullies who verbally and physically abused as many people as possible, were dead. All within a very short period of time."

Lizzy waited for him to catch up. "Two days later, Melony Reed was dead, too. Turned out she slipped and fell on a bunch of knives that happened to be sticking straight up in an open dishwasher. How many people leave their dishwasher open and then go to bed?"

"I have no idea," he said while he wrote.

"Well, go back to your cubicle on Monday and ask a few of your buddies what they think about that."

He looked at her. "So, Melony was number five. Who was the next to go?"

Lizzy got comfortable and went on to give him the details of who was missing and who was confirmed dead. She told him everything she knew.

When she was done, he turned the page of his notebook—a fresh, blank page. "How many members in the club?" he asked.

"Thirteen," Lizzy said with a smile. *By George, the kid is catching on.*

CHAPTER 41

Kitally cupped her hands around her eyes and pressed her face against the windowpane. "I have a bad feeling about this," she told Hayley.

Hayley felt the same way. They had been at the Perdue house for a few minutes already. The old house sat in the middle of about three acres of grass and trees. The next-door neighbors were well hidden behind all the greenery. There was a truck parked in front of the attached garage, but nobody was answering the door. There was also a barn in the back, but it was locked up tight.

"I'm going to go around to the back again," Hayley said.

"I'm coming with you."

Hayley tried the door leading to the garage. She knocked, waited, then turned the knob. Locked.

Kitally knocked on the sliding glass door leading into the back of the house. It was also secure. "Everything seems to be locked up tight. Didn't you say this guy was married?"

"According to the records I found, he's been married for five years." No sooner were the words out of her mouth than they heard a crash.

"That came from inside, didn't it?" Kitally asked.

"Sounded like someone dropped a glass."

"All the blinds are shut tight. It's impossible to see anything." Hayley pulled a pick from her bag, went back to the garage door, and used it to wriggle the lock.

When that didn't work, she pulled out a tension wrench. After she used a delicate touch and a lot of experience, a click sounded and the door opened.

She took a look inside. It was dark. A weird, musty smell wafted out to greet them. She stepped into the garage and felt around until she found a switch. Flipped it up. The place looked like most garages. There were boxes, old bikes, an extra tire, tools, and a Buick Encore.

"Anything in there?" Kitally asked.

"All the usual stuff people keep in a garage, including another car."

"Maybe we should call the police."

"You sound like Jessica."

"Is that a bad thing? I like Jessica."

Hayley came to an abrupt stop. She turned to face Kitally, who had just stepped inside the garage behind her. "Listen. If we call the police and something inside this house is not right, we'll be suspects." Hayley pointed a finger at her own chest. "I don't want to be a suspect."

Kitally nodded. "I get it. What about the crash we heard inside the house?"

"Let's check out the garage first. One step at a time."

"Look at this."

There were four large aquariums on the far wall, large enough to keep a cat in. They were lined with newspaper, and two of them had real tree branches inside.

"I wonder what those are used for?"

"Snakes," Hayley said, pointing to shed skin nearby.

An enormous shed skin.

"Gross," Kitally said.

Hayley started working on the lock to the door leading into the house. She didn't like the idea of finding that skin outside the aquarium any more than Kitally did.

Kitally started to hum, a nervous habit she'd been indulging in more and more often.

"Could you stop that?"

"I don't like snakes. Never have."

"Go wait in the car then," Hayley suggested.

"I'm fine," Kitally said with a sigh. "I'll be quiet."

At the same moment the door clicked open, they were met with a sound from behind that made Kitally jump.

"Is that what I think it is?" Kitally asked.

"Yes, it's a rattler. It's coming from the other side of the garage. You're safe."

Kitally squeezed into the house in front of Hayley. "What happens if we get bit by one of those things?"

"Swelling, internal bleeding, and intense pain."

Kitally started humming again.

They were in the laundry room. "Anyone home?" Hayley called out.

She listened. Heard multiple voices.

Hayley unsheathed a knife from her right leg and held it in front of her as she continued on through the kitchen.

The television had been left on.

Kitally had let her pass and now followed at a safe distance, checking every nook and cranny for more snakes, no doubt.

Two dirty plates, a half-empty glass. On the floor, shards of glass. The other glass had rolled off the table and shattered.

It looked as if the couple had finished dinner, and then what?

Hayley stepped into the family room and had to suck in a breath. She'd never seen anything like it. Mr. and Mrs. Perdue were sitting on the couch.

Kitally pulled up beside her, gasped, and clamped a hand over her mouth.

A ridiculously large python had wrapped itself around Mrs. Perdue's upper body and neck. Her face was a puffy mask—or what was left of her face was. From the looks of it, Mr. Perdue had tried to help his wife and had been bitten several times. There was no reason to check for a pulse. Clearly, they were both dead.

Before Hayley could tell Kitally that they needed to get out of there fast, Kitally screamed. When Hayley swiveled about, she found Kitally standing on a chair. On the floor under the table was a rat being eaten whole by a long, slender-bodied snake with a speckled design.

"Come on," Hayley said. "Let's get out of here."

"I can't. I'm trapped."

"The snake doesn't want anything to do with you," Hayley said. "Not until he finishes eating that rat. Come on!"

"No."

"Look. I'm telling you he won't bother you when he's got that rat to work on. But when he *finishes* . . ." Hayley headed back the way they came. "I'll be in the car. I'm going to call Lizzy."

"You can't leave me here."

"I'm leaving you. You're being ridiculous." Hayley left her standing on the chair, humming a tune.

Another ten minutes passed before Kitally exited the house through the front door. Her face was ghostly white and her spine was stiff as she marched toward the car. She opened the door, slid in behind the wheel, and sat there, blank-faced.

"Lizzy is on her way," Hayley told her. "She's calling Detective Chase. She wants us to wait here."

No response.

"Do not say anything to them about me picking the locks. We'll just say the doors were unlocked. Got it?"

Kitally refused to look at her.

"What did you want me to do? Carry you out of there?"

"I don't like snakes. You could have cleared a path for me."

"Do I look like a snake handler?"

"That thing swallowed that enormous rodent whole. I've never seen anything so disgusting in my life."

"Those snakes are the least of our worries. That woman is taking them all out—one at a time."

"What? What are you talking about? Our woman—the one with the cookies? You think *she* did this?"

"She must have come here last night or the day before and mixed rat poison or something in their dinner. Or maybe she put it in their milk. I don't know much about poisons and crap. I need to do some research and figure out how that all works."

"I think you can safely blame the snakes on this catastrophe," Kitally said.

"Open your eyes. Judging by all the cages and equipment in the garage, that man has been breeding snakes for a while. There's no way his snakes would have been able to get to him and his wife unless they were both incapacitated somehow."

"So you think she just set the stage to make it all look like a crazy snake attack."

"That's exactly what she did. There's no doubt in my mind. The killer must have waited a certain period of time before she came back to let all of his snakes and rodents loose."

"If that's true," Kitally said, "then she's literally running from one city to another. Who's next on the list?"

"Aubrey Singleton and Chelsea Webster."

"How are we going to help them?" Kitally asked.

"I don't know if we can."

CHAPTER 42

Even with the extra blankets, Shelby had never been so cold and scared in her life. The man who'd been holding her captive had just returned to camp. He was acting strange, much different than before. His eyes were bloodshot, his mouth clamped tight. He grabbed the pan and his cooking utensils and shoved them into an old backpack.

Usually when he returned to the campsite, Shelby was able to start a conversation, get him to tell her something about himself, but not this time. He stomped around, kicking dirt and breaking thick branches with his bare hands. For the past few minutes, he'd muttered a string of nonsensical words.

Lizzy always told her students that if they ever found themselves in the hands of an abductor and they couldn't get away, to stay calm and use their instincts. Shelby's instincts told her she needed to get her captor to calm down.

It was midday. She couldn't remember exactly how many days had passed since he'd forced her from the car. He'd held a knife to her throat and threatened to kill her if she didn't do everything he said. He was big and he was strong, and she had believed every word he said, every threat he made.

If she had to guess, she'd say she'd been in the woods for a week now, which would mean it was February. It hadn't rained once since he'd brought her to the woods. She was thankful for that because she was always cold. The lean-to he'd made out of branches and leaves helped a little on the windy days, but not much.

Whenever he left her, he made sure to use a rope or duct tape around her ankles. He would place a chain around her neck and fasten the other end to the oak tree next to the lean-to. Her hands were almost always duct-taped behind her. There was one time during the third day where he'd left her hands unbound, but she'd thought he was testing her, trying to find out early on whether or not she would run for it. He'd then set out for the woods to relieve himself. Her ankles had been bound and she could have hobbled down the hill, but she wouldn't have gotten very far, and she knew trying to escape him would only have made him angry. She'd been taking Lizzy's defense classes for years and knew that in the event a person was abducted, it wasn't wise to make a run for it unless you knew you had a really good chance of getting away.

Still, it was running from him—full speed, her hair flying out behind her, leaving him far, far behind—that she was fantasizing about when he suddenly lunged at her with his knife in his hand.

She let out a shriek, but he didn't seem to care as he cut the duct tape from her ankles. When that was done, he unlocked the chain from around the tree and used it as a leash to pull her behind him, dragging her with him as he made a new path up the hill.

The brush tore at her arms as he pulled her through it. Her legs shook. "Where are we going?"

He didn't answer her, just kept pulling her up the hill.

If she didn't keep up with him, she'd choke. "You said you'd let me go."

He yanked hard, stole her breath.

She was hungry and thirsty, cold and bruised. She wanted to go home. "You promised!"

He turned on her then, fast and furious. He pushed her to the ground and held her there. His eyes were darker than she'd ever seen them. The lines in his forehead had deepened. He didn't look anything like the soft-spoken man who only last night had told her about his little brother and how they used to make up skits that they would perform for family and friends.

"Your stupid whore friends told the police that your secret boyfriend took you. They're not looking for me anymore. They're looking for someone else."

"I don't have a secret boyfriend."

"You're a liar. All bitches are liars."

He got up on his knees and began to undo his belt.

"Don't do this."

"Shut up. I need to. I have to."

Panicked, she knew she needed to turn the attention back on him. "Why are you so angry? You should be glad that they're not looking for you."

"They're taking my glory," he said in a loud voice that cracked with intensity as he worked his belt loose. "Everyone wants to take the glory. First Lizzy Gardner and now your secret boyfriend."

"Raping me isn't going to help matters."

"It's going to be thrilling. You're going to love every minute of it. They all do."

"You need to send them a letter," Shelby said with the conviction of a desperate person in a desperate situation.

"Send who a letter?"

"The police. Tell them you're the one who took me. I'll help you write it. Tell them you have me and demand that they get their facts straight."

His fingers were no longer grasping at his pants. His breathing grew calmer as he seemed to think about what she'd said.

"You're the one with the power. You have full control of the situation," she reminded him. "You have all the glory. They just don't know it yet."

"You're right. I'm in control." He stood up and pulled her to her feet. "Let's go."

"A new campsite?"

"No. I found an old cabin. We'll write the letter there."

CHAPTER 43

Lizzy was on the highway headed for the Perdues, where Hayley and Kitally had found two dead bodies, when the phone rang. The console showed that the caller was her niece.

She pushed Talk and tried to sound cheerful. "Brittany, what's going on?"

"Lizzy, you need to come, quick. Mom and Dad are fighting again. This time it's really bad."

"Are you safe?"

"I'm in my room. I locked the door. Can you come?"

"I'm less than ten minutes away. You stay where you are—you hear me?"

"I promise. Just hurry."

Lizzy got off the phone and cursed. She knew Cathy would be pissed, but she didn't care: she called the police and pretended to be a neighbor reporting a domestic violence case. Then she hung up and made it to the house in ten minutes, just as she'd said.

The moment she stepped out of the car, she could hear screaming. First she shuffled around inside the glove box looking for something sharp. She found a pushpin and stuck it in her pocket. She then went to the back of her car, opened the trunk, and put her gun and holster inside, then locked the car.

Richard knew how to push her buttons. She refused to lose her license because of him.

Her brother-in-law wasn't the only one who knew how to piss people off, which was exactly what she planned to do.

She looked up, saw Brittany peering out the window. Lizzy waved and her niece waved back. She looked so young, reminding Lizzy of the good old days when she and Brittany spent time in the park, talking and hanging out.

When she got to the door, she didn't bother knocking. She just walked right in and made sure to leave the door ajar. Chairs had been overturned. A picture had fallen from the living room wall. Her sister was standing in the dining room, holding a kitchen towel to her nose. Richard stood beyond her, glaring wildly at them.

"What the fuck is she doing here!"

"Your daughter is upstairs, scared out of her wits," Lizzy told him. "She could hear her father beating on her mother."

"Get out of here, Lizzy," Richard said, pointing his finger at the door. "This isn't any of your business. Your sister is a whore. I caught her texting a man at work."

"Well, it's about time."

"You know this man?"

Lizzy looked outside. No sign of the police yet. "You bet I do," she lied. "He's good-looking and charming and everything you're not."

He stomped past Cathy to get at Lizzy, chest puffed out, fingers rolled into fists at his sides—doing everything but thumping his chest like the idiotic ape he was. "Get out of my house," he snarled, "or I swear I'll plant you on your ass."

Lizzy held her ground, didn't budge.

He pushed her.

She stumbled back.

"Leave her alone," her sister shouted.

"I'm fine, Cathy. Go see Brittany. She's scared."

Cathy hesitated before she finally rushed up the stairs.

"Why don't you pull out your gun?" Richard asked. "Makes you feel like a man, doesn't it? You want to kill me, don't you? Hack off my head like you did that other guy. That worked out real well for you, didn't it? You piss off enough people, they come back to get you. And if they can't get you, they go for the people you care about most. I bet Jared never saw it coming, did he? Looking all dapper in his—"

Lizzy heard a car pull up outside. No sirens. *Perfect.* She pulled the pushpin from her pocket, stepped forward, and stabbed him in the leg, then screamed as loudly as she could.

He did what most rage-infested, out-of-control men would do—he punched her in the face right as the door opened.

The cop wrestled him to the ground.

Richard cried out, trying to let the officer know that she'd purposely set out to make him mad, but he made a crucial mistake. His frustration got the best of him and he sort of bitch-slapped the cop in an attempt to get free.

Another he's-so-dumb joke ran through her head as she watched the officer's partner step inside and help him pull Richard to his feet and then hold Richard's arms behind his back so he could cuff him. Figuring they might be more inclined to teach Richard a lesson if she weren't watching, she went to the kitchen to get some ice and a towel.

CHAPTER 44

Jenny was at work, helping to develop a sleeping pill. The company had been waiting years for approval from the FDA on their new sleeping aid when it was reported by a neuroscientist who had reviewed thousands of pages of data that test subjects had been waking up multiple times during the night with dark thoughts. So it was back to the drawing board. There was no way to make a perfect sleep aid without residual effects, but that wasn't Jenny's problem.

There was a tap on the lab window.

She looked up, surprised to see Dwayne standing on the other side of the glass.

Jenny removed her goggles, mask, and gloves and stepped outside the lab. Their date night had worked out wonderfully. They had ended up going to the movie first—an action movie with a wonderfully sappy love story woven in. Afterward, they'd had dinner at Tres Hermanas. She had ordered carne asada and he had ordered chicken mole poblano, and then they'd taken turns feeding each other. It had been silly and romantic and fun.

It would have been a perfect night—except that Dwayne hadn't bothered to kiss her at the door. He'd escorted her all the way to her front stoop and then said goodbye. Worse than that, he hadn't bothered calling her on Sunday.

He doesn't like you. You talk too much. He couldn't get a word in edgewise. Even if he did, you never listen.

Her fingers rolled into fists at her side. She hadn't heard the voice in twenty-four hours. Why now?

She concentrated on Dwayne. He was wearing dark slacks, a white shirt, and a skinny black tie. His long hair was tied back, but if he let it loose, he would look as if he belonged on stage with a guitar instead of in a research lab.

"I saw your car in the parking lot. You got here early today."

She nodded. "I couldn't sleep."

"I wanted to tell you what a great time I had the other night."

"Really."

"Is something wrong?"

Tell him to fuck off and leave you alone.

"The truth is I was disappointed that you left me at the door without a kiss. And then when you didn't call the next day, I figured I must have imagined the connection I thought we had because—"

He kissed her right then and there, a quick peck on the lips, but still a kiss.

They were standing in the hallway. He looked both ways.

This guy is not the one for you. He wouldn't kill a spider if it were biting him on the ass. Milquetoast, that's what he is.

Her adrenaline soared. She smiled up at Dwayne, which prompted him to kiss her again—a little longer, a little better this time. His lips felt soft against hers. His woodsy cologne smelled nice.

He straightened, blushing. "Yesterday I had to go to a family reunion. I thought I told you that at dinner."

She was losing herself in those blue eyes of his, falling under his spell.

"I'm sorry I didn't have time to call. My family is crazy. Do you have any idea how much chaos there is when you round up sisters, brothers, nieces, and nephews and toss them into one room?"

"No," she said. "I'm an only child."

"Really? An only child . . . must have been nice."

"It was fine," she said. Another lie, since she had always wanted a sibling. But so what? He didn't need to know everything about her after only one date.

"I would love for you to meet my family."

She said nothing. Not because she didn't want to meet his family, but because she had no idea how to wrap her brain around what he'd just said. He wanted her to meet his family?

He blushed again. "Too soon, right?"

"Not at all," she blurted. "Not too soon."

He smiled, the genuine kind of smile that told her he truly enjoyed being around her.

Now that she thought about it, he *had* mentioned something about having a family reunion to attend. She'd been too preoccupied with taking dainty bites and chewing with her mouth closed to pay attention to what he was saying. She felt like such an idiot. She'd lost sleep over nothing.

He gestured down the hallway. "I'm grabbing a quick cup of coffee from the lunchroom. Want to join me?"

She stared at him. Another awkward moment ensued, and that was putting it mildly. She was a big dork when it came to communicating with another person, especially someone she was falling for. "I'd love to," she managed.

They walked to the lunchroom together, laughing and talking. A group of three more people was drawn into their conversation about the movie they had just seen. Jenny had never in her life experienced the sort of camaraderie she felt at that very moment.

It felt good. Better than good.

She had always been the loner in the cafeteria, secretly wishing someone, anyone, would sit next to her and strike up a conversation.

For the first time in her life, she felt like somebody.

CHAPTER 45

Not only had Kitally switched cars with her mom; she'd invested in a crazy-ass pair of military binoculars with 160X magnification and high-quality optics. Hell, even parked much farther away, she could see the details of the moth's wings on Mr. Chalkor's front window. An easy-to-use sliding lever made it possible for her to switch from 30X to 160X in an instant. With the touch of a finger, she could sharpen the focus.

Just as she was beginning to get the hang of using her new toy, the Chalkors' garage door opened and a car pulled out. Mr. Chalkor was in the driver's seat. Nobody else was in the car with him.

Frustrated with how much time she was putting into this case, she was determined to get plenty of supersharp, incriminating pictures of him using his supposedly injured arm, and get them *today*. She put the binoculars to the side, turned on the engine, and followed him, careful to stay far enough back so he wouldn't spot her.

He merged onto the freeway. She stayed with him. It was three thirty in the afternoon, and she was scheduled to meet with Lizzy and Hayley in thirty minutes. She decided to follow him for ten minutes. If he didn't exit the highway by then, she would have to try again on another day.

As she drove along, her thoughts drifted to the firestorm at Lizzy's wedding that had nearly killed her and had killed three people and left Jared in a coma. Kitally hadn't known Jared Shayne well, but she knew that Hayley had respected him and Lizzy had loved him.

Life could be so sad. Kitally knew that firsthand. She'd had a little brother once. They were inseparable. Her family used to travel all over the world, so often that they were more than brother and sister—so seldom knowing anyone else, they'd had to be each other's best friend wherever they went, too.

It was on one particular trip that all of their lives changed forever. They were traveling through Buenaventura, the main port of Colombia in the Pacific Ocean. Her father was usually doing business when they traveled, but on this fateful day, their family of four had decided to get out and enjoy the sights, get outside with the people.

Kitally was eight at the time, her brother six. She could still remember the smells of this strange new city as they followed their parents, always two steps behind, close enough to reach out and grab hold of their mother's skirts if need be. Kitally had been hungry that day. While her brother's attention was easily caught by all the barefoot kids playing in the street, Kitally's attention was on the smells: fried rice, chicken and tortillas, savory beans on every corner.

The trouble began when her brother spotted a merchant on the other side of the busy street. The man wore a colorful shirt and he was flinging a handcrafted boomerang into the air. The toy would fly toward the hot sun, almost out of sight, and then suddenly it would be back in his hand again.

It seemed liked magic.

The man yelled something in a language she didn't understand. And then he wriggled a finger at her brother, a gesture that translated well in any language. "Come here," he was saying to her little brother.

Kitally tried to stop Liam, but he was strong for a six-year-old. Stubborn, too. Instead of going after her brother, she reached for her mother, only to be scared out of her wits when she realized she'd grabbed hold of a complete stranger.

The woman had looked at Kitally with dark hollow eyes and then smiled, a wide, toothless grin.

Kitally hadn't meant to scream, but that's what she did. She was eight. She was lost, and she was scared. Screaming at the top of her lungs had done the trick. Both her mother and father were at her side in an instant.

And when they saw that her brother was missing, they went into high-alert mode. Kitally pointed across the street, but the boomerang man was no longer there. She looked to the sky, to the street, back to the sky. Her mother pulled her along as they followed her father. They wove through hot crowds of color-fully dressed people. Hands reached out as they hurried along, screaming for Liam. A street band played music, using old tin pans and wooden crates. Dogs walked around aimlessly, all ribs and wiry hair.

They spent the first day looking in every shop, talking to every vendor. Kitally was interrogated by her mother and father, over and over again until the words coming out of her mouth were robotic and held no meaning.

The police assured her parents that almost all kidnappings ended with a ransom. Her parents took turns searching the city. If her mother went in search of her brother, Kitally was left with her father sitting by the phone. Her father never stopped asking her why she hadn't stopped her brother. She had no answer, so she would just cry. But the truth was, Liam was fast. She spent many weekends chasing after her little brother. She rarely caught him.

But that wasn't good enough for her father. He blamed Kitally. She'd seen it in his eyes the first day Liam had gone missing. To this day, she saw the blame in her father's eyes.

Mostly, she knew better—knew she wasn't to blame, she was just a kid herself—but still, there were times when she felt the weight on her shoulders and blamed herself, too. Her brother had been her responsibility, and she'd lost him.

Chalkor exited the freeway. Lost in thought, Kitally nearly missed the exit. They had been driving for well over fifteen minutes, but she hadn't been paying attention.

They were somewhere in Rancho Cordova. There were lots of warehouses and a few deserted office buildings. He pulled in front of a warehouse. After he climbed out of his car, she lost track of him. She waited a few minutes before she got out of her car, bringing her keys, cell, and her camera and leaving everything else behind.

The back of the building was framed with a chain-link fence. Trash and debris littered the property. She had two choices: climb over the back of the fence and look through one of the windows, or go to the front of the building where Chalkor had parked and risk being seen.

She opted to climb the fence. It wasn't so bad. Took her less than a minute.

She hadn't realized the windows were so high until she got up close to the building. Even on her tiptoes, she couldn't see inside. From the street, she'd seen discarded pallets and other trash on the side of the building, so she walked that way, figuring she could prop one of the pallets against the wall and climb up on it to see inside.

That's exactly what she did. She cupped her hands around her eyes and peered inside. The warehouse looked old and abandoned. Dirty and corroded industrial shelving covered one side of the building. The inside looked dim and dusty. Rusty nails were sprinkled about on the floor. Spiderwebs hung from the ceiling lights like the Spanish moss she'd once seen hanging from trees in South Carolina.

She couldn't see movement, though. Not one sign that Chalkor was even—

A strong hand gripped the back of her collar and yanked her off the pallet, and then another clamped over her mouth. She bit down and ended up gagging on an old rag he had wrapped around his fingers. Although she couldn't see his face, she knew it was Mr. Chalkor.

He dragged her around to the front of the building. She screamed, but the sound came out muffled. Her arms were trapped beneath his forearms. She kicked her legs and flailed about like a newly caught fish, but he continued on, unfazed.

They were inside the warehouse. It was cold and dank. The cement floors were stained with oil and grime. When they reached the door of a small windowless room that looked as if it might have once served as an office, he pushed her in. When he tried to grab her camera, she fought back with a kick to his side and another to his groin.

He ran out the door, slamming it shut before she could catch up to him.

A lock clicked in place. She could hear a chain being dragged across cement.

"Let me out, Mr. Chalkor. You're going to go to prison for a very long time if you don't."

She banged on the door and then kicked it as hard as she could near the lock, hoping to jiggle it loose. "You *will* regret this. I have pictures, proof that you came here. You'll never get away with this."

More kicking and pounding.

"My friends know where I am, Mr. Chalkor. The people I work for will be here in a matter of minutes, so you might want to let me out while you have the chance."

Bang!

That was the distinct sound of the main warehouse doors clanging together.

How could she have let this happen? How stupid could she be?

She looked around. A second look revealed that the room was too small to have ever been an office. It was eight-by-eight at the most. Low ceiling. No windows. She'd left her bag in the car. *Dumb. Dumb. Dumb.*

She pulled out her key and pressed the alarm. She walked the entire room, holding the key at various heights and at different areas of the room, pushing the alarm over and over. Nothing.

To make matters worse, nobody knew where she was. She'd promised Lizzy more than once that she would never follow anyone by car for more than a few miles. She was never to get out of the car unless she called it in and told someone else where she was. She was never to leave her cell phone behind. She pulled her phone from her pocket. At least she had her phone. No service. He must have known that, too. The bastard did his homework.

That's when it dawned on her. Mr. Chalkor had planned the whole thing. He'd led her here.

He had her right where he wanted her.

She was screwed.

CHAPTER 46

"Where's Kitally?" Lizzy asked, looking out the window toward the cars parked outside the downtown office. "Did she know we had a meeting planned?"

"She knew about it. I'll give her a call." Hayley left a message on Kitally's cell, then hung up.

"I have class in an hour," Lizzy said, "and I need to go over a few things, so we'll have to do this without her."

"OK, what's first on the agenda?"

"I have good news and bad news."

"Let's start with the good."

Lizzy opened the newspaper. There was an eight-by-ten picture of Jacque Victoria Mason, her dog, Gracie, and Kitally. The headline read, "New Hero! Pet Detective Saves Pug!"

Hayley smiled.

"The article talks about Kitally being the new pet detective in town. It's great publicity."

"We're never going to hear the end of this from Kitally, you know?"

"I know."

"So, now for the bad news."

"The Dow case," Lizzy said and then watched Hayley closely. Not too surprisingly, Hayley didn't so much as flinch.

"What about it?"

"Mr. and Mrs. Dow have filed a suit against us."

"On what grounds?"

"Mr. Dow claims you ruined his Mercedes and broke his arm. He's claiming damages of over one hundred thousand dollars."

"He's an idiot."

Lizzy tapped her pencil against the desk. "Did you drive your Chevy into his Mercedes?"

"Yes."

"Did you use your stick on him?"

"It's an expandable baton."

"Did you use your expandable baton on Mr. Dow?"

"Yes." Hayley stood. "I'll be right back."

Lizzy nodded. Waited.

Hayley returned with a file and a mini-cassette recorder. She set the recorder on Lizzy's desk and pushed Play.

For the first minute or two, there was nothing more than muffled noises. Then they heard a man scream out in pain.

Lizzy winced.

The next voice was Hayley's. "What did you give her?"

"Nothing, I swear."

"Bullshit. Was it Rohypnol? Tell me what you gave her or I swear I'll break both your legs."

"Gamma 10," the man blurted. "I didn't give her much."

More muffled sounds, car doors opening and closing.

Hayley hit the Off button and then opened the file and handed Lizzy photographs she'd taken of Mr. Dow exiting the club and then Mr. Dow helping Kitally outside the bar.

Lizzy leaned back in her chair. "Why is this the first I've heard of Kitally being drugged and taken captive? Not to mention you crashing into the man's car?"

"You've been busy."

Lizzy eyed her for a moment, then shrugged and said, "I'll give his wife a call, tell her what we have, and see if she wants to come have a listen for herself. We'll see where we go from here."

"Any luck with the Shelby Geitner case?" Hayley asked.

"Not so far. Apparently Shelby has a friend who told Detective Chase that Shelby was spending time with a new boy in town. Nobody seems to know anything about him. As soon as I can figure out who the source of this new information is, I plan to get to the bottom of it. In the meantime, we'll keep the cameras rolling around the perimeter of Kitally's house and see if anything turns up."

Hayley nodded.

"In other news," Lizzy said, "Pam Middleton called today."

Hayley sighed. "How's her daughter doing?"

"Not well. And she's not going to get any better unless a miracle happens and Christina Bradley decides to help her."

"How's Mrs. Middleton holding up?"

"As well as can be expected, I guess," Lizzy said. "It's tough to imagine what that might feel like—having a daughter so sick, and knowing there's one person in the entire world who might be able to save her, but there's nothing she can do to make it happen."

"Maybe we should say screw it and give her Christina Bradley's telephone number and place of work."

Lizzy shook her head. "It would be unethical. And it wouldn't guarantee a happy ending, in any case."

"I have to say, I am surprised," Hayley said. "I really thought Christina would step up to the plate and try to save her little sister. I guess I read her wrong."

Lizzy knew what Hayley meant about reading people wrong. Lizzy had been off her game for a while now. It took her much too long to figure things out lately, even when the answer was right there in front of her, staring at her like an old cat, just waiting to be paid some attention.

The silence stretched out between them until it was deafening. Lizzy tapped her pencil against her desk and then heard herself say, "I miss hearing his voice."

"I know," Hayley said. And for the first time in forever, the tough girl looked slightly uncomfortable. "I miss him, too."

"I don't even know why I said that," Lizzy said. "It does no possible good. *Talk*. Everybody wants me to talk about it." She shook her head. "All I know is it's not real. Not to me."

Hayley gave her a nod of understanding.

"I'm feeling so damned helpless," Lizzy said next. "Shelby's out there somewhere. But where? Here we are, sitting in a warm office while she's out there with some lunatic. And then what about the kill list? Two people on the list are still alive, but for how long? And what are we supposed to do about it? I can't exactly move in with them. I feel as if my hands are tied."

"I still can't believe the authorities fell for the snake scene," Hayley said. "It was *so* obviously staged. Two people don't sit down to watch television and then let their longtime pet snakes sneak up on them. It's ridiculous."

The door to the office opened, and a young woman walked inside at the same moment the phone rang.

Lizzy picked up the call while Hayley went to talk to the woman.

"Is this Lizzy Gardner?"

"This is her," Lizzy said into the receiver.

"This is Sandy, Dean Newman's girlfriend."

"Hi, Sandy. What's going on? Did you hear from Dean?"

"No. He still hasn't come home. I've been looking through his things, trying to find any clue that might tell me where he is. It took me a while to find his passwords. I finally found them, though. Long story short, I found a list of the people he planned to apologize to. I thought you might be interested in seeing the list." The woman's voice cracked. She was crying. "Are you still looking for Dean?"

"I am," Lizzy told her. "The list that you have . . . can you email it to me?"

"Yes, of course."

"My email is on the card I left with you. Do you still have my card?"

"I do. I'm looking at it right now."

"If you could forward the list, that would be a big help."

"You will call me, won't you? You know . . . if you find Dean . . . you'll call me?"

Lizzy cradled the phone. "Of course I will. You'll be the first one I call."

"Thank you."

Lizzy hung up the phone. Dean Newman was dead, and they both knew it.

"Lizzy," Hayley called from the door, "this is Christina Bradley, the person Pam Middleton has been looking for."

Lizzy walked up to Christina and shook her hand. "It's nice to meet you."

"You, too," the young woman said. It was hard for Lizzy to get a fix on her attitude, beyond the fact that she looked as if she hadn't slept in a week.

Hayley said, "Christina just told me that after I paid her a visit at the day care center, she went straightaway to a private lab to have blood work done. She just got the results back from the lab."

Judging by the expressions on their faces, it wasn't good. God, when would all this end? How would she break the news to Mrs. Middleton? How in the world do you tell someone that all hope is lost?

But then Hayley smiled, an occurrence so rare it never failed to take Lizzy by surprise.

"Looks like she's a match," Hayley said.

Chills swept over Lizzy. She looked at the girl standing next to Hayley, peered into her clear blue eyes, and realized she didn't need to ask the question. The answer was right there in Christina's eyes, shining as brightly as the northern lights. Christina Bradley was going to do everything she could to save Pam Middleton's younger daughter . . . her sister by blood.

CHAPTER 47

Kitally huddled in the corner of the room, shivering and humming.

She wrapped her arms around her legs, as though that would actually warm her. She had no idea how much time had passed. She had kicked and clawed at every wall in the room, but these walls weren't made of plaster and drywall. They were solid cinder block.

Mr. Chalkor had apparently gone out of his way to find the ideal place to keep her hostage.

What kind of monster was she dealing with?

Was he going to come back?

Was this his way of teaching her a lesson?

What if he didn't come back?

Was she going to die in this tiny room?

She had no water, no food. She wouldn't last more than three days without water—four or five, if luck was on her side. But how would anyone find her?

Her car.

They'd find her car. That might be her only chance. But then she remembered that she had driven here in her mom's car. Her mom wouldn't know she was missing for another week, when she and Kitally's father returned from their trip.

If Hayley or Lizzy reported her missing and the police found Kitally's car, it would be parked safely at her parents' home.

Nobody would know to look for her mom's car.

She raked her hands through her hair and then fiddled with her dread as though it were rosary beads. Looking heavenward, she realized she might see her brother, Liam, sooner than she thought.

Lizzy tossed and turned. It was no use. She couldn't sleep. She got up, put on a terry cloth robe over her T-shirt and sweats and headed out of her room and down the stairs. On her way to the home office, she stepped into Kitally's room. Looked around. The bed was made. The cat was curled into a ball on the middle of the mattress.

Kitally had not returned.

In the office, she turned on one small lamp on the desk and opened her laptop. As soon as it booted up, she took another look at the list of people Dean Newman planned to apologize to. There were forty-four people on his list—thirty-three women and eleven men.

What the hell did he do to all these people?

Once again she pulled out the list of suspects Melony Reed had given her. Not one person on Melony's list of people whom she thought might seek revenge matched the list of people Dean Newman felt he needed to apologize to.

Damn.

What sort of club would purposely set out to mess with so many people?

She decided to combine the two lists and then, assuming the woman who had called her twice now was the person responsible for the deaths of the Ambassador Club, she would concentrate on the women first.

Joan Liskie.

She typed the name into her database. The woman had a record. Two DUIs and at the moment she was in jail for armed robbery. Joan had no background in anything to do with toxic chemicals or poisons. In fact, she never did graduate from high school.

Lizzy crossed Joan off the list.

An hour later, she had crossed off ten more names.

The twelfth female on the list: Dana Kohl.

Lizzy yawned, kept on typing, searching, reading. Dana had married her high school sweetheart, then divorced three years later. She was a biochemical engineer. Lizzy sat up straight. *Bingo.*

"She's still not home."

Lizzy's head snapped up. Her hand flew to her heart. "You scared me."

"Didn't mean to," Hayley said. "Did you hear what I said?"

"Yes. Kitally hasn't returned. I've left a few messages for her, but her phone must be shut off. I'm not getting a read on the GPS tracking application she downloaded on my iPhone."

"Yeah, her phone is definitely off. Something's not right. I called her parents' number. No answer there, either. I'm going to take a drive to their house in El Dorado Hills."

"It's not even four in the morning. Some people shut their phones off for the night."

"Yeah, some people do. But we won't know for sure until I go there."

Lizzy had never seen Hayley look so worried . . . or so tired. "Give me a call when you get there, will you?"

Hayley nodded and headed out.

CHAPTER 48

Lizzy said goodbye and hung up the phone. Hayley had found Kitally's car parked at her parents' house in El Dorado Hills, but no one was home. What to do about it? Lizzy's mind drew a great big blank, a common occurrence of late.

She was halfway through the combined list of names of possible suspects in the Ambassador Club killings, and still the only name that stood out was Dana Kohl. Lizzy decided to pay her a visit. If she waited until eight o'clock and called Detective Chase, he would simply tell her they didn't have the manpower to send someone to the woman's house. Lizzy couldn't just sit there and wait for the killer to take out another person.

Lizzy rubbed her eyes.

It felt as if she might never sleep through the night again.

Kitally was missing. Shelby was missing. A serial killer was getting away with murder. The entire world had shifted and was crumbling beneath her feet. She pushed away from the chair, grabbed a sweatshirt and her keys, and headed out.

Lizzy's navigation system delivered her to Dana Kohl's house in less than twenty minutes. She climbed out of her car, didn't bother peeking through the windows or checking the backyard.

She just walked up the flagstone path to the front entry and knocked three times.

She heard footfalls and then a woman's voice ask, "Who is it?"

"Lizzy Gardner, private investigator."

"You do realize it's five in the morning?"

Lizzy stiffened. That voice. It was *her*—hearing the killer's voice on the other side of the door jolted her. "It couldn't be helped," Lizzy told the woman as she reached for the gun in her holster. "It's very important that I talk to you right away."

Surprisingly, Dana Kohl opened her door.

Lizzy took full advantage of her carelessness and muscled her way inside. It would be months before Detective Chase decided to do anything about the Ambassador Club killer. Unlike the detective, Lizzy refused to sit on her hands and do nothing. She'd find proof that Kohl was her killer, and she'd find it now.

Asking questions would be a waste of time. Kohl would only lie to her face.

With her gun pointed at the ground, Lizzy went through the house, one room at a time: the living area, the dining room, the kitchen. She opened and closed drawers, looked inside the refrigerator and the dishwasher, anywhere she thought Dana Kohl might be hiding her collection of poisons or toxins.

Kohl had been chattering along after her every step of the way. Now, as Lizzy started toward the hallway to the bedrooms, she threw herself in Lizzy's path. "What the hell do you think you're doing?"

"Oh, I'm getting warm, then," Lizzy said, pushing past her. "I know who you are," she said as she started down the hall. "I know what you've done."

"What are you talking about?"

"The Ambassador Club," Lizzy said, refusing to stop and chat. The first bedroom gave up nothing. "Don't play coy with me."

"I want you out of my house this minute."

"When were you planning on striking again? What were you going to use this time?" She was in the bathroom now. Small quantities of common prescription meds. Aspirin. The usual stuff. No, Kohl wouldn't be stupid enough to store her supplies in there.

Again Kohl blocked her path, this time in the bathroom doorway. "You think I had something to do with those people's deaths?"

"If you didn't, I guess you wouldn't mind if I checked the rest of your house, would you?"

The woman stepped back and pointed toward the front door. "Get out."

"Just as I thought." Lizzy headed down the hallway. She heard the woman pick up the phone and then pretend to call 911. "A woman claiming to be Lizzy Gardner has forced her way into my home. She is carrying a gun. She's clearly out of her mind. Please send help!"

Lizzy opened hallway closet doors as she went. Nothing.

There was an empty guestroom.

Nothing there.

The next room to the right was a home office. Again, Lizzy rifled through drawers, looked under furniture, searched through closets.

Nothing out of the ordinary.

The woman was still on the phone, explaining what Lizzy was doing, step by step. She was almost convincing.

Another closet. Lizzy put the gun in her holster and made quick work of checking coat pockets. She stood on her tiptoes and checked the shelves, rummaged through boxes and a shopping bag. Again, there was nothing unusual—no weapons or wigs, pills or chemicals.

In the master bedroom, she found baby aspirin and sleep medication. It wasn't until she got on all fours and crawled under the bed and found a steel box that her adrenaline kicked up another notch.

She slid it out from under the bed, came to her feet, and used her boot to stomp on the lock. The box came open. Inside was a revolver and enough pill bottles to drug the entire block.

Sirens sounded. Less than a minute later, she heard loud footfalls.

"Drop the gun and put your hands up where we can see them. Now!"

Dana Kohl really had made the call. There were actual cops in the doorway.

Lizzy lifted both hands. "My gun is in my holster."

One of the officers kept his gun pointed at her chest. "I want you on your knees with your hands in the air! Now!"

She dropped to her knees. "Listen to me. That woman, Dana Kohl, is a cold-blooded killer. You're talking to the wrong person."

"Put both hands flat on the floor! One wrong move and I'll shoot."

She started to protest.

"Now!"

She did as he said.

The officer straddled her and patted her down. He took her gun from her holster and then pushed her chest flat against the carpet. She could feel his knee in her backside while he finished his search.

"There's a gun and poisons in that box over there," Lizzy said, her voice half muffled in the carpet. "Those belong to Dana Kohl. You've got the wrong person."

Her hands were pulled behind her back and handcuffs snapped in place.

Another officer yanked her to her feet and escorted her out of the bedroom and down the hall.

Dana Kohl stood in the living room, a trembling hand on her chest.

If Lizzy hadn't seen the gun and enough pills to take out an army, the look in the woman's eyes might have made her question herself.

CHAPTER 49

Hayley knocked three times, then tapped her foot on the welcome mat as she waited.

Tommy opened the door, rubbed his eyes. "Hayley?"

"Mind if I come inside?"

He moved aside to make room and then followed her in. "What's going on?"

"Kitally. Is she here?"

A dark brow shot up. "Kitally? Here?" He shook his head. "No. Why would Kitally be here?"

"I don't know. I had to ask. The past few days have been crazy at the house and there were only two places I thought of that she might go to . . . home to her parents or here . . . to you."

"I haven't seen her since last weekend," he said, "when I helped her with that missing dog situation."

"She's been missing since yesterday afternoon. Her phone has either been shut off or she's in a place where she can't get a connection." Hayley plunked down on the sofa, looked around, tapped her fingers and toes.

"Does Lizzy know she's missing?"

"Yeah, but she can't help me now."

"Why not?" Tommy asked.

"She's in jail."

He shook his head in wonder. "I need to get a pot of coffee brewing." He stepped into the kitchen and started rooting around. Tommy's apartment was basically one big living area with a counter separating the kitchen from the main room. A hallway led to the bedroom. As he filled the coffeepot, he blinked at her. "So now, why is Lizzy in jail?"

"After I left for El Dorado Hills to see if Kitally was at her parents' house, I guess Lizzy went all psycho on a woman she thought was responsible for killing off the Ambassador Club."

"I must really be out of the loop. The Ambassador Club?"

"Yeah, long story short, a woman who was bullied in high school by members of the Ambassador Club, some sort of high-end mean club, is killing club members left and right. She's doing a good job, too, making many of the killings appear as accidents. She's literally getting away with murder."

"So, what did Lizzy do?"

"I don't have all the details, but Lizzy was able to make one call and she called me. After hanging up, I called her friends at *Channel 10 News* and told them what was happening, asked them how in the world anyone could lock up a hero like Lizzy Gardner on a trumped-up charge like this. A woman who has lost everything?"

"Good one. You get shit for sleep, but you're always thinking."

There were more times than not that Hayley wished she could shut off her brain for a few hours, give it a rest, but so far she hadn't figured a way to quiet the beast. "OK, so drink some coffee, Tommy, and try to remember the dognapper case. Kitally tell you anything going on in her life, anything at all that might tell me where the hell she is?"

Tommy left the coffee to brew and sat down across from her. "We didn't have much time to talk. Everything went down pretty quickly. I had just gotten the camera set up when suddenly Kitally saw the guy with the dog approaching the house."

Hayley exhaled as she stood.

"You're not going to stay and have a cup of coffee?"

"No. I can't."

"Before we got to the dog lady's house, Kitally had a lost look to her. Sad, too. I asked her what was wrong, and she said it was her brother's birthday and she always thought of him on his birthday."

"Kitally has a brother?"

"Or had a brother. I didn't ask any more questions. I don't think that bit of information is going to help you find her, though."

"Do you think she went off somewhere to mourn?"

Tommy came to his feet, too. "I really don't know. Do you want me to come with you?"

She shook her head. "I'm going to head home, get on Kitally's computer, see what I can find. I'll call you if I find her."

"Yeah, good. I'd appreciate that. Let me know if I can help."

After he walked her to the door, she surprised him with an awkward hug.

"How's your shoulder doing?"

He straightened his arm, the one that had been injured in their war against Brian Rosie. "It's almost as good as new."

"That's good. I like your place, by the way."

"Thanks. Maybe next time you can stay for a while."

She looked into his eyes, saw a glimmer of hope, and wondered why he even bothered with her. He'd grown in leaps and bounds over the years—opened a second karate school, moved to a nice apartment, helped Lizzy with her defense program. Hayley spent her nights wandering the streets, taking out a thug here and there. She had no tangible proof that she'd helped one other soul. Her future was a dark winding path with no

263

discernible light at the end. Tommy was full of light, too good to follow her trail.

She opened the door and walked away without so much as a goodbye.

"Oh when the saints, go marching in . . . oh when the saints go marching in . . . oh, Lord, I want to be in that number—"

Kitally heard a noise on the little cinder block room's roof. She stopped singing and listened closely. Heard the pitter-patter of tiny feet above her head. It was just a squirrel or a rat—though why would either bother with such a desolate place as this? There was nothing here to sustain life, as she might just be demonstrating.

She plopped down in the corner of the room, clamped her arms around her legs, and sang another verse. Her gaze darted from wall to wall, floor to ceiling. She already knew every crack in all four walls.

She'd stopped walking around and banging the walls hours ago.

Her mouth was dry and sticky. Dehydration was setting in. It hadn't helped that she hadn't taken the time to drink water or eat lunch before Chalkor had shoved her inside this cold, windowless room.

Was he planning on leaving her here?

Yeah, he might be a scumbag trying to collect monies he didn't deserve, but was he willing to kill her for a few extra bucks?

He had to be coming back.

And when he did, she thought, she needed to be ready for him.

She scanned the room for the hundredth time. Nothing. All the rusty nails were in the other room. This room had been swept clean.

Even the shoes she'd decided to wear were worthless to her. If she'd worn her spiky heels, she could have done some damage the second he opened the door.

Think, Kitally, think. She had on a long-sleeved cotton shirt and red stretch pants. She had recently bought a matching bra and panty set.

Her bra! *That's it.* At this very moment, the wire was pinching her skin, making her even more uncomfortable. She pulled her arms out of her sleeves, unhooked the back of her bra, and pulled it off. With her shirt back on, she examined the undergarment. She needed to get the wire out somehow. She crawled over to the door where she'd scratched herself earlier on a ragged metal hinge. She began rubbing the silk against the metal edge until she'd made a hole. The wire slid out. Back in her little corner of the room, she began to twist and bend it.

When Chalkor came back, she'd be ready for him.

CHAPTER 50

Hayley had spent most of the afternoon driving around, visiting every place she could think of where Kitally might be. Unfortunately, she'd had no luck with her search. As she pulled into the driveway, she couldn't help but hope she would find Kitally inside the house, going about her business as if nothing had happened.

Instead, she found Jessica sitting on the front stoop, checking messages on her phone.

"What are you doing here?" Hayley asked.

"Nice to see you, too."

Hayley unlocked the door and left it open for Jessica. "Kitally!" Hayley called out more than once.

There was no answer.

"Where is everyone?" Jessica asked.

"Lizzy is sitting in jail, and Kitally is missing."

Jessica dropped her phone in her purse. "Since when?"

"Lizzy or Kitally?"

"Lizzy. I talked to her the other day and I didn't think she sounded right, so I decided to pay her a visit, see how she was holding up."

"She's a mess."

"You don't look so hot yourself."

"Yeah," Hayley said. "I get that a lot." She anchored loose strands of hair behind her ears. "If you don't mind, I'm going to take a quick shower and then I'll explain everything."

"You live here, too?"

"All three of us—Kitally, Lizzy, and me," Hayley said as she disappeared around the corner.

"Must make for interesting conversations," Jessica called after her.

"That's putting it mildly."

"You didn't tell me why Lizzy was in jail."

"Five minutes. Just give me five minutes."

Jessica secured the front door and then shouted, "Mind if I make myself some tea?"

"Make yourself at home."

Jessica didn't wait for the teakettle to whistle before she poured hot water into the mug she'd found. She walked around the bottom floor of the house as she sipped her tea. So far she hadn't seen any sign of Lizzy's things, not until she walked into the office at the end of the hallway. That's where she found Lizzy's laptop and a couple of very familiar-looking file cabinets, reminding Jessica of all the hours she'd spent organizing and searching through those same files. It was hard for Jessica to imagine Lizzy living with Kitally and Hayley, but these were strange times.

She headed out of the office, made her way down the hall and into the living area. The house was huge. There were more windows than walls. The views were magnificent. As she stared out into the trees, admiring the way the afternoon sunlight slipped through the branches, she wondered again why Lizzy would be in jail. The notion of Lizzy being put behind bars made no sense at all. If Hayley didn't make an appearance soon, she was going to call the station and see what she could learn.

Outside, not too far in the distance, between a regiment of large oaks and light brush, she saw movement. At first she thought it was a deer, but it wasn't.

It was a man.

And he was watching her.

How very peculiar.

Jessica moved her head away from him as she sipped her tea, but she kept him in her peripheral vision.

Her gun felt suddenly heavy upon her hip. A good weight.

From this distance, she couldn't make out the color his eyes, but his hair was light, almost blond. His skin color was on the pale side. He was massive in build and tall, over six foot four.

She took another sip of her tea, didn't taste a thing.

Footfalls sounded as Hayley descended the stairs.

Stay focused.

The man's ears were flat against his head. His neck was half the size of the tree trunk he stood next to. His shirt was plaid. He wore denim, brown boots.

"Looks like you found the tea," Hayley said. "What are you looking at?"

"A man."

Hayley peered off into the same general direction she figured Jessica was looking. "Where? I don't—"

"Not there. Farther to the right. But don't—"

Hayley turned that way.

The man took off.

Before Hayley could run after him, Jessica put her tea down and stopped her. "It's too late. You're not even wearing shoes."

"Why didn't you go after him while you had the chance?"

"Because I was too busy memorizing his features. I need a piece of paper and a pen or pencil. Quick."

Surprisingly, Hayley rushed off to find what she needed, and she was fast.

Jessica began jotting down the description of the man she'd seen: *blond hair, ears flat to his head, full upper lip.*

Hayley took the pencil and paper from her and began to draw on the other side of the paper. "Keep going," Hayley said. "Describe him."

Frustrated, but knowing she needed to describe the man before she forgot what she'd seen, Jessica obliged. With each detail she provided—six-four or six-five, broad shoulders, plaid hunting shirt, heavy brow—Hayley scratched something new on the paper.

Fifteen minutes later, when Jessica picked up the piece of paper, she was looking at the man she'd just seen outside. "This is amazing. I never knew you could sketch."

"You never asked."

"Who is he?"

"A man has been following Lizzy for months, maybe longer. She has no idea who he is, hasn't been able to get a close look at him. Maybe this will help to finally identify him."

"Do we know if he's dangerous, or does Lizzy think it's just another kook who wants to scare her?"

"We know that he's big, strong, and fast. He kicked a truck driver in the face—broke his nose. Definitely dangerous," Hayley said. "Lizzy believes he took Shelby Geitner."

"I've been keeping up on the Geitner case," Jessica said. "I know Shelby. Is she the reason Lizzy is in jail?"

"Mind if we talk about this in the kitchen?" Hayley asked. "I'm hungry."

Jessica followed her into the kitchen, watched her pour a glass of milk and grab a piece of chicken from Tupperware inside the refrigerator. They sat at the kitchen table, and Jessica listened while Hayley caught her up on everything going on, including the reason why Lizzy was in jail.

Jessica sighed. "I'll go to the station and see what I can do, if anything, to help Lizzy, but first let's talk about Kitally. How long did you say she's been missing?"

"About twenty-four hours now. She's not answering her phone and this is the first time she hasn't come home. She's a stickler for checking in."

"How about friends?"

Hayley shook her head. "I checked the only two places she would go—her parents' house and Tommy's place. She wasn't at either one."

"What cases was she working on? Do you know?"

"She had three workers' comp cases, but one particular case was giving her problems." Hayley went still. "Chalkor."

"Who's Chalkor?"

"Just another loser claiming work-related injuries—" Hayley stopped midsentence. "We need to find the file and pay him a visit."

Jessica followed Hayley down the hall to the office she'd seen earlier, watched her open the bottom drawer of the filing cabinet and finger through the files until she found what she was looking for.

Hayley turned the pages. "Here it is. Chalkor lives on Azevedo Drive in Sacramento. About twenty-five minutes from here." Hayley looked at Jessica. "Want to come along?"

The last thing in the world Jessica wanted to do was go for a ride with Hayley. Some of her worst memories were doing surveillance and ride-alongs with her. But they were some of her best memories, too, and she found herself nodding.

CHAPTER 51

If looks could kill, Lizzy would have keeled over and died two minutes ago, right after they brought her into a holding room and shut the steel door with a clunk, leaving her alone with Detective Chase.

"Look at you," he said, gesturing toward the cuffs around her wrists. "What the hell are you trying to prove? I already knew you were a bit of a nutcase, but breaking into people's homes in the middle of the night? I don't get it."

"It was five in the morning when I knocked on Kohl's door, practically lunchtime. If you would quit feeling sorry for yourself and open your eyes, maybe you could show everyone that you really deserved that Top Cop Award that I saw in your office."

"Oh, I see—we're going to talk about me, are we?"

"Yeah, why not? I've seen you more times this past month than I've seen my therapist, and yet I have no idea who you really are. I know you like to throw your weight around and act like a tough guy. I see that you don't get much sleep, but I have no idea why since I sure don't see you hauling in the bad guys. You got *me*," Lizzy said. "Whoop-de-doo. Now what?"

He rubbed the bridge of his nose. When he looked up, he said, "You really do think you're above the law, don't you? You just love being America's sweetheart."

Lizzy sighed. "I don't know what you're talking about."

"Your lucky little pet detective stunt. You and your sidekicks stumble into the dognapper who happened to steal a pug belonging to one of Sacramento's most beloved citizens."

"Jacque Mason is a beloved citizen?"

He grunted. "You're telling me you had no idea who she was?"

"Not a clue."

"Yeah, well, the phones are ringing off the hook. I guess you made your one call?"

Lizzy nodded.

"Did you tell one of your misfits to call the media or did you do the honors yourself?"

"No," Lizzy said, "I didn't call the media."

"Well, somebody told them what's going on, because suddenly I'm getting dozens of calls from fired-up citizens who think you should be given a pass considering all you've been through."

Lizzy said nothing.

"And I don't suppose you had anything to do with the Melony Reed story being leaked?"

"Again, I have no idea what you're talking about." But Lizzy knew that meant Derek Murphy had done his job. The rookie journalist must have pulled through and gotten his boss at *Sac Bee* to publish a story about the Ambassador Club.

"It doesn't matter," he said. "You're not going to be able to break into any more houses or cause any more trouble while you're behind bars."

"I don't care if you let me go or not, Detective. I just want you to arrest Dana Kohl before she kills anyone else."

273

"Because you found a steel box under her bed?"

"Yes. A steel box that contained hundreds of pills and a firearm."

"It's legal to own a gun."

"I understand that, but—"

"She has HIV."

"What?"

"You heard me. Dana Kohl has been taking upwards of eight pills a day for years."

"Why does she keep them under the bed?"

"I don't know. You don't store anything under your bed?"

"She's a biochemist."

"So you want me to go after every person in Sacramento with a major in chemistry?"

"It would be a start."

He expelled a long breath.

"So what now?" Lizzy asked. "We'll both sit here and twiddle our thumbs until another dead body turns up?"

He'd given up on using intimidation three conversations ago. Now he just looked tired. "You need help, Gardner."

"Don't we all?"

"I've already got a call in from your good friend Jimmy. But I could get a call from the president of the United States, and I wouldn't let you out today. I think you need at least one night behind bars to think about what you're doing."

"You're making a mistake."

"So you keep telling me."

"Why not be the hero for once . . . just once. Aubrey Singleton and Chelsea Webster are in danger."

He shook his head and then opened the door. "Take her back to her cell. We're done here."

CHAPTER 52

Shelby's wrists were bound with duct tape behind her back, and her ankles were also secured tightly with tape. She rubbed her wrists against the wood paneling behind her, frantically, like a Boy Scout might rub together two sticks in hopes of making a spark.

The cabin her captor had brought her to was tiny: one room with a built-in twin-sized bed covered by a flimsy mattress that looked as if it had been dragged in from beneath a woodpile. Every once in a while she'd find a bug or a spider crawling up her leg.

Across the room from her there was a sink and a wood counter, but no other appliances.

From far away, when they had trudged up the mountain earlier, the cabin had looked warm and inviting, reminding her of happier times. That was the moment she'd realized they were very close to the place she'd vacationed with Ben and his parents. The moment she recognized the massive rock feature up on the face of the mountain, she knew this was the same exact area. She and Ben had used the rock formation as a landmark to find their way along the trails. They called it Two-Face Rock. If you were west of it, you saw the profile of a rugged man's face; from the east, it resembled a kid with its mouth open as if laughing.

If she could get free, she would know where to go. If she could free herself, she could get off this mountain. Ben loved to hike. He'd taken her all over this mountain, taught her how to boulder hop. They weren't too far from Lake Clementine near Auburn.

Excitement and, best of all, hope made her work faster.

Her captor had left hours ago.

The minute he'd walked out the door to drop off the letter, she'd begun the process of rubbing the duct tape against the rough wood. She could feel the tape loosening. If she could free her hands, she could then work on the tape around her ankles and run.

On their way up the hill, she'd seen tinplates on the roof. It was raining now and each droplet made a loud tinny sound that was annoying as hell.

A section of the tape around her wrists came apart. It happened so fast, it startled her. Adrenaline coursed through her veins as she pulled her arms free.

She wept tears of joy.

And then the door opened.

She jerked upright and swung her arms back behind her.

He stood there looking at her. His eyes fixated on her face and then her ankles, which were still bound.

Had he seen her move? Did he know?

He shut the door and went to the extra trouble of putting a two-by-four in the slots on in the wall on both sides of the door. He hadn't done that last time. Was it to keep her from getting out or to keep other people from getting in?

When he went to the sink to sort through his cloth bag, she used her shoulder to wipe the tears from her face. She then eyed the tape around her ankles. There was no way she could untie herself quickly enough to get through that door and away from him before he caught her.

She gathered the courage to talk to him. "Did you mail the letter?"

He grunted. His grunts usually meant the affirmative.

Facing forward and trying not to move, she did her best to work the tape back around her wrists, hoping he wouldn't figure out what she'd done. She needed to be prepared to run the next time he left on one of his long excursions.

He pulled out the same tin pan he'd been using to heat up soup and began to chop up carrots. When he turned toward her, he was cutting a potato, peel and all.

The dark look in his eyes as he walked her way was freaking her out. "Are you going to peel them first?" she asked.

"What does it look like?"

She could barely swallow. She was shivering again. "Are you making stew?" Her voice sounded all quivery and scared. She needed to get him talking like she'd done before. If she could just stop her voice from squeaking and make it appear as if she were confident, maybe she could get him to relax.

He put the knife up close to her face. "I think you're far too pretty for your own good. You need a scar right here to give you character."

The sharp tip of the knife cut into her skin.

She cried out as she grabbed his hand and tried to push him away. It was no use. He was too strong.

"I knew it," he said. He stormed back to the kitchen and then came back to her side with the duct tape in his hand.

"No, please, don't."

"You said I could trust you." He put down the tape so that he could wrap one of his big hands around her throat. He squeezed until she could hardly breathe. Then he forced her mouth open and inserted the potato, which was worse than being strangled. She tried to cough it up, but she couldn't. He was wrapping tape around her hands again, so tightly she thought he would cut off her circulation. He shoved her head close to his chest while he worked. He smelled like a wet dog. She gagged.

"Too tight," she tried to say, but the words came out muffled.

He pushed her head back against the paneling, then leaned down and brushed his jaw against her neck.

She tried to wriggle free.

He did it again.

She tried to scream out and kick her legs, but under the weight of him, she couldn't move an inch.

His hand slid under her shirt, his callused fingers brushed over her skin. His breathing grew ragged right before he ripped the shirt from her body and simply stared.

She shivered, tried not to cry out again, knowing he would only grow angrier if she did.

She couldn't breathe.

She closed her eyes tight and pretended she was somewhere else, somewhere safe.

CHAPTER 53

Jenny was running out of time. She'd left work thirty minutes early, told her boss she had a dentist appointment.

Jenny had seen the commotion on TV. The media's darling was in jail for going after Dana Kohl. What a joke Lizzy Gardner was turning out to be.

Dana Kohl was harmless.

The private investigator will not give up. You need to listen to me. She'll come after you next. You must slow down . . . think things through.

Although Jenny had personally never talked to Dana, she knew *of* her. She knew the Ambassador Club had gotten their claws into her, too. Jenny had always been relieved when they focused their attention on Dana instead of her. She knew that wasn't right, but it was the truth. It was how she'd felt back then. There wasn't anything she wouldn't have done in high school to get them to stop. She would have handed over her china doll, both her parents, the entire farm, everything she had if they had told her they would leave her alone.

But that's not what happened.

And now Jenny was forced to make them all pay.

Today was Aubrey's day to die.

Aubrey Singleton had recently moved into a brand-new house. Lucky girl.

During high school, Aubrey Singleton always seemed to end up in Jenny's PE class. Aubrey used to love to take Jenny's clothes from her locker so that after Jenny showered, she'd have nothing to wear. Aubrey would take all the towels, too, and then invite the boys to come take a peek.

That was how Jenny had learned that even though the boys didn't want to date her, they sure liked to look at her naked.

Aubrey used to pass Jenny notes, too, sinister notes saying how she fantasized about the two of them being together some day, but then the next note would talk about how she planned to kill her while she slept. Aubrey would draw pictures of a cross with Jenny nailed to it. Blood dripping from her arms and legs.

She was a strange one.

But somehow Aubrey went on to marry a doctor. They had two kids and they lived in one of the nicer areas on the outskirts of Sacramento. The house was brand-new, and, although there were security signs poked into the grass, front and back, the alarms had yet to be turned on. She knew this firsthand. Breaking into someone's house sounded like a big deal, but if anyone tried it, they would see that it was easy. Most people left a window unlatched or a door unlocked. Walking into someone's house unnoticed was like taking a stroll through the park. Jenny would talk to kids in the neighborhood, wave at the cars as they passed, make people think she belonged. If they ever did question who she was, she had wigs and glasses and enough makeup to disguise herself. But nobody ever questioned her or stopped her from making her rounds. It was the same everywhere she went.

If you smiled and dressed up, looked as if you belonged, people believed that you did. Confidence. All you needed was a cheerful expression and a little confidence.

After work, five days a week, Aubrey picked up her kids from day care and arrived home at approximately six o'clock.

Jenny looked at her watch. It was only four. She had plenty of time. The last time she'd walked through Aubrey's house, she'd taken her tube of toothpaste. Today, she planned to replace it. Aubrey and her husband had two separate sinks. Cluttered with lotion and feminine products, her side had been easy to identify. Jenny was certain she'd stolen the right toothpaste.

Aubrey should be dead before morning.

Jenny walked up the driveway, lifted her hand over the side gate, pulled the chain, and let herself through to the side yard. Last time she'd gone through the garage, but today she decided to see if the back door was open.

The French doors came right open. It was as if someone were waiting for her.

No alarm. No problem.

She smelled something cooking in the oven, thought that was odd, and looked around.

She could smell a roast.

Something dropped in the other room. A woman cursed.

Turn around this minute! Come back tomorrow.

Jenny took slow, careful steps out of the kitchen and into the dining room. Not too far from where she stood, Aubrey Singleton was hanging pictures . . . or at least, she was trying to hang pictures. She had a nail in her mouth, a hammer in her right hand, and she used her left hand to blindly reach around behind the little picture, trying to loop the wire or hook around the nail head.

Jenny thought about the toothpaste in her purse. She'd put a lot of work into making it look and smell just right. She'd lied to her boss and had gone to a lot of trouble to get here today. She was about to turn around and walk back the way she'd come when

Aubrey dropped the picture. It was a small one and it fell to the couch without so much as a clank.

No harm done.

Except that Aubrey had leaned over to pick it up and was now looking at her with wide-eyed wonder. "Who are you?"

"You know who I am."

The woman straightened and narrowed her eyes. "Jenny?"

Jenny smiled.

"They warned me that someone might be coming after me. I thought of you, Jenny Pickett. In my mind, you were the only one it could be, but I pushed the warning aside, didn't even tell my husband, because I didn't think you had it in you."

Confident, holding her shoulders high, Jenny walked forward.

Aubrey raised the hammer, but the woman looked as if she weighed about ninety pounds. Her arm wobbled from the weight of it.

Jenny stopped and sighed. "Do you really think I came here to hurt you?"

Aubrey took a backward step and then another. "Why did you come, then?"

"I wanted to talk to you about what you did. I want to know if you feel any remorse."

"Of course I do. We all do. We were young, Jenny. Each and every one of us would take it all back if we could go back in time."

"Oh Aubrey." Jenny put a hand to her heart, as though overcome—and took another step closer. "You have no idea how happy that makes me. I didn't think any of you cared about what you did to us."

Aubrey's shoulders relaxed. "I wish there was something I could do to make up for it."

ALMOST DEAD

"Give me the hammer, Aubrey, so we can sit down and enjoy a cup of tea together. Just knowing you would take it all back if you could is all I needed to hear."

Aubrey played it out for a few seconds, even made it appear as if she might put the hammer down. Instead, she turned and ran for the front door.

Jenny caught up to her and wrestled the hammer from her hand. Then she swung hard and fast before the bitch could get away.

The look on Aubrey's face when she fell to the ground said it all: *You really came after me. You really got the last word, didn't you?*

"You bet I did," Jenny said.

Having no desire to hang around, Jenny dropped the hammer inside her bag, used her foot to nudge Aubrey's arm out of her way, then headed outside, right through the front door. She walked a block, shoulders back, head held high. After another three blocks, she sat on a bench that the community had built for people who wanted to sit and catch their breath, maybe view the beautiful lake-sized pond or feed the ducks.

Slowly, determined not to call attention to herself, she slid off the blood-splattered sweater, one sleeve at a time, leaned over and wiped the streak of blood on her right shoe. She then rolled the sweater up into a nice little ball and slid it into her purse on top of the hammer.

A kid, riding his bike on the walking path, picked up speed as he passed by, didn't make eye contact, had obviously been told not to talk to strangers.

Ten minutes later, she climbed into her car and drove off.

283

CHAPTER 54

"Just like old times," Hayley said to Jessica as they pulled up to the curb outside Chalkor's house.

"Yeah, just like old times."

"How's Magnus doing?" Magnus Vitalis was a DEA agent and a man Jessica had been very fond of even before he'd thrown himself in front of her at Lizzy's wedding and taken a bullet to the spine for his efforts.

"He's not adjusting well," Jessica said. "He's angry. The doctors have told him he'll never walk. He's not ready to accept that prognosis."

Hayley shook her head and listened.

"Some days I find myself babying him, doing every little thing for him, but on the other days I do my best to practice tough love. The physical therapists told me to let him do things. They want him to keep his muscles strong. The joints need to stay limber, and they want Magnus to keep active. So when I insist he do things for himself, we fight."

"I'm sorry. That sucks."

"Yeah, it does."

With nothing else to say, they both exited the car.

The house looked well kept, the trees trimmed and the walkway swept. The grass was weed-free and newly mowed.

"Here we go," Hayley said, then knocked on the door.

"Who is it?" The woman answered immediately, as though she'd been waiting for them right on the other side of the door.

"My name is Hayley. It's very important that we talk to Mr. Chalkor."

"Go away."

"If you don't talk to us, we'll have no choice but to make a call and get the police involved."

The door inched open. "What did he do now?"

She was heavyset. Blonde. Deep grooves made from her permanent frown were plastered across her face.

"Is he inside?" Hayley asked.

"No, but I'm his wife. Tell me what's going on."

"A friend of ours is missing. She drives a new Ford Escape and—"

"The girl who's been parked across the street off and on for two weeks taking pictures?"

"That would be her."

"I have no idea where your friend is."

Jessica flashed her badge. "FBI."

"Shit."

"I guess that means you know something?"

The woman looked down and away and locked her arms across her stomach. Then she released a sharp, tense breath through her nose and looked up at Jessica. "I just know that he was gone for most of the day yesterday," she said in a low voice. "He needed to get some tools from the warehouse. I also know I haven't seen the girl in the past few days."

"Does he work at a warehouse?"

"Oh, no. The warehouse is a run-down building that we invested every penny into when we were first married. If he had sold it when I told him, too, we'd be living the good life about now."

"Could you give us the address?"

She looked suddenly pensive. "You don't seriously think my husband would have anything to do with your missing friend, do you?"

"Why don't you give us the address," Jessica said, "and let us check it out."

"What if I refuse?"

"We'll be forced to call for backup and they'll haul your ass down to the station for further questioning," Hayley told her. "It's up to you."

Hayley also knew she could do another Internet search and find out any and all properties the Chalkors had ever owned, but that would take precious time they didn't have.

"It's 11500 Sunco Drive, Rancho Cordova."

"Do you have a key to the place?"

"My husband is the only one with a key, but he's not home."

"When will he be back?"

The woman sighed. "Your guess is as good as mine."

CHAPTER 55

Ever since being warned that almost every member of the Ambassador Club had died in some sort of bizarre manner, Chelsea Webster had been unable to eat, sleep, or do much of anything at all . . . except stare out the window, jump at every sound, and pour herself another shot of Jack Daniel's. With a trembling hand, she brought the glass to her lips, took a sip, winced, then downed the rest in one swallow.

That's why she'd left her boyfriend a note at their apartment in Orangevale and then had driven out of town. She was scared, and she didn't want to put him in any danger. She was staying in a Motel 6 off of I-80 in Auburn. Where else would she go?

Certainly not to her family. Most of them had disowned her when she was only seventeen after she'd kicked her grandmother in the shin, cutting through skin and hitting bone, causing swelling in Grandma's leg that she'd heard from a cousin still bothered her to this day. Not that that was the only awful thing she'd done. It had just been the final straw.

Chelsea didn't know why she'd been such an angry teenager. Looking back, it didn't make much sense. She'd been spoiled since birth. But lots of kids in the world were spoiled and somehow they turned out all right.

Maybe if her parents had disciplined her every once in a while, given her chores, things would have turned out differently. When she used to get angry with her mother, she would dump the contents of her mother's purse onto the floor and then take cash and credit cards. Her mother never stopped her.

She poured herself another glass, swallowed the contents in one gulp.

To this day, she didn't like waiting in lines, had zero patience, and did not like to share. The world hadn't made any sense at all until she'd met Adam. He was the most caring, patient, understanding individual she'd ever met. He loved her for who she was, and yet he didn't take her shit, either. He stood up to her. She'd never had anyone do that before.

It sounded corny, but it was the truth: love had opened her eyes to so many things—the good and the bad, although the bad all had to do with her past. No matter how hard she tried, she couldn't seem to shake all the nasty things she'd done back in high school.

She looked at the gun sitting on the nightstand.

One more drink for courage, she told herself.

Adam insisted she needed to let the past go, told her she needed to forgive herself. But would he say that if he knew everything she'd done? Sure, she'd told him about taking her mom's credit cards. She'd even swallowed her pride and told him about the time she'd kicked her grandmother. But she couldn't tell him everything. The things she'd done while she was a part of the Ambassador Club were so horrifyingly awful, she couldn't begin to imagine telling him. If she couldn't forgive herself, how would Adam ever find it in his heart to forgive her?

She put the entire bottle to her mouth and guzzled.

The amber liquid drizzled down over her chin as she reached for her gun.

It was time to end the pain.

She lifted her cell phone. The names in her contact list were blurred. It took her a moment, but she finally hit the right button. Adam answered on the first ring.

CHAPTER 56

The thick bulletproof glass window slid open, and Lizzy's things were passed through to her: wallet, gun, ID, money, purse. She signed a form, then followed Jessica out the station door, but not before giving Detective Chase a smug look.

As soon as she climbed into the passenger seat of Jessica's SUV, though, she said, "How the hell did you get me out of there?"

"It wasn't me. Jimmy Martin worked his magic. He has a soft spot in his heart for you."

The first time Lizzy had met Jimmy, he was special agent in charge of the Samuel Jones aka Spiderman case. Jimmy and Lizzy had been like oil and water back then. But Jared had been their common denominator, and they had quickly grown on one another. Now she thought of Jimmy as a father—the doting, caring father she'd never had. "I'll have to give him a call and thank him."

"I'm sure he would appreciate hearing from you."

They were silent for a long moment as Jessica drove, and then Lizzy said, "Sorry I wasn't at the house earlier to greet you."

"Not a problem. It gave me time to bond with Hayley. Why didn't you tell me she was living with you?"

"I figured you would find out next time you were in town, which is exactly what happened."

Jessica pulled onto the freeway, heading west. "Where are we going?" Lizzy asked. "I could really use a change of clothes and some coffee."

"No time for that at the moment."

"What's going on?"

"Mr. Howard Chalkor is what's going on. There's a possibility he might be holding Kitally hostage in a warehouse over in Rancho Cordova. When we got the call saying you were being released, Haylcy and I decided to split up. She'd get Tommy, I'd get you, then we'd all meet there."

Jessica floored it up the HOV lane. Lizzy had a tight grip on the grab-handle.

"How are you holding up these days?" Jessica asked.

"Great. Never been better." Jessica didn't deserve her sarcasm, but Lizzy was in no mood to apologize.

Jessica seemed to shrug it off. "Good. Maybe we can talk more later after you've gotten some rest."

"How long are you planning on hanging around?"

"A few days. I need to get back to Magnus and training. It's amazing I've gotten this much time away." She looked over at Lizzy. "Do you think Kitally will mind if I take one of those empty rooms in that giant house of hers?"

"I'm sure she'll invite you to stay for as long as you'd like. We just have to find her first."

As Jenny drew closer to her house, she noticed a car parked outside her front walkway. It looked like Dwayne's. What was he doing here? She looked at the wig sitting on the passenger seat on top of the bag filled with a bloody hammer and sweater.

If Dwayne hadn't climbed out of his car just then and waved, she would have turned around and driven off. Instead, she hit the remote to open the garage, pulled in, and shut the garage door before he could get to her.

Her hands shook as she put the key in the garage door leading to the house and ran inside. She shoved the bag inside her closet and then ran to the bathroom and washed her face. She looked in the mirror. *Shit!*

Her blouse was stained with blood. She pulled her shirt over her head, tossed it in the closet with her bag, and grabbed a clean blouse. Her hair was a mess. She finger-combed it, tried to make it look presentable.

By the time she opened the front door to let Dwayne inside, he looked concerned.

"Is everything all right?"

"Of course. Why, what's going on?"

"I heard that you left early to go to the dentist, and I thought I'd surprise you." He held up a bouquet of flowers and a small tub of gourmet soup.

She took the flowers and the soup from him and headed for the kitchen. He had completely thrown her off guard by showing up. She couldn't think straight.

He was right behind her. "What's this in your hair? Are you bleeding?"

"Here," she said, handing him the flowers. "Do you mind finding something to put these in while I go to my room and wash up? The dentist hit a nerve. I had blood on my shirt and my face. I didn't want to worry you, so that's why I rushed into the house before saying hello."

"Sweetheart," he said, his expression filled with concern. "Let me take care of this. You go get comfortable, and I'll warm you up some soup. Are you allowed to eat this soon after?"

"I don't think I should. But bringing me soup and flowers was very thoughtful of you."

He took her into his arms and gave her a gentle squeeze. She closed her eyes and prayed he couldn't feel the frantic beating of her heart.

She was finished, she realized. She couldn't bear the thought of losing Dwayne.

Dwayne is a pussy. You need to focus. You have one more person on your list. Dwayne doesn't love you. I'm the only one who cares about you. Chelsea Webster cannot get away with all of those horrible things she did to you.

"Dwayne," she said, looking up into his eyes.

"What is it? What's bothering you?"

"We haven't known one another very long, but I was wondering if you thought that maybe someday you could ever fall in love with someone like me?"

He smiled. "Someone like you? Are you kidding me? You have no idea how beautiful you are, inside and out. Every morning I wake up and wonder if this will be the day Jenny Pickett realizes she's way too good for me. And then I see you and you smile at me and in that moment I know Jenny Pickett is my girl, my one and only. I've loved you since the first moment I laid eyes on you."

"I love you, Dwayne."

"I love you, too."

Oh, for Christ's sake.

Tires sent gravel flying as Hayley pulled her Chevy in front of the warehouse on Sunco in Rancho Cordova. Tommy had followed her on his motorcycle. He killed his bike's engine as Hayley hopped out of her car and immediately began to dig around in her trunk. Too many damned tools. She quickly found her set of lock-picking tools, but was damned if she could locate the crowbar. At last she unearthed it, though, and headed for the main door into the warehouse.

Jessica and Lizzy pulled into the driveway as Hayley reached the roll-up door. It was a heavy affair, with a white rusted frame. The door was banged up good.

She put the crowbar underneath it and hauled up on it. Nothing happened the first time, but the second time did the trick and she threw open the door.

They charged into the warehouse as a pack. The place was dank and dark and empty except for a rat skittering across the cement toward the back corner. There was a low-ceilinged room back there—an office by the rear receiving door. If Kitally was here, that's the only place she could be. They hurried over to it.

"Kitally," Hayley called, "are you in there?"

The door was locked. There was no answer.

Hayley used the tools she'd brought to try to pick the lock, but this lock wasn't like anything she'd seen before.

"Let me try," Tommy said. Using a pick gun and a tension tool, he had the door open in a little over a minute.

"Nice job," Hayley said.

"I've been practicing."

When Hayley opened the door, Kitally was already lunging at her, but she managed to stop herself in midswing, the wire device in her hand mere inches from taking out Hayley's eye.

Kitally's pupils had dilated. Her hair stuck out in every direction, making her look as if she'd been trapped in the tiny room for weeks instead of twenty-four hours.

"Are you all right?" Hayley asked.

Kitally stepped out of the room without a word, just kept walking through the warehouse toward the light. Jessica grabbed

Kitally's camera and phone from inside the windowless room, then followed the rest of them out into the open air.

"What's this?" Lizzy asked, taking the wire from Kitally.

"I made it. I wanted to be ready for Chalkor when he came back."

"Did he tell you he was coming back?"

"No. I just didn't think he'd really leave me in there to die." Kitally looked around the parking area. "Where is he? How did you find me?"

Before Lizzy could answer, a car came roaring into the lot, spraying gravel. A heavysct man jumped out. "What the hell is going on? This is private property!"

Kitally walked up to the man and shouted, "Ay Yaah!" before anyone had a clue what she was up to. A powerful thud sounded the moment her foot connected with Chalkor's gut. Panicked, he turned about and tried to get back in his car, but another one of Kitally's kicks shut the door, almost taking his hand.

He turned to face the crowd. "Help me," he said. "She's crazy."

Nobody said a word.

"I could have died in there, you son of a bitch!" Kitally chambered and snapped her leg through a vicious front kick that drove her heel into his side.

Chalkor grunted and doubled over, clutching his side. "I was coming back to let you out."

"Liar," she said, driving a sudden knuckle blow into his throat.

Tommy looked at Lizzy and said, "Don't worry. She's going easy on the guy. If she wanted to kill him, she'd already have popped his nose into his brain."

"Great. I feel better now."

When Kitally advanced on him then, there was something darker in her movements, as though she'd taken Tommy's remark as an instruction.

Chalkor cowered against his car. "Somebody stop her."

Tommy stepped up behind Kitally, hooked an arm around her waist, and held her back.

"Let me go, Tommy. He tried to kill me."

"Don't worry," Lizzy said. "You've got four witnesses. Mr. Chalkor is going to be spending some time behind bars."

"You're all crazy," Chalkor moaned. "I'm going to sue you for everything you've got."

"Get in line," Lizzy said. "Get in line."

CHAPTER 57

Kitally's house looked like Grand Central Station. Everywhere Lizzy looked, there was coffee, pizza, and soda. Not to mention stacks of files, notebooks, and enough laptops to supply everyone in the room with two computers each.

Tommy had run off hours ago to instruct classes at his karate business, and Lizzy and Jessica had followed Hayley and Kitally home.

A giant whiteboard was propped up against one of the windows. In big bold letters Lizzy had written: *Identify the man following Lizzy. Identify the Ambassador Club killer.*

It was past nine and nobody showed any signs of slowing down.

Kitally wasn't talking much. She was pissed off after spending two hours filling out a police report and leaving with nothing more than a promise that they would look into the matter further since it ended up being his word against theirs. After the police finally showed up, Chalkor insisted that they had broken into his warehouse because they were angry they hadn't been able to find any evidence incriminating him in the workers' comp case. It hadn't helped Kitally's case that she'd beaten the crap out of him.

Kitally sat on the biggest couch in the room. She had fabrics and a sewing kit spread out as she worked on a new project. Nobody went near her.

Hayley and Jessica had taken over the kitchen table.

Lizzy had lists, papers, and maps spread out across the floor, where she did her best work.

"How many mug shots have we looked at?" Hayley asked.

"At least a thousand."

"Any possibilities yet?" Lizzy asked.

"Three maybes."

Hayley kept right-clicking, keeping the pictures moving at a good pace. "Wait," Jessica said. "Go back."

Hayley clicked the left button until Jessica said, "Him—I think that's our guy!"

In less than a minute, all four of them were staring at the man on the screen in front of Hayley. Hayley didn't look convinced. "Are you sure?"

Jessica had used Kitally's copier in the back room and made copies of the sketch Hayley had drawn that morning. She took one of the copies and handed it to Hayley. Then she handed her a pencil and said, "Can you give him a beard and make his hair darker?"

As soon as Hayley finished with the drawing, they were all nodding in agreement. "Those two men are identical," Kitally said.

"What's his name?" Lizzy asked.

"Frank Lyle. He served ten years for aggravated assault, rape, attempted murder."

"I know that name," Lizzy said. "He was the convict who was more than happy to take credit for Spiderman's victims. For a long while everyone thought he was Spiderman and the media went crazy for him. He was—"

The sharp report of a gun outside cut Lizzy off. She grabbed for her weapon, but she wasn't wearing her holster.

Jessica ran to the door leading to the backyard. "There's someone out there."

Lizzy ran down the hallway and up the stairs, put on shoes, and grabbed her gun. By the time she ran outside, Kitally was at her side with her machete in hand. They found Hayley standing over a man who lay bleeding on the ground. Jessica was kneeling over him, and barked orders at Kitally to call 911 and get her something to stanch the flow of blood. Kitally ran back to the house.

Lizzy took off her coat. She bent down and made a makeshift pillow for Detective Chase's head. He'd been shot in the chest. He was bleeding bad.

"You were right," he said, his voice weak.

"What are you talking about? What are you doing here?"

"Not a phantom," he said in a whisper. "Your guy is real."

"What about Shelby's other boyfriend? What happened with that?"

"Turned out"—he paused for a breath—"the kid made up the entire story."

"They're on their way," Kitally told Lizzy as she bent down and moved Lizzy's hand that was pressed over the detective's wound. Kitally made quick work of cutting open his shirt and using clean cloths and lots of gauze to stop the bleeding.

"The girl's parents dragged her to the station, made her apologize," Chase said, his voice clear, as if the shock was wearing off and he'd gotten a second wind. "She was jealous of the attention Shelby was getting, wanted a piece of the action. Can you imagine?"

"So you came here? Why?"

"I came to tell you what I knew, thought I'd let you gloat a little. I parked a few blocks away, figured I'd take a look around, keep an eye out for this phantom of yours. And lo and behold, I saw a shadow moving through the trees, heading this way. I thought I could catch him unaware. Turns out your guy has eyes in the back of his head. I had no idea he knew I was there. He wheeled around and shot me and then took off through those trees."

"It's Frank Lyle," Lizzy said. "That's his name."

A flicker of recognition crossed his face. "No kidding?"

Chase didn't look good. He'd lost a lot of blood. Lizzy wanted him to stay conscious. "Stay with me, Detective."

"I'm not going anywhere," he said.

"You've been shot before?"

"Nah," he said, wincing. "I've been doing this for thirty years and not a scratch. I had a feeling my first time would have something to do with you, Gardner."

CHAPTER 58

It was seven in the morning. Lizzy sipped her coffee as she watched the men working outside. Last night, crime scene investigators had squared off a large area around the spot where Detective Chase had been shot. A bullet casing had been found. Tests were being done, footprints photographed and documented.

Where the perpetrator's footsteps ended at the edge of the wooded area behind Kitally's home, an official police search was about to begin. A group of officers and dogs were going in search of the shooter.

A light drizzle was not helping matters. Everyone was dressed in parkas and rain ponchos. They wore heavy boots.

Thirty minutes ago, Lizzy had been told that Detective Chase was in stable condition. That was a relief. Despite their somewhat hostile relationship, she liked the man. It was obvious he had his own demons to deal with, but who didn't?

As Lizzy headed outside, she only got a few feet before Jessica came up from behind and grabbed hold of her arm. "Frank Lyle dropped a letter off at the news station on Broadway," Jessica said in a low voice. "The letter has been turned over to authorities. Jimmy Martin is taking over for now, and he wants you to take a look at it."

Lizzy knew the drill. Because it was a kidnapping case and probably due to the possible connection to a past serial killer, a joint task force had been formed. For that reason, and because Chase was out of commission, Jimmy Martin, FBI, was now in charge. Despite Jimmy's continuous attempts at retirement, one more case always seemed to pull him back into the fold before he could make the final leap to sandy beaches and pristine golf courses. Lizzy didn't ask questions. She just followed Jessica around the house to her car.

The morning air was crisp, her body chilled. Sticks snapped and leaves crunched beneath her feet. A feeling of déjà vu washed over Lizzy. It was happening again. Different players, different surroundings, but in a way nothing had changed.

She couldn't remember ever feeling as if she was in control of her life.

Life happened to her, not the other way around.

She and her sister used to talk about fate. Cathy believed everything happened for a reason. If that were true, what was all this madness about? What more could she possibly learn from Shelby's abduction? The girl had been missing for well over a week now. That didn't bode well for her.

Jessica unlocked the car and opened the passenger side to her SUV.

Lizzy climbed in, then waited for Jessica to start the engine before she said, "We need to find her."

"I know. We will."

"I can't let him get away with this. You know that, right?"

"What do you mean? Are you talking about Frank Lyle?"

"These monsters can't just do whatever they want. Roam around until they find another victim. Time after time."

"Lizzy, I'm not sure what you're trying to say."

"It never stops. Never."

"Should I take you home? You don't need to look at the letter right now. It can wait."

"No," Lizzy said, an intense look in her eyes. "I need to see that letter."

Lizzy read the letter for the third time.

Across his desk from her, Jimmy was talking on the phone with someone at the crime scene behind Kitally's house. From what she could overhear, they had yet to find more than a few footprints and one shell casing.

Jessica had left a few minutes ago to get them both a cup of coffee.

Every five minutes, someone stepped into the office. This time, Jimmy gestured for the person to go away. Every time the door opened, it sounded as if shit were hitting the fan on the other side. Now that the Shelby Geitner case had been pronounced an official kidnapping, the police department was crawling with federal agents. She knew from working with Jared that the FBI had the ability to tap into resources at a moment's notice when there was a big case such as this.

When she and Jessica had arrived, there were outside broadcasting vans and production trucks at every corner. They all wanted to know the latest scoop on Shelby. And how exactly was Lizzy involved? They heard there was a shooting. Had they found Shelby?

Lizzy pushed her thoughts along with the noise out of her mind.

Focus.

She read the very last line.

Shelby Geitner is alive. She rote most of this leter.
She didn't know it yet, but she will be ded soon.

Lizzy felt nauseous, took a sip of water, and started at the beginning.

> *I did it. I took Shelby Geitner. The news people are*
> *all idiots. When we met before, I told you I was*
> *responsible for the deaths of so many girls, but you*
> *did not believe me. You stupid journalists treated*
> *Spiderman like a god. He was nothing compared*
> *to me. This time you will see what I am capable of.*
> *You will see. You will all see.*
>
> *I told you. I warned you all and what did you*
> *do? You ordered your men in blue to open the*
> *gates and let me out.*
>
> *I sit here now with a lost soul at my side. It is*
> *easy to see she yearns for attention. We both think*
> *it is sad that it had to come to this.*
>
> *Am I invisible? Shelby says NO. I am in con-*
> *trol. I have the power. I think she is right.*

Lizzy took a breath before reading the next paragraph, the paragraph that stopped her every time. She read each word slowly.

> *Shelby wants me to tell her parents she is fine.*
> *She is happy and there is joy in the world she says*
> *and also she thinks it is important to teach me the*
> *words to ~~Gerammia~~ Jeremiah was a bullfrog. She*
> *is verry annoying at times. She makes so many*
> *promises.*

The letter went on, paragraph after paragraph—the rambling words of a crazed man. And yet it was obvious which parts Shelby had helped him with. Shelby was trying to tell them something. Which was why Lizzy kept going back to that fifth paragraph. Shelby had been taking her defense classes for five years. She'd been there the day Lizzy brought in a special guest, a woman who had been held captive for months before she'd convinced her captor to write a letter. The woman had told the class how her captor had felt as if nobody would listen to him, so she'd suggested he write a letter and send it to the media. Not only had he written the letter, he'd unwittingly allowed the woman to include clues that led the authorities right to her.

Shelby was a bright student—an exceptionally smart girl.

Lizzy stood. When she looked across the desk at Jimmy Martin, he hung up the phone and said, "What is it?"

"We need to talk to Shelby's boyfriend, Ben. You need to bring him here now. He needs to see this."

Jimmy didn't question her. In the past, there had been far too many moments like this one for him to bother with mindless interrogations of her or time-wasting uncertainty. Instead, he pushed a button and made the call.

CHAPTER 59

It was late by the time Lizzy got home. She had stopped at a restaurant and asked for a grilled cheese sandwich to go, but by the time she'd arrived at the hospital, they weren't allowing visitors. Even if her timing had been better, it wouldn't have done any good. Detective Chase had gone from stable to critical.

She put the wrapped-up sandwich in the fridge, surprised to see Hayley and Kitally still up, grinding away on the Ambassador Club killer case. "Where's Jessica?"

"She went to bed," Kitally said.

"Smart girl."

"Any news on Shelby?"

"No."

"Every news station is talking about the letter he sent to the media. I know you can't say much about what they know, but do they think she's still alive?"

"I have to believe she is."

The room fell silent for a long moment except for the clacking of Hayley's keyboard.

"Eighteen of the thirty-three women on the list of Ambassador Club killer suspects," Kitally said, holding up a list, "have degrees in something that could be considered connected to the medical field."

She stood and handed Lizzy the list. "Here. I'm going cross-eyed."

It was easy to see that Kitally's night in the abandoned warehouse had done some damage—taken some of the light out of her eyes and the kick out of her step.

"Go to bed," Lizzy told her. "I'll take over from here."

Kitally yawned. "We should all call it a night."

"I'm not tired," Hayley said without looking up from her computer.

"You do realize," Kitally said before she disappeared down the hallway, "that this person could have a degree in mathematics for all we know. Hell, she could be self-taught."

Neither of them responded.

"It's a matter of crossing one person off at a time," Lizzy said under her breath.

Twelve o'clock the next day, Hayley strolled into the kitchen. She found the grilled cheese sandwich inside the refrigerator and shoved it into the microwave to heat it up. After the microwave beeped, she grabbed a paper towel and took a seat at the table across from Jessica. "Where is everyone?"

"Good morning to you, too. Or should I say, good afternoon?"

Hayley shrugged and took a bite.

"Lizzy left a note." Jessica slid it across the table.

Hayley read as she ate.

> *Girls—I wanted to get an early start on the Ambas-*
> *sador Club case. I decided to take the four names*

*at the bottom of the list that Hayley and I came up
with last night:*

*Jenny Pickett
Kat Remington
Julie Smith
Latochia Bell*

*The rest of you pick a couple names and see what
you can find out. Let's meet back at the house at
six p.m. to see where we're at. —Lizzy*

Hayley took her time finishing her sandwich, then tossed the paper towel in the garbage. "I'll grab my bag. Are you ready to go?"

Jessica looked behind her before saying, "Who, me?"

"You don't have anything else to do, do you?"

"True, but—"

"And I don't see Kitally around."

"She went to get her car in El Dorado Hills. Tommy took her."

"OK, then," Hayley said. "I'll be ready to go in five minutes."

Lizzy had already crossed three people off her list.

She went about things a little differently this time. Instead of barging in like a maniac and making accusations, she rang the bell, introduced herself, calmly told whoever answered the door why she was there, and then proceeded to ask questions.

So far, so good.

If she hadn't been running on adrenaline and caffeine when she'd paid Dana Kohl a visit, she might have seen that the woman wasn't who she thought her to be. She'd gone to the woman's house with her mind already made up.

She'd made a mistake. She'd been making a lot of them lately. But not today. She knew what needed to be done. Today she would proceed with care and professionalism. If she had done the same when she'd first met Melony Reed, the woman might still be alive.

It turned out that Latochia Bell had a husband and three kids. She was clearly overwhelmed. She didn't have time to feed the baby, let alone plan a murder.

Julie Smith was newly married with a baby on the way and was quite possibly one of the sweetest ladies Lizzy had ever met—she was not a cold-blooded killer.

Lizzy had just left the third woman on her list five minutes ago. Kat Remington had turned out to be a major yapper. Lizzy had nearly fallen asleep listening to her stories about how the Ambassador Club members only did what they did because they were insecure. Apparently, Kat believed strongly in forgiving those who she believed didn't know any better. After her lecture on forgiveness, she spent the next forty-five minutes complaining about how her impossible mother-in-law told her what, when, and how to do everything, including how to make a bed, iron a shirt, and cook a proper dinner for her husband.

The woman was beyond exasperating, but no killer.

Jenny Pickett was next on the list.

The only Picketts listed, though, were Ophelia and James Pickett in Elk Grove.

It was just past five.

Lizzy was tired, but she was only fifteen minutes from the Pickett pig farm, and she figured she might as well get this over with so she could cross one more person off the list.

■ ■ ■

"Third time's a charm, right?"

"Sure," Hayley said. "Next person on our list is Tracy Carson."

"I wonder how Lizzy is doing. I don't like the idea of her going out alone. She's obviously exhausted. Otherwise she never would have stormed into that woman's house."

"She needs time."

"And a break from all of this."

"I agree," Hayley said.

There was a long pause before Jessica said, "I can't begin to imagine what Lizzy is going through. When do they actually take Jared off life support?"

"I guess you haven't heard."

"What?"

"Jared's parents have petitioned the court for guardianship of Jared's health care."

Jessica sighed. "It just goes on and on."

Hayley nodded.

"Poor Lizzy." Jessica pulled the car to the curb across the street from a small Victorian house. "Let's go," she said. "I'll do the talking this time."

"Sounds good to me."

As they walked up the pathway, Jessica felt a droplet of rain hit the top of her head. She looked heavenward. The clouds were gray and rippled.

Hayley knocked and a woman opened the door. She was short and frumpy, with thin, disheveled hair and a moth-eaten sweater two sizes too large.

"We're here to talk to Tracy Carson," Jessica said.

"Why? What is this about?"

"My name is Jessica Pleiss, and this is Hayley Hansen. We're doing a story about the Ambassador Club. We were told that Tracy attended Parkview High School. Is she in?"

The woman blinked at them, then sighed. "I'm Tracy," she said. "And, yes, I did go to Parkview."

The thirty-year-old woman looked much older than her age. "Any chance we can come in and talk to you for a few minutes?"

"It depends."

Hayley and Jessica exchanged a quick glance.

"On what?" Jessica asked.

"It depends on if you're telling the truth or not. Are you really writing a story about that group of good-for-nothing assholes, or is this about something else?"

"No," Hayley said, speaking out before Jessica could answer. "We are not writing a story at all. The truth is we're doing an investigation."

"Why did you lie about it?"

Hayley gestured toward Jessica. "It was her idea."

Jessica rolled her eyes. "People are usually more open to talking if it's for a story."

"What a load of shit that is," the woman said. "Truth. Always start with the truth."

Hayley smirked.

The woman crossed her arms and gave Jessica the once-over. "Come on in," she finally said.

Tracy Carson moved the newspapers from her tattered couch in the front room and pointed, which meant take a seat.

Jessica noticed that the weeks' worth of newspapers were all folded to various stories having to do with the recent accidents. "Looks like you've been following the Ambassador Club story pretty closely."

"You bet I have."

"Do you remember the Ambassador Club?" Jessica asked.

"How could I forget?"

The woman disappeared. They could hear cupboards being opened and closed in her small kitchen. She came back minutes later with a plastic pitcher filled with some god-awful-looking foggy-yellow concoction and three glasses.

Jessica leaned back into the couch as if the pitcher were filled with acid and Tracy might suddenly toss it at them.

Hayley took over. "Are you aware that more than half of the thirteen members of the Ambassador Club have perished recently?"

"I am," Tracy answered with a smile. "I can only hope that the person responsible finds a way to get all of them."

"Are you saying you're not disturbed by any of this?" Jessica asked.

"That's what I'm saying. Every time I turn on the news and see that another member is gone, I celebrate. I kick my shoes off and do a little jig right here in this very room."

"What did they do to you?" Jessica asked.

"You wouldn't believe me if I told you." Tracy Carson pulled her sweater tight around her waist and then took a seat in a La-Z-Boy close by. "But I won't talk about it. Not to anyone. Most times I make believe it didn't happen at all. The memories, though . . . the memories live in me like a tumor that's too close to vital organs, so it can't be cut out. When every member of that club is dead, the tumors will still be there." She placed a hand over her heart. "But I'll sleep like a baby when it's done."

Jessica scooted to the edge of the couch. "Do you have any idea who might be responsible?"

"If I did, I wouldn't say."

"So you do have an idea of who might be responsible," Jessica said.

"You look parched," the woman told her. "Go ahead and have some lemonade. It's nice and cold."

Jessica looked at the particles swirling about inside the pitcher. Was this their killer?

"I made it myself. I have a lemon tree out back."

"No, thanks. I'm not thirsty."

"I am," Hayley said and proceeded to pour herself a glass. Before Jessica could stop her, she guzzled it down, then wiped her mouth with her sleeve and said, "Delicious."

"You knew that was a test, didn't you?" Tracy asked.

Jessica couldn't believe what Hayley had done. "A test?" she asked.

"Tracy believes we might think she's the killer," Hayley said.

A perfectly reasonable assumption, Jessica thought. "You have a degree in chemistry," Jessica told her. "For four years, you were abused by one, maybe more, of the members of this club. Of course you might be on our radar."

"Well," Tracy said, "I'm flattered. I only wish I had the nerve to pull off something as delicious as this. But I don't. She's bound to get caught, and when she does, she's going down. Prison and me, that's not a good mix." She grinned. "I just hope she finishes the job before they get her. You think she'll go after the ones who moved away?"

Jessica and Hayley looked at each other, then turned back to her and shrugged. "Hard to say," Jessica said. "What makes you think the person responsible is a woman?"

Tracy lifted a brow. "Why are you here talking to me?"

"All righty, then," Hayley said, pushing herself to her feet.

Jessica joined her and thanked Tracy Carson for her time. While there was no arguing the woman was a little strange and overly excited about the Ambassador Club deaths—that in itself was no crime. But still . . . Tracy Carson made her uneasy.

On their way to the car, Jessica turned to Hayley. "How can you be so sure she's not the killer?"

"That woman can hardly see. She has uveitis."

"Uveitis?"

"An inflammatory problem that causes swelling and destroys eye tissues."

"How do you know this?"

"While you were watching Tracy, I was looking around the room. The cane was my first clue, the medication for uveitis was the second."

"How does she read the newspaper?"

"You didn't see the magnifying glass on the table?"

Jessica sighed. "Are you feeling woozy yet?"

"Not even a little," Hayley said. "If anything, she might have put some sort of energy drink in that lemonade. I've never felt better."

Jessica snorted and then opened the door and climbed in behind the wheel.

CHAPTER 60

Lizzy had never been to a pig farm before. From what she'd read online, the Pickett Pig Farm had five hundred sows that each produced about twenty-five piglets every year. The Pickett farm handled the breeding and marketing and allowed their piglets to grow organically. They did not use hormones or antibiotics. The pigs were free to live outdoors and roam around.

As she drove up the long, graveled lane toward the farmhouse sitting in the middle of the lot, she thought the place looked lonely and neglected against its backdrop of gray skies.

Lizzy cut the engine in front of the house and climbed out of her car. The stairs leading up to the porch had seen better days. Her sneakers squeaked against the wood wraparound porch as she made her way to the front entry.

It had rained earlier in the morning. Instead of getting a whiff of fresh hay or even manure, something damp and moldy wafted her way.

She knocked.

When no one answered, she walked a third of the way around the porch before she heard a woman call out, "Can I help you?"

Lizzy hurried back to the door. "Hello. I'm Lizzy Gardner. I was hoping you might have a few minutes to spare."

The woman wiped her hands on an old tattered apron strung around her tiny waist. "We haven't been to church in a while, but you can tell the pastor we'll be back as soon as Jim is feeling up to it."

"I'm not with the church. I'm an investigator."

The woman was petite and birdlike. Beneath the apron she wore faded jeans, a moss-green T-shirt, and a pair of brown tie-up boots with worn soles that looked as though they'd walked five hundred miles and then some. Her gray hair was pulled back away from her face. "What would an investigator want with us?"

"It's about your daughter, Jenny Pickett."

The woman licked her thin, dry lips.

"When Jenny was in high school, do you remember if she ever mentioned the Ambassador Club?"

She shook her head thoughtfully. "Never heard of it before now. Jenny was and is very bright. As far as I know, she never joined any clubs, though."

"Have you heard anything about what's going on with some of the graduating class of 2002?"

"You mean at Parkview? Jenny's school?"

"Yes."

"We don't get the newspaper or own a television set. Never have. My husband often quotes somebody or other: 'Without hard work, nothing grows but weeds.'" Ophelia Pickett held the door wide. "Why don't you come in and tell me all about it."

Lizzy stepped inside.

"I just made some stew if you're hungry."

"I already ate," Lizzy said, "but thanks for offering." The floorboards creaked beneath her feet as she followed the woman across the main living room.

Not one light was on, and the windows were covered with a hodgepodge of fabric that looked like a patchwork quilt, but not the kind you might find at a craft show. These curtains looked as if they had suffered the same trauma as Mrs. Pickett's boots.

Every available surface in the house had a doily on it, most of them faded to a dingy yellow. Dust mites and spiderwebs had made a home in every high corner of the ceiling. The kitchen was a medley of furniture—a picture of both hominess and thrifty chic.

The woman grabbed a dirty rag and wiped it across the vinyl seat she had pulled out for Lizzy. "Go ahead—get comfortable while I finish up this stew."

Lizzy did as she said.

"Now tell me," Ophelia said as she struggled to get a thick wooden spoon through whatever was in the tin pot on the stove, "what is the name of the club you asked about?"

"The Ambassador Club."

"And what is it exactly that's happening to the class of 2002?"

"Members of the club seem to be running into a bit of bad luck. Most seem to be accidents, but not all."

"Are you saying that they're being murdered?"

"We're not sure. We still have a lot of questions."

"Well, I'm glad my Jenny wasn't a part of any clubs," the woman said without looking away from her stew.

Lizzy watched the woman work, couldn't pinpoint what was wrong with this scene, but this was no Norman Rockwell painting she was looking at.

"I do hope the police have rounded up a few suspects."

"Not even close at this point."

"And why would any of this matter to me or my wife?" an old man asked from the door, his walking stick pointed at Lizzy. He had a square face with a large, bulbous nose in the middle of it. His hair, what little was left, stuck out like a porcupine's quills.

Without his stick to hold him up, he was bent so far over she thought he might topple.

Lizzy stood and offered her hand, ready to introduce herself, but Mrs. Pickett told her to sit down and pay him no mind.

"What is Mindy doing in our house?" the old man demanded of his wife.

"It's not Mindy, dear. This is Lizzy Gardner. She's an investigator."

He grunted and walked off.

"Mindy who?" Lizzy asked, knowing the name sounded familiar.

"Mindy, Cindy, Windy," Mrs. Pickett said. "Don't pay any attention to him. His mind gets a bit muddled at times, but he's a good man with a good heart."

"I don't mean to cause any problems."

"I'm sure you don't." She used a ladle to fill a bowl and then slid it in front of Lizzy, along with a spoon and a cloth napkin that looked as though it had never been washed. "Eat up," she said.

Lizzy made the mistake of looking into the bowl. It was not a pretty sight—lumpy with something sticking out of it, something that looked a lot like a claw or maybe a beak. She almost gagged. "I'm really not hungry. Do you think I could use a bathroom?"

"Sure," the woman said, frowning as she took the bowl to the stove and poured its contents back into the pot. "Follow me."

They walked down the hallway and through a bedroom to get to the bathroom. "This is the only one that's working."

"Thank you."

Lizzy stepped inside and quickly locked the door behind her. She didn't hear the woman walk away, but she couldn't worry about that. She opened the toilet seat and threw up everything she'd eaten that day. After two flushes, she splashed her face with water from the sink and washed her hands.

She took another minute to collect herself before she headed out. The room she had to walk through to get back to the kitchen was one of the strangest-looking bedrooms she'd ever seen. The mirror on the wall was cracked and framed with bird feathers and rocks. The dresser was covered with old playing cards and lined with glass jars, the kind with screw-on lids. Inside the biggest jar was a china doll. Something wriggled its way out of the doll's porcelain eye.

"Are you OK?"

Lizzy jumped.

"Didn't mean to scare you." Mrs. Pickett stood in the doorway fiddling with her dirty rag, but she didn't seem to be using it for anything. "I meant to ask you what the Ambassador Club did. I know kids join all sorts of clubs these days, but the Ambassador Club is an odd name. What did they do?"

"They were mean kids," Lizzy said.

"So they picked on other kids?"

Lizzy nodded. "Do you know if anyone ever picked on Jenny when she was in high school?"

"Nobody ever picked on Jenny. She wasn't the most popular girl in school, but she had friends. She was always ahead of her class. I never ever had to worry about Jenny."

"So, she did have friends?"

"Well, she didn't bring any of them over, but that was mostly because we're so far out here in the boonies."

Lizzy looked back at the doll in the jar and shivered.

"Jenny loved books. She liked to read. One year, she read four hundred books."

"That's impressive. So she never came home crying or upset?"

"No. Never. She was always happy."

Behind her, her hatchet-faced husband appeared. "You shall not take vengeance or bear a grudge against the sons of your own

319

people," he intoned, "but you shall love your neighbor as yourself: I am the Lord."

"That's enough, Jim." She looked at Lizzy. "He likes to memorize verses from the Bible."

"Why is Mindy here?" he asked again.

Mrs. Pickett ignored her husband. "I'm sorry I can't be of more help to you."

"You've been a big help," Lizzy assured her as she followed Mr. and Mrs. Pickett back to the kitchen.

Ophelia sat her husband in the same chair where Lizzy had sat earlier. "You sit right there and I'll get you a cookie." She smiled at Lizzy. "Our daughter comes home for dinner quite often and always brings us homemade cookies."

Lizzy watched her go to the freezer and pull out a Tupperware container filled with cookies identical to the ones Lizzy had sent to the lab for testing. "I know I said I wasn't hungry," Lizzy told her, "but those do look delicious. Mind if I take one for the ride home?"

Ophelia Pickett placed a cookie in a napkin and handed it to her.

Lizzy walked over to where she'd left her purse on the table. She had to lean low over the table to reach it. Mr. Pickett grabbed the purse strap and wouldn't let her have it. "You shouldn't be here, Mindy," Mr. Pickett said. "We don't like bullies."

CHAPTER 61

Jenny had one more thing to do. She had gathered the wigs, gloves, shoes, anything that might incriminate her if it were ever found in her house, including the bloody sweater and the hammer, and put it all inside a garbage bag.

Then she put everything in the trunk of her car and went for a drive.

So much had changed in such a short period of time.

She felt like a newly blossoming bud. A beautiful flower. A butterfly that had just metamorphosed. Corny but true.

Ten minutes later, she parked as close as she could get to the apartment complex in Orangevale and realized this might not be as easy as breaking into a house. As far as apartment buildings go, there appeared to be a good amount of people coming and going. It didn't help matters that for the first time, she wore no disguise.

She felt vulnerable, and she didn't like it.

But she had to do what she had to do. She climbed out of her car, gathered the bag from the trunk, and headed for the main door.

Confidence, Jenny, confidence. She straightened her spine as she stepped inside the building. The place was decent enough, well kept. The actual apartment she needed to visit was on the fourth floor. She took the steps, passed a young couple carrying bikes over their heads on the stairwell. They smiled. She said, "Hi."

No big deal.

Once she was on the second floor, the only floor without a camera, she hit the alarms and then waited for the chaos to begin.

It didn't take long. She made her way up two more floors, weaving her way through fleeing residents, concerned expressions on their faces as they left their belongings behind them. One man, the man she'd hoped to see, was helping a woman who was having a difficult time getting three small children down the stairwell.

On the fourth floor, her gloved hand on the doorknob, she smiled when the door opened.

Two minutes later, she was rushing down the stairs with the rest of them, even helped an elderly woman when she tripped in her haste and almost fell.

As Jenny opened her car door and climbed behind the wheel, she realized she couldn't remember the last time she'd heard the voices in her head.

She smiled.

The smell of freedom wafted through the open window. Starting today, she would begin her new life, a life filled with friends and family and endless possibilities.

The past was in the past. She was letting it all go.

She was ready.

Lizzy was in the car when the phone rang. It was the rookie reporter, Derek Murphy.

"Hey, Murphy. I've been meaning to call you and thank you for writing the story and getting the mucky-mucks over there to run it."

"You're welcome. But that's not why I called. Guess who they're bringing in for questioning in the next thirty minutes."

She perked up. "Who?"

"I heard this through the grapevine, but I figured with your connections you might be able to finagle a way inside and get the scoop."

"What's going on? Who's being questioned?"

"Jenny Pickett."

A shot of adrenaline coursed through Lizzy's body. "When did this happen? The investigator I talked to told me that my cookie connection theory was flimsy as best."

"It wasn't the cookies. They found Dean Newman. Seatbelted in his car at the bottom of the canal near Carmichael. Where are you? It's all over the news."

"I'm in the car on my way home."

"Well, it shouldn't surprise you that Dean Newman's death looks like suicide, but he had an envelope addressed to Jenny Pickett tucked inside his pocket."

"Had the letter been opened?"

"I don't think so . . . not sure. But the GPS on his phone and in his car pointed to 55 Glen Tree Drive in Citrus Heights. Guess who lives there?"

"Jenny Pickett?"

"Yep, and I guess between the letter and the fact that Newman had been to her street, it was enough to bring her in."

"Thanks for the call. I'm all over this."

Lizzy pulled to the side of the road and keyed in the Citrus Heights address. It was 7:34 p.m. It would take her twenty minutes to get there. She made an illegal U-turn and headed for the freeway. If luck was on her side, she could get to Jenny's house before they hauled her to the station. She would love to look Jenny Pickett in the eyes when they handcuffed her, let her know that sometimes justice really did prevail.

CHAPTER 62

Jenny reached over and rested her hand on Dwayne's leg.

He kept his eyes on the road and his hands on the wheel, but she could see a hint of a smile playing on the corner of his mouth. After work, he'd picked her up and taken her to an early dinner at Moxie on H Street in Midtown. They had lingered overly long. It was almost eight.

A police cruiser passed by. Jenny's chest tightened. A week had gone by since her visit with Aubrey Singleton. The local news stations hadn't said much at all about Aubrey's death, which Jenny found odd since she was one of the few people who was obviously murdered. Being struck in the head with a hammer was no accident.

After Dwayne had come so close to catching her in bloodied clothes, Jenny had come up with a new plan. Although her plan had required her to break into one more building, the deed was done. Despite there being one name left on the list—two if she counted Lizzy Gardner—every moment spent with Dwayne made her realize she'd made the right choice. Her job was finished. The kill list had been burned and the computer destroyed. Every incriminating item had been removed from her home.

Other than the two lucky Ambassador Club members who had moved, Chelsea Webster would be the only one on her kill list to survive. Chelsea had always seemed like such a miserable, tortured soul. She was a mean one. Rumor had it that her family disowned her after she beat her grandmother. What sort of person beat up her own grandmother?

Jenny sighed. She would have to make do with the hope that Chelsea's depression and misery only deepened as the years wore on.

Dwayne pulled his car into the driveway and killed the engine.

"Are you OK?" he asked. "You've seemed distant lately."

She looked at him and said, "I'm just happy."

He leaned over the center console and gave her a kiss. His lips felt divine. Then he climbed out of the car and came around to open the door for her.

She loved that he took the time to open doors for her. She would never tire of being pampered by Dwayne. He was a gentleman, and they adored each other.

Before they got as far as the mailbox, three police cars were speeding down the road toward them. Tires screeched as the vehicles pulled up to the curb.

"Jenny Pickett," one of the officers called out.

Jenny looked at him and said, "I'm Jenny Pickett."

He pulled his gun from his holster. "Stay where you are, and put your hands in the air where we can see them."

"What's this all about?" Dwayne demanded.

"Sir, you need to step to the side. Now."

"What's going on?" he asked Jenny.

"I don't know. You didn't call them, did you?"

"Of course not. Why would I? What do you mean?"

"Nothing," she said.

Not too far up the road, she saw two more cars pull to the curb. Lizzy Gardner climbed out of one of the vehicles and led a pack of uniformed officers her way. The street had been blocked off. Strobe lights swirled everywhere she looked.

An officer came forward, handcuffed Jenny, and put her in the back of his vehicle.

Lizzy looked at the officer, and he dipped his chin, allowing her one moment with Jenny before he shut the door.

"It took some work," Lizzy told her, leaning in so no one else could hear, "but it looks like you weren't as clever as you told me you were."

"Are we being taped?"

"No."

"All but one is dead, but I'm afraid you have the wrong person. They won't be locking me up anytime soon."

"What do you mean 'all but one is dead'? Chelsea Webster was found in a motel room with a bullet in her head."

Jenny rocked back in the seat. "You cannot be serious." She couldn't have planned it better if she'd tried. "Did she leave a suicide note?"

Lizzy gave her a dubious look. "Are you trying to tell me you didn't kill her?"

"I absolutely did not kill Chelsea Webster. Like I said before, you have the wrong person."

Lizzy stepped away and shut the door.

From behind tinted glass, Lizzy watched as the investigators took turns interrogating Jenny Pickett. It was late, and she found herself wishing Detective Chase was the person doing the interrogating. The investigator asking all the questions didn't have half of Chase's intimidation factor working for him.

The investigator pointed to a video showing a blurry image of a redhead walking away from an apartment complex. "It all started here, didn't it? You knew Terri Kramer."

"I already told you. Terri Kramer and I were college friends. I was devastated when I heard about what happened to her."

He read off a list of names, members of the Ambassador Club. "Do any of those names mean anything to you?"

She shook her head. "I recognize a few from high school. Is this why I'm here? Did something happen to them?"

His mouth tightened. "We'll sit here through the night if we have to, Ms. Pickett."

"You have no grounds on which to keep me here. I've done nothing wrong."

"Chelsea Webster, your last kill, named you personally in the note we found next to her body."

"That's ridiculous. That woman made my high school life a living hell, but I never once considered doing her harm. You have the wrong person. This has gone on long enough. I would like to call my lawyer."

Lizzy heard a small commotion behind her as the detective she was sitting with was called out of the room. When he returned, he said, "Looks like she gets to go home."

"How? Why?"

"They searched Pickett's home and came up empty. There's nothing there. She doesn't even keep insecticides or rat poison in her garage. And that's not all. We got a call from a guy named Adam Lamont, Chelsea Webster's boyfriend. Apparently he was on the phone with her when she blew her head off. He said nobody else was in the motel room with her. Nobody made her do it."

"This doesn't make any sense," Lizzy said. "What about all those other people?"

"Chelsea's boyfriend found a bag in their bedroom closet. It was filled with shoes, wigs, bloody clothes—enough evidence to put the woman away for a very long time. Apparently she couldn't live with the guilt. So first she killed the rest of the Ambassador Club members, and then she took care of herself."

Lizzy couldn't believe what she was hearing. Jenny Pickett had thought of everything.

He headed inside the interrogation room.

She watched him unlock the cuffs from Jenny's wrists and tell her she was free to go. By the time Jenny Pickett was allowed to leave the interrogation room, Lizzy was standing by the door waiting for her.

Their gazes locked.

The self-satisfied look on Jenny's face would've been bad enough. But as she walked down the hall, she looked back over her shoulder and said to Lizzy, "There *is* justice in the world, isn't there?"

CHAPTER 63

"I'm here at the house now," Jessica said into her phone as she pulled up to the front of Kitally's house. "We'll be on our way in five minutes." She clicked off, cut the engine, and jogged to the front door.

Kitally answered the door.

Jessica stepped past her. "Where's Lizzy?"

"She's upstairs. First bedroom on the left. What's going on?"

Jessica ran upstairs. She found Lizzy sitting on a mountain of fluffy bedding, papers strewn and covering the entire mattress.

Lizzy looked up, her eyes sunken and tired. "What is it, Jessica?"

"They found her."

"Shelby?"

Jessica nodded. "You were right. It took him some time, but Ben, her boyfriend, thought he knew what she was trying to say in the letter. Shelby taught him to sing 'Joy to the World' when Shelby vacationed with him and his family. She would sing every time she heard the croak of a frog. Shelby and Ben took a lot of hikes when they were there. Ben and his parents led us to the place. It's near Auburn. It didn't take them long to find them. It was right there—a tiny cabin—off the beaten path near Two-Face Rock."

"Is she safe?"

"No. He still has her. We believe Shelby is tied up. He has a gun."

"Were we right? Is it Frank Lyle?"

Another nod.

Lizzy had no words.

"He wants to talk to you, Lizzy."

"Me?"

"Yeah, *only* you. Says he'll kill her if we don't bring you there now."

Lizzy was already on her feet, grabbing her jeans and T-shirt. She started to put on her holster, but Jessica stopped her. "No weapons."

Kitally had been standing by the door the entire time. "Wait!" she said to Lizzy, "I have something for you." Then she ran off, her footfalls skittering down the stairs in record time. By the time she was running back up, she passed Jessica on the stairs going down.

"I'll be in the car," Jessica shouted, clearly annoyed. "Try to hurry!"

Five minutes later, Lizzy jumped into the passenger seat.

Jessica didn't wait for her to buckle up. She put her foot on the gas pedal and gunned it.

Once they were on the highway, Jessica asked, "What was Kitally's problem?"

"No problem," Lizzy told her. "She was concerned, that's all."

"You two have grown close."

"You'll always be my first assistant," Lizzy said with a smirk, hoping to change the subject.

"Thanks. I was worried."

Awkward silence followed. They were both worried about Shelby, but they had a fifteen- to twenty-minute ride in front of them, too, and it wouldn't do much good to sit and stew in fear of what might lie ahead when they arrived at the scene. "How's the FBI program working out?" Lizzy asked.

"All is well. No regrets."

There was a moment's pause before Jessica said, "What about Hayley?"

"What about her?"

"Still wandering the streets at night?"

"Not so much," Lizzy lied. "I think she's finally moving on."

"How so?"

"She registered at the local community college."

"Really? What class is she taking?"

"Art."

"The Art of Weaponry?"

"No, smart-ass. Painting and drawing."

"Hmm."

And that was it. That's all the chitchat they could handle considering the circumstances, both knowing that a young girl's life was at stake and that anything could happen.

Going well over the speed limit, it still took them twenty minutes to get to the area in Auburn where it seemed every media van and emergency vehicle in Placer County had set up camp. A long line of dark sedans and police cruisers dotted the area.

"SWAT has been set up," an agent said in greeting as soon as they climbed out of the vehicle, "but there's only one window, and they can't get a visual. Perpetrator said he'll shoot her if anyone throws a smoke bomb. He's not going out without a fight."

They were on foot now, ignoring the journalists who shoved microphones in front of their faces.

The federal agent held up the crime scene tape and led them up the hill. They stayed on a path for a while until another agent took over and led them off the trail, through trees and thick brush that had been marked with small white flags. The ground was thick with dead leaves and pinecones, but the flags were easy to see.

The grade got steeper as they went, and they hiked for much longer than Lizzy had anticipated they would. It was cold and drizzly, but by the time she got within a hundred yards of the cabin, she was sweating. It was good to see Jimmy Martin at the front of the group, talking on his radio. He clicked off as Lizzy reached him.

"I thought you retired a long time ago," Lizzy said.

"So did I."

Jimmy gave Lizzy a hard look. He didn't like this one bit. "He wants to talk to you. Wants you to walk up to the cabin, knock three times, and then say your name."

"Let's do it, then."

"Are you sure?"

"Yeah, I absolutely want to do this."

Another man, a guy in a helmet dressed in black, the upper half of his body covered with a thick bulletproof vest, looked at her and said, "Ready?"

"Ready."

"No weapons on you, right?"

"That's right." She'd left her gun with Jessica. She held up her arms. "I'm clean. Let's do this."

They set off.

Lizzy followed the nameless man in black.

Behind her, she could hear Jimmy Martin back on his radio, barking orders. She glanced over her shoulder, made eye contact with Jessica before she slid out of sight behind a tree. She'd managed a smile, but it was tenuous at best.

Stay focused, she told herself. Despite the drizzle, the leaves on the forest floor had been protected from the rain by the trees and crunched beneath her feet.

"Just the woman," a man shouted from the cabin as they approached.

She didn't recognize the voice, but she knew it was *him*.

It felt as if Spiderman were back from the dead, his copycat wannabe trying to make a name for himself.

"Step back!" he ordered the man in the vest. "All the way back until you're with the rest of your guys."

The nameless man hesitated.

"I'll be fine," Lizzy told him.

He turned and followed the same trail back.

The sound of birds surprised her for some reason. Lizzy inhaled a breath of fresh pine air and continued on toward the cabin. She made her way to the door and was about to knock three times as instructed, but then she heard wood scratching against wood. The door had hardly opened before he had her arm and yanked her inside, tossing her across the room so violently there was nothing to do but roll with it until she crashed into the wall, her head and the back of her neck striking hard enough to leave her momentarily dazed.

And then she saw Shelby—sitting on the edge of the narrow bed against the far wall, her eyes wide and scared. The girl had been beaten down and bruised, hardly looked like Shelby at all. Her hands were behind her back. She was gagged; her ankles had been bound with duct tape.

Lizzy pushed herself to her feet.

Before she could go to Shelby, Frank Lyle stepped between them with his gun trained on her. "Stay right where you are."

She did as he said.

"Take off your clothes."

She hesitated.

"Now!"

She took off the hooded sweatshirt Jessica had handed her in the car on the way there and laid it on the floor.

"Kick it over here!"

Her eyes never left Shelby's as she did as he asked. She wanted Shelby to know that everything was going to be OK. They both needed to stay calm. Needed to keep clear heads.

"Everything!"

She took off her shoes and then her socks. She purposely slowed down the process in order to give herself time to take in her surroundings. Her breathing calmed. She looked at the bed, took a closer look at Shelby's ankles. Her feet weren't secured to the bed, which meant Shelby could use her legs if she needed to.

Lizzy slipped off her pants, slowly, then kicked them over with everything else she'd removed so far.

Her T-shirt came off next.

She was down to her bra and underwear. She wrapped her arms around her waist, stood there barefoot and half-naked, shivering and praying he wouldn't make her remove anything else.

He checked the pockets of her pants and then kicked the pile of clothes to the side.

Lizzy continued to keep eye contact with Shelby, trying to convey that they were not going to give up easily.

She thought Shelby understood. She looked frightened but determined, too. Shelby hadn't given up the fight yet. Lizzy could see it in the rigid set of her jaw.

Frank Lyle stepped close to the bed and brushed his hand over Shelby's leg as if he wanted to let Lizzy know he could touch her where and whenever he wanted and there was nothing she could do about it. His fingers continued up and over Shelby's stomach.

Shelby closed her eyes for just a second, then found Lizzy's gaze again.

"So, what do you want?" Lizzy asked him.

"It's not obvious?"

"No."

"I know how you hate to watch others suffer," he said, "so I thought I would bring you here so you could watch me kill the bitch." He moved the gun to Shelby's head.

Shelby cried out through the gag.

Lizzy started forward, and he let her come, swinging the gun toward her and raising it until he pressed the muzzle against Lizzy's forehead. "Move another inch and I'll kill you first and *then* take care of her."

"You're not going to get out of here alive," Lizzy told him.

"Step back," he said.

Lizzy did as he said.

He laughed. "You're not as smart as I thought you were. Why couldn't any of those guys take you down?"

"Do you mean Spiderman?"

His eyes were bugged out and bloodshot. His smile was crooked. "You don't get it, do you?"

"Why don't you fill me in?"

"You're only here because I wanted you here. I bet every news van in the country is out there right now, everyone wanting a piece of the action, a piece of me!"

He hooked an arm around Shelby's neck and pulled her so close her face was pressed against his body.

Shelby's eyes were open. Her breathing had slowed. She was focused again. She didn't struggle to get away, just locked her eyes on Lizzy's. She was ready for whatever was about to happen.

"I wanted you here because I wanted to show the world that I'm the guy." He let go of Shelby and slapped the palm of his hand against his chest.

Lizzy's heart was racing, beating hard against her ribs.

"I'm it! I'm the guy everyone is talking about—the one who finally took Lizzy Gardner down. And guess what?"

Lizzy pretended to shiver from the cold, willing him to believe she posed no threat to him.

"After the two of you are dead," he went on, his gun flailing as he talked, "after I've had my fun, I'll walk out of here, head held high. And yeah," he said with a laugh, "I might spend ten or twenty years behind bars—better yet, the rest of my life! And then everything will be how it should have been all those years ago, before you came into the picture and ruined everything. People will know my name again. There will be interviews and whole books written about me—*Frank Lyle, the predator who did things his way.* My face will be on every news station across America."

Lizzy shot a look at Shelby, used her chin to gesture. *Now.*

Shelby picked up both feet and slammed them hard into the backs of his legs, sending the big man sprawling toward Lizzy.

She ripped the Velcro from the lining of the bra Kitally had given her, grabbed the thin metal shank Kitally had fashioned in her warehouse cell, and jammed it into the side of his neck.

The gun dropped from his hand.

He fell to the floor, blood spurting from his neck.

Lizzy dropped to the ground, scrambled around on her hands and knees, looking for the gun. It was under the bed. As she reached for it, Lyle turned, managed to grab hold of her arm and twist hard.

Lizzy shrieked in pain.

Shelby raised both legs again and drove her heels into the man's face, busting his nose wide-open.

He let go of Lizzy's arm. Blood was spraying everywhere now. Lizzy stretched out for the gun, but it was just out of reach. As she struggled to close those final inches, she felt Frank Lyle's hand grip the arm he'd already injured. The electric jolt of pain launched her away from him. Using her other hand, she reached for the gun, then twisted and fired—once, twice, three times—before his body went still.

Keeping the gun aimed at the man, she checked for a pulse.

Frank Lyle was dead.

Lizzy used the edge of the cot to pull herself to her feet.

She pulled the gag from Shelby's mouth before working on removing the tape from around her wrists. Between sobs, the girl tried to catch her breath.

At this rate, Lizzy knew it would take forever to get the tape off. She got up and made her way to the sink, careful not to slip on the blood-slicked floor, and found a knife. On her way back to Shelby, she removed the wood slat from the door.

"You'll be free soon," she told her as she cut at the tape.

Jimmy was the first to enter the cabin. He saw that Frank Lyle was dead and put a hand up to stop anyone else from entering.

Lizzy continued to saw at the tape, finally cutting through.

Shelby rubbed her wrists.

Lizzy looked at Jimmy and held up the knife for him to take.

He knew what to do. He went to work on the tape around Shelby's ankles while Lizzy put a blanket and her arms around Shelby.

"We did it," Shelby said between sobs as they held one another tight.

"You did it," Lizzy said.

"Was it the letter?" she asked, her voice hoarse, her body so frail within Lizzy's embrace.

"Yeah," Lizzy said. "Ben figured out what you were telling us. I've never been so proud."

A few minutes passed before Lizzy pulled away and looked over her shoulder at Jimmy. She was about to ask him if he was almost done there, but he'd lost his cool. Jimmy Martin was having a difficult time cutting through the layers of tape with a blunt knife. One of the tough guys, he was also having a difficult time holding it together. His eyes were red and brimming with something that looked a lot like tears.

Lizzy took the knife from him, finished what he'd started. Then she put a hand on his shoulder before returning to Shelby and helping her to her feet. She and Jimmy had known each other for a while now. He had two daughters. He'd taken down his share of monsters. Hell, he'd survived cancer. But she knew why he was getting a little sentimental. He'd come to the hospital the other day to see Jared. And for the past ten minutes, he'd worried about Lizzy, too; she'd seen it scrawled in every line of his face before she'd walked off toward the cabin.

The nameless man in black who'd brought Lizzy halfway up the hill came inside then, made sure Lyle was contained/dead, and then told a dozen people behind him to hold off.

"How the hell did you take him down?" he asked Lizzy.

"Teamwork," Lizzy said.

He lifted a questioning brow.

"This brave young girl caught him off guard, kicked him my way so I could use the shank hidden in my bra."

"I thought I told you no weapons."

"I believe you did."

"It's OK," Martin told the man. "You didn't know who you were dealing with. Lizzy Gardner doesn't listen to anyone."

CHAPTER 64

"How long are you planning on keeping me here? Holding me hostage in my own apartment?"

Hayley watched her smoke ring float upward. It made it within two inches from the ceiling before it disintegrated. "This apartment does not belong to you," she told the scumbag.

"Then why are all of my belongings in here?"

"Because the law-abiding citizens of Sacramento pay taxes, this apartment belongs to the taxpayers." Hayley took another long drag on her cigarette and then said, "I pay taxes, so we'll just agree that this is *my* apartment. And I want it back."

He chuckled. "You're going to get caught, and they'll put you behind bars where you belong."

"And who, exactly, is going to catch me?"

"My probation officer," he said smugly. "She has a thing for me."

"Is that right?"

"Yeah," he said with a nod, "that's right. What day is it?"

"Thursday."

He licked his lips. "She'll be coming around later today to get laid. She likes it hard and fast, right against the wall over there."

"Too bad for her."

"Why's that?"

"Unless she has a key to your place, she won't even realize you're home."

"She'll see my car parked outside. That'll be enough to make her kick the door down if she has to."

"Your car isn't out there. Remember the underage girl you were going to rape before I interrupted your little party?"

"You're talking gibberish. That girl was at least twenty-five, and she climbed into my car of her own will."

"You are so full of shit."

"It's the truth."

"Well, good, because the truth shall set you free," Hayley said, then coaxed out another smoke ring and watched it roll up toward the ceiling. This time it made it all the way before it vanished. When she looked back at him, he seemed uncharacteristically agitated. "What is it?"

He was trying to wriggle free, but that wasn't going to happen. Hayley had used his own personal roll of duct tape that she'd found in his car to bind him to the radiator.

Thank God for old buildings. Nothing like a cast-iron radiator to anchor a hostage securely.

His ankles were also duct-taped, but they weren't attached to anything, and he kept kicking the floor, which was why she'd also duct-taped his calves and feet to a pillow. The hollow thumps he raised with all his thrashing were comical.

"Where are the keys to my car? If you did anything with my ride, I'll be forced to fuck you in the ass." His face reddened; his brow scrunched as he struggled to get loose. "I'm going to make you pay, you motherfucking bitch of a whore."

Hayley smiled. "You are a ballsy one, aren't you? All tied up and making threats."

"You're going to regret ever showing your face to me. I'll make sure of that."

"That's my line." She stood and made her way into his bedroom. On top of all its other odors, the room smelled moldy. The stench was nearly unbearable. She needed to step up her pace and get this over with. On top of his dresser she found another roll of duct tape, ropes, a dildo the size of a small cannon. *What a fucker.*

"You never told me what you did with my car! Get back in here right now and tell me where it is."

He was becoming belligerent. She never should have removed the duct tape from his mouth.

She left his room and made her way to the kitchen, grabbed a plastic bag filled with a few random grocery items, dumped everything out into the sink, and then realized the plastic bag was too thin. She looked through a few more drawers until she found a thicker bag used for weeds and debris. She walked back into the room, where he was still thrashing about, and then pulled up a chair in front of him and took a seat.

"OK," she said. "Let's start. Tell me: Why do you rape people?"

"You are fucking insane. Let me go right now, and I'll consider not pressing charges."

"You've said it yourself," Hayley went on. "You're easy on the eyes; you know a thing or two about carpentry. Overall, I think we'd both agree that you could have a decent life. Is it about power?"

"Fucking cunts—all of you. Every woman I've ever fucked wanted it. Wanted it bad, enjoyed every minute. You're no different than the rest of them."

"You know damn well that no woman would want you. That's why you have to drink and do drugs and go for the women you know you can easily manipulate and control."

"You're as stupid as the rest of them. You think I care what you say?"

"I'm going to give you one more chance to explain why you do what you do. Make it good, because somebody needs to stop you from raping women, and I really don't want it to be me."

"I don't do anything the guy next door doesn't do. I've never hurt anyone in my life. Go fuck yourself."

"Tell that to the eighty-two-year-old widow you left with broken ribs and bite marks. According to the newspaper, you kicked the shit out of her and spent three hours forcing her to carry out perverted sex acts."

"That stupid bitch loved every minute of it. You should have heard her. She kept begging for more, practically wept with joy."

"You really are one of a kind. And you've made it very clear. You'll never stop degrading women, hurting people, making everyone else pay for your inner pain. You deserve to die."

Hayley took in a sharp breath as she came to her feet and readied the bag.

"What's that for?"

"You've given me no choice."

"I do it for the fucking thrill," he said, panic lining his voice. "There. I answered your question. Happy?"

Hayley set the bag to the side and ripped off two pieces of duct tape. She put one piece of tape over his nostrils.

"I didn't kill anyone," he said. "People have sex all the time."

"Rape isn't sex."

"I bet you've been raped. And you liked it, didn't you? I saw you watching the other night. You could have stopped me sooner, but you were enjoying yourself."

"You've said enough." She pressed the other piece of tape over his mouth.

The man was almost dead the minute she'd watched him carry the young girl into this dump, but he didn't get that. He didn't understand that Hayley didn't have a choice. It had taken her years to come to grips with the fact that the police wouldn't or couldn't do anything about scumbags like him. It was up to her to stop him. She put the bag over his head and sealed it tightly around his neck.

He was screaming now, or trying to. His high-pitched shrieks were muffled beneath the tape. She forced herself to watch, waited until the deed was done, until he fell silent once and for all.

She wasn't proud of what she'd done, but he needed to be stopped.

After she cut him loose from the radiator, she made sure everything she had touched was wiped clean and in its place, keenly aware of her actions, knowing she was walking a very fine line between reality and insanity. Between life and death. Between good and evil. But it couldn't be any other way. She'd known that when she was twelve and her mother's boyfriend had curled up next to her in bed and taken away her innocence along with her choice to choose a different path.

Deep down, she'd known all along that it couldn't have ended any other way.

She stepped out into the night, didn't pause to take a breath. She walked onward, head held high as she let go of the past—the burning anger that came with sadness, hurt, and blame flittered away like moths. It was time to move on.

CHAPTER 65

Lizzy sat in the corner of the hospital room where she had been for the past three days, ever since Dr. Calloway had called to let her know that Jared's family had indeed gotten a second and third opinion and had decided to no longer fight Jared's directive.

All ventilators and equipment had been removed from Jared's room that same day. No more IV. No more tubes entering and exiting his body.

From that moment on, the warring parties had laid down their arms and shared their vigil at Jared's bedside. Few words were spoken, but they'd treated each other gently over the past three days, bringing each other food and coffee, taking turns in the bedside chairs.

They were all there this morning: Jared's father, mother, and sister in the chairs surrounding his bed, and Lizzy watching on from her seat in the corner.

Lizzy hadn't realized until they unhooked Jared from the machines that she, too, had been hoping for a miracle—they all had. But now it occurred to her that perhaps the miracle was that she and Jared had found each other at all.

And then, after all the long waiting, it happened.

A heart-wrenching sob broke from Michael Shayne. Jared's father stood so abruptly his chair fell over behind him as he bolted from the room. Jared's sister followed her father out.

Jared's mother brushed her son's hair back from his forehead and kissed him lightly there, then looked across the room at Lizzy and gave one subtle nod of her head.

Was it over? It couldn't be.

Eyes wide and fearful, heart pounding, Lizzy made her way across the room. She slipped her hand into Jared's. He looked so peaceful, so beautiful.

She felt a hand on her shoulder. And then, without a word, his mother left Lizzy alone with the only man she had ever loved. She crawled into the bed with Jared, wrapped her arms around him, and held him close.

Thirty-six hours after Jared's passing, Lizzy pulled up to the house she and Jared had once shared, turned off the engine, and sat quietly for a moment, hoping the chill coming through her open window would freeze her insides and put her into an unceasing state of numbness.

She hadn't been back to the house since her wedding day.

It didn't feel right coming here.

The house felt like sacred grounds, and she was about to trespass.

Jared had always been fond of telling her she was the strongest person he knew. For the first time since he'd fallen into a coma, she saw him in her mind's eye. He was smiling at her, his eyes glimmering. She saw him clearly, so clearly she reached out to touch him, her heart beating rapidly against her chest.

But the tips of her fingers brushed against cold glass.

His image disappeared as quickly as it had come, but she was grateful to have seen him again, reminding her of happier times, if just for an instant.

She exited the car, her feet heavy—each step wearisome.

A white iris had bloomed despite the wintry cold—more than one. Somebody had been watering the plants.

She inhaled, aware of the air filling her lungs. She wanted nothing more than to turn around, get into her car, and never come back here. But this had to be done. Now. She couldn't allow anyone else to go through Jared's things. It took her a moment to find the right key on her ring. Her fingers clamped tightly around the handle, she pushed the door open.

Filtered daylight came through half-open blinds.

She stepped inside, expelled a long breath as she shut the door behind her. Not only had someone watered the plants outside; they had cleaned the inside of the house, too. The carpet was marked with perfectly even streaks from a vacuum. The house smelled like lavender, the kind that came from a can of room freshener. Nothing could cover up the familiar smell of *their* house, though, the house she and Jared had shared together.

They had sat on that very couch, drank wine, nibbled on cheese and crackers, and talked through the night. She could hear his voice, the laughter they'd shared. There had been many serious talks, too, conversations about what the future might bring.

She swallowed.

After setting her things on the coffee table, she made her way upstairs.

The bed was neatly made. More vacuum lines.

The closet door had been left open. Jared's shoes were lined on the shelf above a row of starched buttoned-up shirts.

She walked to his side of the bed, pulled his pillow out from under the covers, and held it to her nose, trying to breathe in his scent, praying she would find some small remnant that told her she wasn't imagining anything . . . the two of them, for a short moment in time, had had it all.

"Jared," she said, her legs quaking before she fell to her knees by the side of the bed. "I can't do it," she cried. "I can't go on without you."

Tears held back for much too long came flooding forth.

Jared Shayne meant the world to her.

Jared understood her.

The fact that dreams of the life they would share together would never be fulfilled was too much to comprehend. She gulped for breath between sobs. Her arms curled around her waist, and she rocked.

While a future without Jared was not something she could consciously envision, in her dreams, she could see that world very clearly, and it was not a pretty sight. The world Lizzy inhabited had always been dark, but without Jared it was colorless—a vast expanse of scorched hillsides and splintered trees, a world without hope.

Lizzy wasn't sure how long she remained on the floor, wrapped in grief, but it was quite a while before she could breathe normally.

She pushed herself to her feet, using the bed frame for support, and barely made it to the bathroom in time to puke until she had nothing left. She rinsed her mouth and washed her hands.

She walked back into the bedroom, glanced at the row of Jared's shoes in his closet and then at the bed. Leaving the pillow where it lay on the floor, she worked the key to the house from her key ring and dropped it on top of the bed.

She left the bedroom, couldn't stand to see any more.

With quiet steps, she made her way down the stairs, grabbed her bag, walked out the door and across the pathway to her car. She made no effort to extend so much as a backward glance before she climbed in behind the wheel.

They could do whatever they wanted with the house.

Burn it down.

She didn't care.

With no clear idea of where she was going, she drove off. Not into the sunset but into the unknown—a black hole where no light could be found, only bleakness.

CHAPTER 66

Hayley stopped at the bottom of the stairs, looked at the closed door at the end of the hallway.

Every day for the past four days, Lizzy had sat inside that room. Hayley could hear the clacking of the keys on the computer from where she stood. If Kitally or Hayley tried to talk to her, Lizzy ignored them. It was as if nobody else existed. Papers, books, and notepads were piled high on the floor around her feet. The eraser end of a pencil was permanently lodged between her teeth, another pencil tucked behind her ear. Lizzy never used pencils, but she always kept one close.

Lizzy had eaten little. She had turned down every meal Kitally cooked up and offered her. She hardly ever came out of the office for food or water—at least not during the day. Usually Hayley heard her rustling around in the kitchen sometime around three in the morning.

Hayley and Kitally knew that Lizzy had stayed by Jared's side until the end. They also knew she'd been to the house she'd once shared with Jared. They saw her the day she came home, looking close to death herself: her hair a tangled mess, her eyes swollen and red. They were worried about her, and Hayley had had enough.

Hayley marched toward the door, entered the office, and took a seat in front of the desk where Lizzy had been parked for too many days.

Then she waited.

Five solid minutes passed before Lizzy looked up at her.

"It's been long enough," Hayley told her. "You're not eating, sleeping, or doing anything but clacking away on that stupid keyboard. What's going on?"

"I know what I've got to do."

"What do you have to do, Lizzy?"

"I need you and Kitally to take over the investigative business. At least for now."

"Why? What will you be doing?"

"I'm tired of people hurting me and the people I care about. I'm tired of being a victim. I think you've had the right idea all along."

"I don't know about that," Hayley said.

Lizzy ignored her. "I've been researching those who have been naughty and those who have been naughtier. From here on out, I plan to work on keeping them from hurting anyone." Lizzy held up a piece of paper—a list of names.

"What is that?"

"Ten known criminals I need to watch."

"Why them? What did they do?"

"One guy was recently released, and within hours he raped a young girl who was walking home from school. He's back inside, but we both know they'll let him out again. My plan is to keep an eye on him. I'll make sure I know the moment his feet hit the streets."

"And then what?"

"I'll do what you do—I'll make sure he doesn't hurt anyone else."

"How do you know what I do?"

"Trust me—I know."

Hayley wasn't sure she liked where this conversation was going. It was one thing for *her* to go out at night and take out the trash, but something else altogether to see someone like Lizzy get involved. Lizzy was one of the good guys. One of the few people left in this world who cared more about others than themselves. After all she'd gone through as a teenager and then as an adult, she'd still somehow found a way to claw her way out of death and destruction. She had volunteered her time to teach young girls how to defend themselves. She had also opened her heart to love. Lizzy had been afraid to love Jared unconditionally—to do so had been like walking into a battlefield without weapon or armor—but in the end, she'd done it. She'd given her heart freely to Jared. And in return, she'd lost everything in an instant—on her wedding day, of all days. Lizzy had paid the ultimate price.

Hayley made herself finish traveling where her thoughts had taken her. What would she have Lizzy do? Lie down and die—or fight back?

"Jason Walker," Lizzy said next, pointing to someone else on her list. "He's in prison, too. He's been there for ten years, but now his release date is coming up. If he so much as looks inside his neighbor's window, I'll be ready to take action."

Hayley exhaled. "Boundaries? Limits?"

"No boundaries. No limits. I'll do whatever it takes."

"There are too many scumbags out there, Lizzy."

"I'll go after one bastard at a time."

"What did this Jason Walker do?" Hayley asked.

"He raped an eighteen-month-old baby."

Hayley frowned. "And they're letting him out?"

"He served his time and was a model prisoner."

Kitally barged into the room just then. "What's going on in here?" She looked at Hayley. "She's talking to you?"

"She wants us to take care of business while she does her own vigilante thing."

"Bullshit," Kitally said, then turned to Lizzy. "I'm in."

Lizzy kept her gaze on Hayley. "I'm not going to discuss this with Kitally."

That pissed Kitally off. "What the hell? Can you see me here in the room with you? Am I invisible? Talk to *me*." She glared at Lizzy until Lizzy finally looked at her. "I thought we were a team," Kitally said to her. "A family."

"You're nineteen years old, not even old enough to order a drink."

Hayley snorted. "That's a stupid thing to say. Age has nothing to do with anything. Kitally has more life experience than most fifty-year-olds. Whatever your plan is, whatever direction you're going with this, we're going along for the ride."

"Damn you two," Lizzy said. "We cannot get caught!" She pointed a finger at Kitally. "That means you can't peer into warehouse windows without knowing where all your players are, got that?"

Kitally crossed her arms and didn't say a word.

"If we get caught, it's all for nothing. They'll lock us in a cell, throw away the key, and it's over. Do you both get that?"

"I've got more experience with this sort of thing," Hayley said. "I've got a few ideas how this is going to work."

Lizzy leaned back in her chair. "Go on."

"The three of us work together. No going rogue. It'll be a team effort."

"What about Lizzy Gardner Investigations?" Kitally asked.

"The business will continue on as if nothing has changed."

"That will be our cover."

"Yes."

"We do our research, make sure these idiots are deserving of our wrath. We don't use violence unless absolutely necessary, and, like Lizzy said, we don't get caught."

Now that she'd starting talking to them like this was really going to happen, Hayley wasn't happy about this newest turn of events. *She* had stepped over the line—she'd made her choice—but Lizzy and Kitally were wired differently. They cared about people, went out of their way to help others. It wasn't too late for them.

"Ultimately," Lizzy said, her tone resolute, "we do whatever it takes to get the job done."

The silence in the room was thick and raw. It was clear in that moment that nothing would ever be the same again. But still, Hayley couldn't help but wonder if this was only a temporary lapse of judgment on Lizzy's part, so she looked at Lizzy and said, "This doesn't sound like you."

Lizzy lifted her chin. "That's because the old Lizzy Gardner no longer exists. You don't know me any longer. Nobody alive knows me."

ACKNOWLEDGMENTS

David Downing must be acknowledged first for his editing expertise. He literally morphs into my characters as he edits. It's sort of scary and also fascinating at the same time. Thank you, David.

Alan Turkus. You've been on this crazy publishing journey of mine since the beginning. I can't thank you enough for your constant enthusiasm and support. You're always calm under fire, a trait I greatly admire. And you haven't steered me wrong yet. Thanks!

Kjersti Egerdahl, Jacque Ben-Zekry, and Tiffany Pokorny. Thanks for always having all the answers.

Jana DeLeon, Denise Grover Swank, and Jane Graves. Without providing me a continuous means of procrastination, I would go nuts. Thanks for the laughs.

Vincent and Tony Rolandelli, two of many nephews. Thanks for forming the band Almost Dead, and thus providing me with an awesome title for my book. You rock!

ABOUT THE AUTHOR

New York Times and *USA Today* best-selling author Theresa Ragan grew up with four sisters in Lafayette, California. She has garnered six Golden Heart nominations in Romance Writers of America's prestigious Golden Heart Competition for her work. After writing for twenty years, Theresa self-published in March 2011 and went on to sell more than one million books. In 2012, she signed with Thomas & Mercer and is having the time of her life. Besides writing thrillers under the name T. R. Ragan, Theresa also writes medieval time travels, contemporary romance, and romantic suspense. To learn more about Theresa, visit her website at www.theresaragan.com.